CONSENSUS AT ADITI

FIRST CENTURION KOSNETT, BOOK 2

BLAZE WARD

KNOTTED ROAD PRESS

Consensus at Aditi
First Centurion Kosnett, Book 2
Blaze Ward
Copyright © 2021 Blaze Ward
All rights reserved
Published by Knotted Road Press
www.KnottedRoadPress.com

ISBN: 978-1-64470-234-5

Cover art:
Illustration 208792938 © Philcold | Dreamstime.com

Cover and interior design copyright © 2021 Knotted Road Press

Reviews
It's true. Reviews help. Even a short one, such as, "Loved it!" So please consider reviewing this book (and all of the ones you've read) on your favorite retailer site.

Never miss a release!
If you'd like to be notified of new releases, sign up for my newsletter.

http://www.blazeward.com/newsletter/

Buy More!
Did you know that you can buy directly from my website?

https://www.blazeward.com/shop/

PROLOGUE: KOSNETT

Philip S. Kosnett. First Centurion. *Republic of Aquitaine Ambassador with Plenipotentiary Powers in the Galactic West.* The stars far beyond that gap of darkness that was only occasionally broken with lights and civilizations until one reached the nebula of young stars known as the Balhee Cluster.

Looking in his morning mirror, he would have asked how he'd gotten here, but Phil could plot every decision point, every choice that had landed him at this moment. And at present, he wouldn't have changed any of them, but some mornings were a little rough.

He put it down to the day. After a month of everyone settling back down from near catastrophe, he was finally going to depart *Vilahana*. Head deeper into the hollow sphere of stars and gas that hid the cultures from the greater galaxy and let this realm develop into some of the oddities it had expressed.

That was really it. The casual way folks just shrugged off what looked to him like rampant piracy as a way of life, rather than seeing something that should be crushed.

Entropy. Plain and simple. If the system wasn't supported and rebuilt constantly, it risked falling completely apart. *Aquitaine* and her four primary neighbors were all much better at that. Granted, *Salonnia* and *Corynthe* had both had to have their moments of realization, but Jessica Keller had taken the throne of the latter and cracked together the heads of the survivors until they understood.

And Vo *zu* Arlo had personally conveyed to the criminal oligarchs of *Salonnia* that they had one year to get their act together, before he did it for them. They had even supposedly beaten that deadline, but even a few years afterwards Phil was taking a generational view before committing to an opinion on their success.

So far.

Arlo would win them over to his way of thinking. Or crush them. Nobody really gave that man credit for the depth and strength of his foundations. When you pissed Arlo off, you apologized, and then the smart folks went back and tried to figure out where they'd gone so horribly wrong to get into that situation in the first place.

Phil rubbed his face once to clear his mind and emerged from the bathroom, dressed and ready to face the day. Then out into the main portion of his suite. Markus Dunklin was sitting in the chair just inside the front door, reading a slab with two travel mugs of coffee next to him.

He looked up as Phil emerged and jumped to his feet, tossing the slab onto a nearby chair and grabbing Phil's coffee.

Markus put it right into his hand wordlessly and stepped back.

"Do I look that fierce?" Phil asked.

Maybe he felt that way.

"Yup," Markus replied. "Hungry, angry, spring-time bear. Bring a really long stick if you're feeling that ambitious."

Trust Markus to put it in such colorful terms.

Phil nodded and stepped to the comm on the wall, keying it and typing in the number he needed.

"Good morning, Phil," Heather replied. "What can I do for you?"

She'd seen the number calling and knew he was in his quarters rather than his office or the flag bridge.

"Meet me at the airlock," Phil said. "I want to have a chat and a stroll."

"Be right there," she said and cut the line.

Markus was quiet, as he did when he wanted to be.

"You stay here so I can find you when I get back," Phil decided, keying the door.

Markus nodded and slid back into the chair to read and sip coffee. The man had been with him clear back to the Age of Piracy, and knew how he thought these days. And as long as Markus kept all ten fingers, he could remain in the job as Phil's Personal Assistant. His *dog robber* to use the ancient term.

Markus was known to play with heavy machinery and high explosives, so as a threat to be careful, losing the job if he lost fingers was better than anything else in the galaxy.

Phil sipped his coffee as he made his way aft. The Survey Dreadnought *RAN Urumchi* had a number of Ambassadorial suites forward, in the space freed up by removing the *Reversed Field, Pinch, Plasma Implosion Generator* down the centerline. Lady Moirrey's (in)famous *Bubble Gun*. By itself, the weapon mount was nearly the size of a small corvette, so there was a lot of free volume.

He had commanded that an arboretum to come into being, as well as space for parties and guests. Because everyone had heard the stories of the famous Science Officer, Centurion, and later Pirate Warlord Javier Aritza. Not a true admiral in that sense, the man had made the second half of his life one of diplomacy and exploration.

Phil still found the man a useful role model, especially as the Republic had one of Aritza's best friends available at *The Library at Alexandria Station*, now on the planetary surface instead, to ask. Six thousand years later, and she remembered all the things she'd done with him, as well as the men and women he had immortalized

Heather was waiting at the airlock into the arboretum when Phil approached.

"You angry at anything in particular, or just wake up on the wrong side of the galaxy this morning?" she asked, only half-jesting from her own look.

"A little of both, I think," Phil replied as she keyed the hatch to open.

Once they passed through the airlock, the atmosphere was much wetter and warmer. Sergey, the Master Gardner and civilian in charge of this space, had his plants in high summer now. In a few months, he would cause about half of the space to traverse into fall, lowering the temperature, adjusting the daylight strength and length, and adding rain to move the temperate areas forward seasonally.

The desert and jungle sections didn't really change much. Still like the Science Officer himself, Phil had plants and seeds he could swap, anywhere he went, on the assumption that not everything, like not everyone, would have survived the thousand years of darkness after the war.

"So why are you so gruff?" Heather asked.

She could. He'd picked Command Centurion (CC) Heather Lau because she was an old shipmate, an old First Officer, and an old friend who had been there with him in the piracy days.

Ground Control.

"Having one of those crises of conscience, I think," Phil replied, sipping some of the excellent coffee Markus had prepared. "Trying to decide if us being here will result in the Cluster becoming a better place, or falling to pieces because I want them to change and have the firepower to make that happen if I demanded it."

"Too much piracy?" she nodded.

"Too much everything," Phil said. "We model ourselves on the Romans. Everyone knows that. Fine engineers and vicious warriors when roused, but also willing to absorb culture from others and use it. They gave history roads, trade, and culture."

"So who would you compare the Balhee Cluster nations to?" Heather asked as they made their way down a path of dirt and grass, surrounded by more species of real trees than Phil could identify. "Three Kingdoms China of roughly the same era? Or maybe the Italian City-states of the mid-Renaissance?"

"Today, I feel like Perry sailing into Tokyo's harbor with black ships and a list of demands," Phil said. "Not the most pleasant feeling on my part, even if it triggered the Meiji Restoration and eventually turned Japan into one of the great industrial powers of the age. A lot of wars had to be fought and people killed to get there."

"I thought that was why we were headed to *Aditi* itself," Heather noted. "Find the folks most likely to help raise the technology of the entire cluster up, and hopefully bring about some peace. You'll never end piracy as a thing, except to throw overwhelming force at the problem with orders to use unnecessary brutality. We'll need carrots as well as sticks."

"Aye," he agreed. "Trade. Technology transfers. Cultural transfers. Scholars and students exchanged between sides so they can learn our ways and then take them home and explain to others. This is a generational thing, and I'll be dead before it fully bears fruit."

"Meanwhile, you'd like to be hunting pirates," she grinned.

He grinned back.

"*Viking* is currently having all the fun," he nodded. "Quietly surveying places for signals we can explore later. Lost colonies are rare, but illegal ones appear to be pretty common, and parsing those out separate from pirate bases requires a lot of effort."

"All those colonies, legal or not, won't go away, Phil," Heather laughed. "Certainly not if we spend six months in the *Aditi Consensus* showing the flag and making friends. You can always go after them later."

"You're right," he sighed, pausing to turn back now. "I guess I just needed to hear it from someone else. Someone I trust to have the best interests of the *Republic* and not just themselves."

"Hey, that's why you hired me," she said with a grin. "*Ground Control.*"

He grinned back at her.

They were all pirates, the five of them. Him, Heather, Markus, *Stunt Dude*, and even Sam Au.

A little diplomacy first, and then maybe he could go after the *Zen-Mekyo Syndicates*.

And make the Cluster a happier place. And the galaxy a safer one.

EXPLORER

ONE

Phil was seated at his command table on the flag bridge, with Harinder Abbatelli, his Flag Command Centurion, across from him with her staff all around the room at stations, faced in and ready.

He did like this design, where Bedrov had folks looking inward at him, even if most of the time they were staring at screens. They could always look up and see him, or others, instead of just a wall. That built all sorts of camaraderie. Bedrov had said that not having that view was a mistake on an older *Corynthe* hull. He was bringing that same design philosophy to the rest of the galaxy, one ship at a time.

Because that reformed pirate was currently designing the future, and people were listening. And Bedrov listened when Phil had wanted to bitch about shortcomings in his old designs, making them better.

Survey Dreadnought *Urumchi*, for instance. The thing Bedrov had designed before making an even better one for Jessica to take on her honeymoon cruise.

This wasn't a honeymoon. It was only exploration, but he'd been at *Vilahana* long enough.

It was time to move on.

He drew a breath and Harinder smiled. But she knew how he worked and had patiently waited while he got to the place she'd probably been at when she woke up this morning.

"Open a squadron comm," he said quietly.

Faces appeared around his table as holograms, but lifelike enough to treat as people. All seven of his command centurions on the corvettes. Barnaby Silver off *RAN Viking*, back from another survey run to join the team just a few hours ago and already set to head out again.

And Kaur Singh. Commander of the *Aditi Consensus* Cruiser *Aranyani*. Unlikely friend they had first met on arrival, and who had pretty much become part of his force, at least until she escorted him to the *Consensus* homeworld of *Aditi*. Then who knew what might happen.

The Balhee Cluster was mostly populated by folks genetically drawn from the ancient geography of Southern Asia on Earth, filtered out to various colonies before it had been destroyed. They all had local tongues, but a modern variant of the ancient Hindi was the common trade language here, and Phil had even adapted his accent enough to sound like a local.

Kaur smiled as he looked at her projection, aware of the honor that the *RAN* was doing by including her as one of them, when a month ago there had been a pitched battle to see if the man who had nearly destroyed *Vilahana* would get away with it.

He'd gotten away, but only after getting his ass singed pretty good and Phil had subsequently let the entire cluster know that Captain Utkin was on his shit list.

Phil would deal with him after making friends at *Aditi*.

"This is Kosnett, I have the flag," he announced. As if anyone was surprised or unprepared for this moment. "*Aranyani*, I show all vessels are ready for transit to JumpSpace. You will take the flag and lead us out."

"This is Commander Singh, aboard *Aranyani*," she replied formally. "Ahead one quarter acceleration and form up in three lines astern. Stand by to jump."

Phil leaned back and muted his line so he could listen. The *Aditi Consensus* was the single largest political entity in the Balhee Cluster, but not that much bigger or more powerful than any of the others. Part of that edge was their geographical location almost at the physical center of the cluster, in the hollow sphere formed by several ancient supernovae and a couple of stellar nebulae twisted around into something that reminded him of an enormous egg in space.

The *Dalou Hegemony* might have been next in pure size and power, but they were fractured along clan lines much like the ancient Japanese Shogunate Culture of pre-industrial Earth that they had consciously emulated, just as *Aquitaine* drew from the ancient Roman Republic. Those folks built powerful vessels with weird, plasma-powered missiles called firebirds that were slow to charge and capable of being destroyed if you had enough escorts with rapid-firing mounts.

Across from the *Hegemony*, the *Gloran Empire* was much more warlike, but so wound up in themselves and their personal honor that they spent more time on duels and petite civil wars so hardly ever threatened their neighbors.

Technically, he was about to fly through space belonging to both on his way to *Aditi*, but again, everything was messy, as colonies might be randomly dispersed, loosely aligned, and subject to change with the winds of fortune.

Beyond *Aditi* and the *Consensus*, Phil had heard about the *Ewin Principality* and a somewhat secretive place called the *Yaumgan Domain* that had apparently surprised the *Consensus* by sending an ambassador to *Aditi* for the express purpose of meeting with Phil.

And all around them the *Zen-Mekyo Syndicates* roamed. Something more than armed merchants, but supposedly technically less than outright pirates, when there was always someone willing to issue *Letters of Marque and Reprisal* to someone else as a bribe or so they could fence stolen goods.

Basant Utkin, Commander of the *Ingham* Enforcer *Tango*,

was the man who had apparently committed the *Ingham Syndicate* to war with *Aquitaine*, however unknowing the rest of their Board of Directors might have been. *Tango* and the Salvager *Wulfa*, under command of one Andrea Liefan, were the ones he planned to hunt down.

That was non-negotiable.

"All vessels, we will transition to Jump in five seconds," Singh announced now as everyone was up to speed.

Urumchi and her normal escorts could make the sail to *Aditi* almost two full days faster than *Aranyani*, even over this short of a distance, but again, Bedrov-designed hulls manufactured by either *Aquitaine* or *Fribourg* were at least a century more advanced than anything in the Balhee Cluster.

At least for a few more years. Phil had no doubt that better drives, better engines, better guns, and better shields were on everyone's list, either to buy, steal, or design.

And then they were in JumpSpace. All the screens went blank as everyone was in their own portable time/space bubble until they emerged to join up and let *Aranyani* keep up with the rest, so she could escort them into harbor when she got home. A hero's welcome she deserved.

"Harinder, grab Aliza and you two join me in my office," Phil said. "In fact, have Heather come as well. I feel like a planning session."

He grinned as she rolled her eyes at him. Over the last year, the two of them had hardly done anything but have planning sessions. However, all that work had showed its worth when things went sideways and his people could react fast enough to save the day.

Nobody else in the galaxy could say that.

TWO

Heather studied the group as she arrived, last because she'd been coming from the bridge. Phil at his desk like *The Professor* he was occasionally nicknamed. CC Harinder Abbatelli, Phil's left hand, she supposed, if that made Heather the right hand. Fist. Something.

CC Aliza Babatunde, Fleet Ambassador and the woman responsible for wrangling the fifteen or so Command Diplomatic Centurions that had already been sent home with various folks to start the process of knitting all this messiness into something a little more coherent.

And her.

Heather knew why she was with Phil on this mission. And supposed that planning for the next step would be part of that as well, since they were about to sail into the main orbit of one of the biggest political entities in the Cluster and say hello.

At least they had a formal invitation, warmly transmitted by Director Danyal Narang, the rough equivalent of a Fleet or First Centurion from *Aditi*, before he had left on his Ship of the Line to brief everyone ahead of them.

"What are we facing?" Phil began as soon as her butt settled.

Heather looked at the other two women, as they'd been

closer to the diplomacy side of things. Heather had spent time on *Aranyani* with Kaur and Nam, meeting her crew and even training with them, but those folks were the warriors in the fleet.

Not the talkers.

"You're going to be the belle of the ball, Phil," Aliza replied, her dark face crinkled into a sarcastic smile. She'd let her hair grow longer now, into bigger ringlets, but everything underneath was coming in gray and white.

Heather looked forward to something similar. Probably by the time they got back to *Ladaux*.

"That's Day Two," he replied grimly. "What's Day Five?"

"How serious are you about scalps?" Heather asked before either of the others could speak. "How soon do you want to put all this firepower to use breaking *Ingham* and routing the survivors so hard that they scrape off their membership tattoos with knives?"

She'd carried out the previous threat to herself in the last month, going down to the surface to find the right local. The guy with an exceptional reputation who had imprinted on her a tattoo of the logo of the *Fribourg Empire's* Seventeenth Imperial Police Protectorate, inked just above her left shoulder blade, with a bar added underneath indicating the encounter at *Vilahana*.

It was still a little tender, though nobody could see it unless she stripped her sports bra off in addition to her tunic. Hopefully, she'd never have a reason to add a second bar. Not that she believed it for a moment.

Phil studied her face. The mention of tattoos had apparently spurred him down some rabbit hole. But a lot of pirates tattooed themselves to indicate who they belonged to. And it cut both ways. Cops always knew who they were dealing with.

He turned to Aliza.

"What do we know about the sort of legalisms around offering a bounty and then getting that transmitted to everyone in the Cluster?" he asked.

Heather turned to the woman who had spent the most time around the locals.

"The merchants of *Vilahana* have already done something along those lines, declaring all trade with the *Ingham Syndicate* ended under threat of ouster," Aliza said. "*Dalou* and *Gloran* might not care enough to listen, but neither of them really meet the minimum bar for what I would call an organized political state, either. The others are not much better. *Yaumgan* is about as insular as you can get, and *Ewin* almost as internally riven with politics as *Dalou* or *Gloran*. Individually, they work taking on as pirates and marauders, but only *Aditi* is really coherent enough to form fleets and do big things."

"And if they did that, everyone else might get their heads out of their asses and gang up on *Aditi*," Harinder reminded them now. "The entropy is mostly static, but we could cause all the wrong fractures to split and drive some of the edges into a long-enough unity to fall on *Aditi* from all sides."

Phil nodded. They'd chewed that particular bone over and over again. It was pretty dry by now.

An idea struck Heather.

"Aliza," she said now. "Who does collect bounties like that, if we put up a big enough one?"

"Define big enough?" Aliza replied.

"Dunno," Heather shrugged. "Maybe technology transfer of the old Type-1-Pulse we don't even use anymore because we have the Two and the Three. We did a number on those firebirds, and a wing of ships with Pulse-1s would probably cause *Ewin* to implode socially or turn their entire culture upside down to the point that they embrace one of the technologies of their neighbors. Worst case scenario they have to completely rebuild their current fleet and cease being a threat to any of their neighbors for a decade."

"Are they a threat now?" Harinder asked. "They border *Yaumgan* on one side, as much as that matters when the *Domain* keeps everyone out. *Dalou* on the other, with that wide zone of neutral stars where so many pirates happen to hide. *Ewin* always struck me as kind of the loud-mouth kid at the back of the room clowning for attention."

"And *Yaumgan* was the kid who blew the grading curve for everyone else," Phil said. "What do we know about them?"

"I've read Kaur's notes," Heather replied. "And followed up because the design honestly said giant robots that fly through space. And apparently they are. But the culture behind it reads almost like someone mixed Plato with the realities of the Ionian/Dorian culture of late Bronze Age Earth. Supposedly timocrats, so rulership by an elite group who are identified young and trained up, while others are generally born into a caste and remain there unless something special happens. *Buran*, without them being quite such assholes about it. But they consider everyone else in the Cluster barbarians."

"Are they native?" Harinder pressed. "The Dorians came down from the mountains of Central Europe, if I remember, and just injected themselves as a ruling aristocracy atop an existing culture they had conquered."

Heather shrugged.

"They didn't come from the east, if they are outsiders," Phil said, referring now to that long beach of stars in the galactic arm that contained *Aquitaine, Fribourg,* and even the former *Holding of Man* that Keller and Kermode had finally smashed. "What's farther west?"

"Earth," Aliza spoke up. "Or rather, that solar system and some of the oldest colonies known. Do we give credence to the Dorian theory?"

"We do not discount it," Phil said, placing his hands flat. "But ask whoever you assign to *Yaumgan* to listen for clues. Same with *Aditi.*"

"I was hoping for *Aditi* myself, Phil," Aliza said.

He nodded.

"And I have to overrule you," he explained. "For all the reasons we've just touched on. You are the senior diplomat, with all the other ambassadors having the rank of Command Diplomatic Centurion. If I let my only Fleet Ambassador be assigned to the *Aditi Consensus*, I'm obviously playing favorites and that might get the others riled up to the point that it is counter-productive."

"So I'm stuck here with you?" she asked with a sarcastic smile.

"Hey, it was good enough for Harinder and Heather," he laughed back. "And maybe later we can adjust things, but right now I feel like we are inching along an edge in a storm so bad we can't see where the fall might be, so I feel like erring short of the cliff on just about everything."

"Except *Ingham*," Heather said.

"Those people attempted to destroy an inhabited planet with a mechanical bolide weapon," Phil nodded. "Nothing they can say after this makes that go away. *Aquitaine* law comes into place if I find them. When I find them."

Heather shuddered, but didn't argue. Along with treason itself, that was the only other capital crime on the books.

As it should be.

THREE

ADCON CRUISER ARANYANI

Kaur Singh sat in her quarters and read the daily reports. She preferred doing this in her personal evening, rather than during the day, just because she had other things she did then.

The front room was comfortable, with a small couch more like a chaise lounge she could turn sideways in, stuffed thick enough to sleep on if she felt like it. A coffee table in front of her held an empty bottle that had been water. A spare chair for when she had guests. Not art in here on the walls, but that was because this was her quiet space. She had a few watercolor prints in the aft section, where she slept.

A rap at the door caused her to look up. She rose and keyed the hatch open, stepping back as Arya Chaudhari, her First Officer, entered. The woman's face showed the concern she would never let the crew see, but only after the hatch was closed behind her.

"Spill," Kaur ordered her as they sat, Kaur back on her chaise and Arya on the chair.

"*Ingham*," Arya said, subsuming whole conversations and private arguments in that one word.

"What about our piratical and soon-to-be-destroyed dipshit friends?" Kaur asked.

"I'm worried about a general war breaking out, Kaur," Arya said. "Phil and Heather might not intend such a thing, but that might be the obvious and logical outcome of his intent to bring *Ingham* before a judge."

"You're assuming they'll ever see the inside of a court room, Arya," Kaur chided her. "They might decide to go down fighting when cornered."

"That's their option," the woman said. "What happens afterward?"

"What do you mean?" Kaur asked.

"What does Phil order the Republic forces to do about the fences that worked with *Ingham*?" Arya asked. "Or the bases and drydocks that provide services in quiet systems without asking a lot of questions or looking too closely? Does Phil decide to clean up the whole Cluster?"

"He can't do it alone," Kaur reminded her.

"No, but what if he catches the dreams of all those folks back home who had been itching for a reason to throw the military at such a task?" Arya fired back. "What if the *Consensus* itself comes around to finally doing something about the sorts of lawlessness that we have all taken for granted for so long, right up to the day *Urumchi* dropped out of jump? We were just at *Vilahana* to rescue a freighter because it had an ambassador aboard. And all we did was recover it, letting *Saluki* off with a warning. Phil destroyed the ship to the point that they ended up scrapping it for parts in one of the local junkyards when he was done."

"I don't know, Arya," Kaur replied. "Director Narang didn't share anything with me about the higher politics involved, other than to praise us for doing the right thing in an impossible situation. He's gone home to explain it all to them, and I expect we'll be welcomed with kisses on both cheeks and then quietly shunted off the stage, going back to patrol somewhere out of the limelight."

"Should we go quietly?" Arya asked seriously.

She could do that, here in private. Kaur had always made sure that the woman had a safe spot to ask impertinent questions of her Commander. Better to be slightly offended now than surprised later.

"We don't have a choice, Arya," Kaur said.

"We could offer Kosnett our own naval ambassador now," Arya said now, having apparently worked her way around to the topic that really brought her here. "Someone who could explain a few things that they might not grasp. They are polite and friendly folks, but they are still aliens to the Cluster."

Kaur fell silent and absorbed such a concept. It wasn't entirely unheard of to offer such a thing. At the same time, they were largely operating on instinct, because none of the manuals covered something like this. Officer exchanges had been done in the past, mostly when various treaties were in force, at least until they were broken again. Or when a group of ships needed to work together for some task, such as hunting down pirates that had gotten out of hand.

"You and I can't go," she reminded the woman. "Who might you suggest we offer up to Phil, if we broached the subject?"

"Nam," Arya said immediately, so she had planned this out. "Senior enough to be important and listened to. Junior enough that most Directors likely won't get their noses bent out of shape when they find out."

Kaur considered it. Senior Officer Namrata Nagarkar was in charge of Weapons on *Aranyani*. Everything *Aranyani* had was certainly antiquated by the standards of *Aquitaine*, but that actually worked in her favor. And Kaur's.

The *Consensus* would need people who better understood the new systems that they could hopefully trade for or purchase, and weapons would be at the top of the list. As would the types of defensive arrays that *Aquitaine* used, since they had never bothered inventing the Shield Projector.

Having Nam aboard *Urumchi*, or maybe even one of those deadly corvettes, would give the *Consensus* a leg up on everyone else, because she would already understand the best practices that the Republic had worked out.

"Have you mentioned this to her?" Kaur asked.

"Negative," Arya replied soberly. "Figured the odds of it actually happening were extremely long, once you took into account all the players."

Kaur nodded.

"And it might even give us a reason to see *Urumchi* again," she noted. "If we had to rendezvous with them somewhere to recover one of our officers."

"And it puts us at the top of the list, if the Directors need a cruiser to sail with Heather somewhere," Arya smiled. "We'll already have multiple, organic connections to the situation."

Kaur nodded and smiled.

"Just remember this sort of thing when you are sitting in this chair in a few years, youngster," Kaur said.

Arya was a decade younger, but had been promoted rapidly while Kaur had been kept in command of *Aranyani* longer than was usual, because she had been so effective. If the *Consensus* liked what Kaur had accomplished at *Vilahana*, she might even be promoted to Director soon and given a squadron of ships to let her go root out some of those troublesome pirates that hadn't gotten the news.

Because there really was a new sheriff in town.

FOUR

Phil listened to the explanation again in his head, just to make sure he'd understood it the first time correctly. Nothing changed the second time.

He turned to Harinder, seated across from him in his small office.

"They really have found a way to call my bluff, haven't they?" he asked.

They were alone in his office, reviewing the message *Aranyani* had sent when they joined up with his squadron, a day out from *Aditi* itself.

"Were you bluffing, Phil?" she asked with the faintest grin.

"Apparently," he nodded, grinning lopsidedly. "I mean, we've sent diplomats home with everyone who could be trusted to play nice later. But nobody was sharp enough to offer me one in return. Even *Aditi* had been waiting for us to arrive there, and presumably would have suggested someone. That's why I have all that space forward, so I could house them in luxury. Kaur's the first one to offer me a warrior to train with my crew, instead of a talker to spar with Aliza."

"Glad to know someone can still surprise you," she grinned.

"Not funny, woman," he fired back. "Nobody is supposed to

be able to really do that, remember? We're supposed to have plans for *everything*."

"You're not Jessica Keller, Phil," she said, sobering. "That woman really did have plans for every combat scenario she could come up with. But that's all she did in her spare time, according to Enej. At least until Captain Wald came along, but by then she was as much in the politics of high command as the tactical assessment of *Buran*."

He nodded. Many of his people aspired to being the next Keller, but he quietly knew that those days were over. The war with *Fribourg*, and the next one with *Buran*, and then the near-civil war after that, had cured a generation of folks from wanting any more. Even the broken *Holding of Man* was slowly consolidating along roughly sector lines now, and would hopefully be at least a century before any major powers arose that were a threat to the rest of the galaxy.

No, Phil Kosnett might be the single biggest menace available right now. At least until Casey's first daughter applied to go to a naval academy. Would she prefer to go to *Aquitaine*, like her mother, or remain in *Fribourg* to break down more barriers was the single question unknown right now.

"Do we like Nam that well?" he asked now.

"She got along with Heather's crew when they interacted," Harinder nodded. "I don't see any personality issues there, but you'll have to ask her, as this isn't in the *Phil Kosnett Everything Playbook*."

She laughed and he had to force himself to do the same. He hated surprises. Even good ones.

"Okay, can you swap for Heather then and I'll pick her brain?" he asked.

Harinder rose and exited. Markus stuck his head in.

"Two coffees," Phil said, letting the man know that the next meeting might be one of *those*.

Markus nodded and departed, leaving Phil to think.

What could he do with the rough equivalent of an officer

right at that point where a Centurion might be promoted to Senior Centurion? She wouldn't know the weapons, but that was her job on *Aranyani* now, so it made sense to send her over and start training her, if Phil really was serious about the technology transfer of something like a Type-1-Pulse.

Nam and Hào Boyadjiev, his current Gunner, were about the same age, as he remembered.

Lots of unknowns.

Heather opened the door with a mug of coffee in each hand.

"Markus was laying in ambush," she said, sitting immediately and handing him one.

"Kaur Singh just surprised me," he said without preamble. "She offered to send over Nam Nagarkar as something like an Exchange Student for a while, to help learn our systems and probably prepare both sides for the future."

Heather was quiet for a few moments. Contemplative.

"Makes sense," she replied finally, after a sip of coffee. "Not quite the favoritism that you were concerned about with Aliza, but it opens the door for others to make the same offer."

"And they'd have to be cleared," Phil said. "I still expect a round of Ambassadors from everyone else, but Kaur has worked with us long enough and close enough to be that far ahead. And we can blame it on her when someone asks."

"She can handle it," Heather laughed. "How deep do we want to slot Nam in?"

Phil leaned back now and sipped. If Heather wasn't saying no, then it could move forward.

He was in command of the entire operation, but *Urumchi* was her ship. Her crew.

"I'd like to keep her here," he decided. "Rather than *Viking* or one of the escorts. We know she's smart and competent, but she'll need to retrain almost from scratch on our policies and procedures, so we'll have to crash-course her through the 90-day-wonder stuff. Assign her someone like her own Markus to help with everything. Enlisted but sharp. Chief or a Yeoman destined for a commission. You'll decide if she can qualify up to command one of the Pulse-Two batteries, but by then we'll have a much better feel."

"Will they let her remain aboard?" Heather asked. "Will we land at *Aditi* and someone will jerk her chain back, or Kaur's, just as soon as they process the right paperwork?"

"Not without pissing me off," he smiled. "It would be exceptionally disrespectful to the visiting aliens to do that without a complaint from our end, which I don't honestly expect, once they sent over Nam."

"Okay," Heather nodded. "So what do you really want me to do with her?"

Phil smiled. If it was a bit cruel, she wasn't the target of his ire.

"I want you to do to Nam what Jessica did to Casey Weigand, once upon a time," he said, watching the woman's eyes grow a little big and surprised. "I want you to make her into one of us."

FIVE

RAN URUMCHI, DETACHED DUTY

Nam looked up as the door to her spacious cabin opened and *RAN* Yeoman Elaheh Kovach stuck her head in.

"You ready for lunch?" the woman asked quietly.

Kovach did a lot of things quietly, Nam gathered, which was why she'd drawn this duty. Short. Dark-skinned like Nam and unlike much of the crew. As Nam understood the *RAN*, they might be grooming Kovach to become an officer if she wanted. Alternatively, she might be ready to become a Chief. *Aquitaine* did that weird.

Nam nodded, unsure she could actually eat anything, but needing to get out into the crew spaces and start meeting people. Doing things.

She glanced quickly around the room she had been assigned to make sure she hadn't forgotten anything, but she'd barely been here long enough to do more than set her bag down. This whole thing of being a visiting officer on exchange to *Urumchi* was still a little unsettling and quick. However, according to both Arya and Commander Singh, it represented the sort of lateral transfer/semi-promotion that might qualify her for her own command, and sooner than she would have.

Or set her up to go into Fleet Operations back at a base somewhere.

All doors were suddenly beckoning invitingly, if not taunting her. She just wasn't sure where she wanted to go with it, but didn't have to decide today.

Right now, she had to take baby steps, as there were already several weeks of homework set up on a special tablet for her to read and study.

But she wanted this, whatever *this* was.

She followed Yeoman Kovach into the hallway and walked beside the woman. The corridors were nearly a meter wider on *Urumchi* than Aranyani, so it was almost like being on a movie set. Kovach was just a little older than her, but an enlisted woman who had reached a stage where she would be making her own career choices soon

Like everything else weird that *Aquitaine* did, they were much more flexible about how one reached officer rank than the *Consensus*. Some went through their Academy, those who tended to be identified when they were about thirteen and offered scholarships to prep schools. They were the ones that people expected to make it to supreme ranks.

Others might come out of a college training curriculum with a reserve commission, and then get it activated. Some enlisted before being promoted later and given the choice if they proved themselves exceptional sailors.

There was even the infamous Trinidad Mildon, aka *Stunt Dude*, who had spent a lot of time training actors in martial arts for video roles with retired sailors when he was young, before enlisting himself and being directly commissioned as a Centurion.

Weird, but eerily effective, when you considered the wars that they had been fighting to the death for more than a century.

She wanted to learn from them. They represented at least half a dozen futures for her.

Unlike *Aranyani's* single mess, *Urumchi* served food in

several sections of the ship, with folks coming in to one of several lunchrooms, depending on where they slept or were on duty. And officers and crew mingled easily, not just within departments but across any range of things.

At least this crew was fairly evenly divided by gender. Nam had wondered about *Fribourg* or some of the places where men were the entirety of the fleet. Wasn't that stupidly inefficient?

Inside, the space was thus much smaller than Nam was expecting. Almost like a restaurant instead of a convention center floor. Low ceilings and only three rows of picnic-style tables with benches. You went down a line as you entered, filling a tray from communal troughs with more options than Nam was used to.

Lunch today was something similar to a long, round samosa, but they called it a *chimichanga*, drawing on the distinct Hispanic roots of their own culture. Wheat dough fried flat and rolled around a filling with cheese and things before being fried in oil. Meat or just vegetables. Cheese from cow and spicy sauce available as desired.

Water or reconstituted juice to drink. Various side dishes, some of which she could identify and some she could not. Dessert if she chose, but nothing like keer. At least not today.

They got filled up and found a space to sit. Nam tasted everything, uncertain but open-minded. Yummy, filling, and tasty. *Aquitaine* ate well, and made sure that the whole crew was healthy. Always a good sign.

"What's *Aditi* itself like?" Kovach asked as they started to dig in.

Nam had to stop and consider. None of the places in the Cluster that *Aquitaine* had seen were comparable.

"Warmer than *Vilahana*," she decided. "At least as a rule. *Vilahana* is a little cold, a little dry, and not particularly heavily populated, while *Aditi* was one of the worlds that survived the long darkness. Something of a paradise world, since people had so many to pick from in the ancient times. The current population is about two billion."

Nods, not just from Kovach, but a few others that had casually assembled around them as they ate. Folks wanting to learn. She didn't know names yet, but had faces and would make a point to remember. *Urumchi's* crew was huge compared to any ship she'd ever been on. *Aranyani* had a crew of just over four hundred. *Urumchi*, if she'd heard right, had nearly three thousand.

"The *Consensus* was formed there, when several close worlds and young colonies decided to organize for trade," Nam continued. "We like to say we are beset on all sides by lunatics, pirates, and enemies, but most of them tend to stay to themselves and not threaten shipping or commerce. *Aranyani* had to chase *Saluki* clear to *Vilahana* because they had kidnapped an ambassador of ours accidentally."

"Good thing you were there," Kovach offered. "Can only imagine what would have happened if one of those fool pirates had gotten up in the First Centurion's face."

That elicited laughter, but Nam understood. Phil could be terrible in his wrath, and had the means to execute it. Those pirates would have been annihilated and most likely *Vilahana* would have been captured as a forward operating base for *Aquitaine* forces. Phil's relationship to the cluster would have been markedly different.

"You suppose we'll draw leave?" someone asked in a general way without pointing it at her.

"Doubtful, Han," Kovach replied. "Too many diseases to prepare for on a planetary surface. Plus, we don't have money and they won't necessarily want to put up with sailors roughhousing in their port until they know us better."

"That sucks," the man, Han was his name, replied.

"Oh, they'll probably assign us something like a cruise ship in dock eventually," Kovach laughed. "Or send a request home for someone to deliver an R&R base we can tuck into orbit so we don't offend the locals."

Nam nodded at that. It made perfect sense, as they would be strangers. And these sailors seemed to take it perfectly in stride that they would not be allowed on the surface.

But as Phil had said, *Aquitaine* modeled themselves on one of the most successful military cultures in history. Discipline was a key factor to their success.

"What about you, Centurion?" Kovach asked, but glanced around in such a way that Nam could talk to the group around her, allaying fears and giving them something to tell all their friends.

"I'm here to learn, Kovach," Nam said honestly. "We are so different that it will take a while to get there, but we'll figure it out."

Nods and grunts. Good folks, if strange and alien.

But she had a job to do.

SIX

Heather studied the layout of orbital space. From here, *Aditi* looked like any other oceanic world. Mostly blues and greens, with a lot of clouds floating by. It was their current destination that was interesting.

Someone had cleared out a sizeable chunk of orbital volume, trailing one of the biggest stations in orbit. Their prime naval base, she had figured, but not pressed too hard. Nam was still figuring out what to share and what to hold, but that was fine.

They were here by invitation.

As before, *Aranyani* was in the van, leading *Urumchi* and *Viking*, with three corvettes in lines down each side and *CC-501* bringing up the rear.

"And there's *Khandoba*," Senior Centurion Leyla Ekmekçi, Science Officer, muttered under her breath. "They take phalanx combat seriously around here."

"You knew that, Leyla," Heather replied.

Still, it was impressive. One Ship of the Line, sailing along in orbit with two Cruisers in front of it and five smaller vessels leading, all in a single row like a shield. If you were facing that, all their weapons would come into range at about the same

33

moment, meaning you were facing main guns, titan bolts, and Power Taps.

If you tried to sail around the line while remaining on the same plane, the whole formation would turn with you, with the flanking cruiser and escorts accelerating across the formation to intercept you, even as the other two big vessels kept pounding. Heather found it telling that their smallest vessels, the so-called **Moat**, came in two flavors, classified as wolverines and porcupines, depending.

Buran would have eaten them alive with Capriole drives, but they would have done that to anybody not flying an Expeditionary design specifically intended to kill sharks.

Being able to kill everyone else in the galaxy was just a bonus.

Heather could see four such squadrons on her screens, but none nearby. A lot of firepower, but this was their homeworld and they had just invited dangerous aliens over for tea.

"Pilot, bring us in but make sure we are a little high, in case we suddenly need to run for the edge of the gravity well," Heather called out.

Centurion Bozhidar Virág nodded and kept tapping keys.

"In fact, that is a standing order," Heather decided. "Any time that a squadron seems to be maneuvering to put themselves above us in the gravity well, the ship comes to alert status."

More assents. More nods. Paranoia, but there was a lot of risk here. *Urumchi* was big and deadly, but they could still be overwhelmed by enough ships coming at them.

The *Aditi Consensus* hadn't given her any reason to suspect, but she was a long ways from home.

"Governor's Salute transmitted to both *Aranyani* and *Urumchi*," Leyla said now. "Welcome and all that jazz."

"Acknowledge in Phil's name and everybody hopefully prepare for another round of parties," Heather said.

This was why they'd come. The chances of someone trying

another assassination attempt like *Vilahana* were low, but never zero.

Ingham would be like rats trapped in a corner, one of these days.

SEVEN

INGHAM ENFORCER TANGO

Basant Utkin studied the tactical display with a sour taste in his mouth. The thing he was looking at was nominally a *Wisym Syndicate* base. Oh, they'd trade with anybody, but they preferred their own. Today, that had meant denying his request for docking and resupply.

They'd even had the gall to call him a pirate.

Outlaw, maybe, but they were all buccaneers around here.

"Status?" he asked loudly.

"*Wulfa* is hanging back," Johanic Raast replied from his station scanning things. "*Atlas* and *Maddog* have our flanks. The station currently has their shield projector centered on *Tango*."

Basant nodded. Neck or crown, wasn't that the old saying? If you went in for a coup, you better win, or your life was forfeit.

The *Ingham Syndicate* was still wavering, torn just about down the middle by his actions at *Vilahana*. *Hamath* was making friendly noises his way, while *Gilas* retained more of their loyalty towards *Dalou*.

Wisym had apparently decided to be assholes about things.

"Push the wolfpack wider," Basant ordered. "Get them to the edges of the Shield Projector cone so they can force the station's hand. Stand by all weapons for combat if they don't back down."

Heads nodded around him, everyone looking away, as was appropriate. If nobody was able to see who or what their commander was looking at, they couldn't betray him at a critical juncture.

Like facing down a once-friendly station with unlocked weapons systems.

"I have a red shift detected," Raast called. "One of the Pickets on the far side just undocked and looks like they are running."

"Whose?" Basant snarled.

He had his Enforcer, plus a Raider and a Picket. Even against the station, an enemy Picket couldn't do much.

Except die gloriously, he supposed.

"*Jakro* hull," Raast said. "*Cicada*."

"Are they fleeing or fighting?" Mati asked over the noise.

Matvei "Mati" Ignatiev. Pilot of *Tango* and someone who had been with Basant for years. Knife-fighter, so fast and deadly in close. He flew an Enforcer hull like a Picket, most days.

"Fleeing right now," Raast answered. "All red shift and accelerating away."

"Ignore him," Basant said. "Most likely he's running somewhere to try to collect a reward for sighting us. I don't plan to be here long enough to matter."

Basant studied the arrangement. His wolf-pack had maneuvered now.

"Order *Atlas* to launch a firebird," he spoke to Raast. "And have *Maddog* hit them with both titan bolts. Keep our crane charged and ready to launch if he doesn't back down now. I can always destroy this platform and find another to trade at, if they give me enough reason."

Raast spoke into a microphone and Basant watched the effect. Two bolts flickered at once and exploded on the station's inner shields. *Atlas*'s falcon-sized firebird raced down-range.

The station shifted their shield projector around to cover

against the firebird, and opened up on it with several main guns, but didn't otherwise reply.

"I'm getting signals from the station," Raast called. "Honor has been satisfied. Surrender offered under usual enemy terms."

Basant nodded. Covering their asses. If asked later, they had been attacked by the terrible *Ingham* renegade Utkin and surrendered after a hard and terrible fight, but he had not destroyed the station in the process.

Thin, but sufficient in any court of law.

Assuming the *Republic of Aquitaine* honored Cluster law. Basant could see them just destroying anyone in their way. That could work in his favor, too, as the other Syndicates would assume they were next and both help him out and gang up on anyone else.

If not, the Cluster might see its first ever pirate civil war.

"Order them to lower shields and prepare for docking," Basant ordered. "Uncharge the crane but keep everything else handy in case they try to pull a fast one. We're only going to be here for two days at the longest, so make sure you have your lists updated on what we need to buy. Our credit is probably shit after this, but we'll be away and hiding where they'll never find us."

He leaned back and let his crew work.

Yes, he could see a Syndicate civil war coming.

Basant Utkin would just have to win it.

EIGHT

Phil still wasn't used to the *Aditi* way of doing things, in spite of the time he'd spent around them. Even the Ships of the Line separated off a boom section to transport senior officers and diplomats to the surface of the planet, although around here he'd guessed that there was enough orbital traffic to ride a transport shuttle down from one of the stations.

The *Aditi Consensus* was treating him like the Ambassador, so Phil was in one of his own shuttles now, on final approach to the surface and watching the terrain below.

Aditi itself was quite similar to *Ladaux*, but that wasn't a surprise. Some worlds were just about perfect, in terms of surface gravity and location around the right stars. Like Earth had once been.

They were coming north along a long, sinuous coastline now. Ahead, Phil could see where the Nawa River emerged from the last batch of hills onto a coastal plain and started the long run to the sea, with Deshanpur at the edge of the hills and Jhapuri the port where the river mouth belled out into a harbor.

Roughly between the two, on the south bank, was the main naval base and fleet operations headquarters at Burhande, but

Phil wasn't going there right now. Presumably later, but this was a civilian thing today.

He glanced over at Kaur Singh, riding down with him. He'd suggested it, as one more way that they couldn't just order her off the stage, because she didn't have transportation to her ship if they did.

Phil didn't figure his hosts would be that rude. At least without a reason. Mostly, he wanted to be friendly, but not too friendly. A fine line to cut.

"First Centurion, we are sixty seconds out," the pilot called from up front. "Weather is adequate but looks like some rain blowing in from the northwest, so you'll probably want to be indoors pretty quick."

"Noted," Phil answered.

He was just the guest here, but hopefully they wouldn't insist on ceremony if things started getting wet. Like Kaur, he was in one of his better uniforms. Not the full dress thing he wore at home for major events, but nicer than usual. All the medals and ribbons would get in his way of just talking to people, as he'd be busy explaining why some of them were the wrong size compared to the rest.

That would lead to conversations about *Fribourg* and all his experiences as a pirate, and…

No, better let that slide. Director Narang had been briefed by Kaur and her people, and Phil had a pretty good idea how much they had been told.

"Nervous?" he asked.

"Unsettled," Kaur replied. "I've been pushing my luck in a variety of ways for several months, and it's likely to come back and bite me eventually. Karma's like that."

"Know the feeling," he nodded.

Like waking up to the sound of the JumpSails failing explosively, still way behind lines and without any of his friends.

He looked the other way as Harinder slipped a bunch of documents into a travel bag and Aliza tugged her tunic into place. A lot of years planning and preparing, and it kind of all came down to today.

Phil Kosnett, Explorer Extraordinaire.

The shuttle shifted to a hover now with a smooth transition. Out the porthole, he could see the clouds and it looked like a squall line was moving this direction.

"First Centurion, I am being rerouted to a nearby hangar for landing," the pilot spoke up. "Call the ball."

"Go ahead and land," Phil said.

Last minute paranoia. The pilot was nervous about potentially being trapped inside, but rain was rain, and he'd rather not be wet right now.

As the shuttle moved, he saw lines of troops in dress uniforms double-time to cover, with all the politicians madly piling into vehicles as well.

Good. That meant today was much less likely to be stuffy. Receptions like that were necessary and important, but just detracted from the ability to *talk* to people.

"Landing now," the pilot announced as the skids touched. "They ask for a few minutes to reorganize."

"Acceptable," Phil said.

It was a mess, but an organic one. He got to watch everyone move around and reset themselves from the shuttle, via cameras and windows.

Lots of uniforms, but even more civilians in every manner of fashion he could think of, from saris to blazers. Again, good.

The *Aditi Consensus* had started as four main worlds and expanded to dozens over the last couple of centuries. Still mostly that South Asian ethnotype like Kaur and a few of her crew, with not many of the other colors, either lighter or darker in tone.

Homogeneity had some benefits, when you were constrained, but Phil was obviously much lighter skinned, and more red. At least all of Earth and most of her children were represented somewhere in his crew.

He turned to Kaur.

"Do you have legends where all of the Cluster was originally populated from a single colony world, either before or after the Fall?" he asked.

She squinted and fell into thought.

"Some of the usual," she offered after a few moments. "Generally, each of the major players in the Cluster came from a culture already resident, but I'm not a historian, and it's been about eight centuries since Baudin's JumpSails arrived as a technology. Before that, we had some primitive, low-accuracy jump drives. Good enough to get around, but not to go anywhere."

He nodded and leaned back. Island archipelago, as it were. Small ships that could get between the islands, but nothing sturdy enough on a normal day to cross hostile seas.

He made a mental note to ask for a historian at some point. Or maybe a good scholarly treatise on the known history of the Cluster. There would be a lot of myth and legend wrapped up in anything he might just buy off a shelf in a store.

"First Centurion, they say they're ready for you?" the pilot spoke up now.

Looking out a window, Phil understood his slight disbelief at that statement, but folks were here, and more or less organized.

He turned to the other women and caught his usual security detail in that glance, including Xochitl Dar, his petite security Centurion who had even faced down Basant Utkin at that one party. Hers was an ancient, Nahuatl name that meant *flower* and was pronounced *SHO-cheech*. She was anything but delicate. Dar was also exactly the minimum height and weight to enter and graduate the Academy.

And tough as nails if he needed something done to someone.

"We're going down casual," Phil announced. "Dar leads, then me, then everyone else, raggedly rather than parade. Questions?"

He could lots of questions in eyes, but none came to mouths, so he nodded to his killer and she opened the hatch.

Phil followed her down as folks were more or less in lines and politicians were looking as much at each other at him.

It was easy to pick out Speaker Mhasalkar. The man was at least half a head taller than much of the crowd, even taller than Phil. Extremely corpulent as well. Not quite round, but well past the maximum amount of squishy that a serving naval officer was allowed.

He had a round face with a fake smile. Deep-set eyes twinkling with intellect, but not particularly hostile as Phil approached.

It was his hair that caught the eye. Long and poofy, like a lion's mane almost. And a mono-shade of black that told Phil he had just had it dyed in the last day or so. Must be a visual signature from when he was a younger man.

Most of the rest were average in height and mass. High-end politicians, but the *Aditi Consensus* was a mercantile place, so you went into business if you wanted power and wealth.

Salonnia, with better laws, if you will.

Phil enjoyed the way faces got a little apprehensive as he stepped close and stopped, rather than being all formal. He bowed a reasonable amount to everyone and smiled. They generally returned it.

Phil turned enough to gesture at the open bay door of the hangar, and the utter monsoon currently blasting the tarmac.

"Thank you for doing this indoors," he said with a smile.

That got some laughs. His accent was as good as theirs now, with so long to practice. And a few vids Kaur had sent over to watch when nobody was listening.

A woman stepped out from next to Mhasalkar and bowed more formally now. While the Speaker was in a pair of baggy taupe pantaloons and a blue jacket with about fifty buttons down the front and a lot of gold embroidery, she was in a delicate, silk saree in a red somewhere between pink and salmon.

The sort of color Keller's old Flight Commander *Neon Pink* might have worn.

Impressive and athletic, she was almost as tall as Heather and nearly as broad-shouldered. Beautiful even, when Phil had found that politics seemed to be the industry you went into when you weren't attractive enough for the entertainment industry.

"First Centurion Kosnett, I am Roshni Jayanti Mishra, Herald to the Speaker," she announced in a voice loud enough to fill most of the hangar. "In his name, we welcome you and your people to the Balhee Cluster and the *Aditi Consensus*. And to our world of *Aditi* itself."

Phil bowed equally to her. Kaur had warned him that politics tended to be a little stuffy and prosaic. The rain breaking up the original welcoming program had probably saved him several hours of speeches, for which he was thankful.

"Thank you, Herald Mishra," he replied, not as loud. He gestured to his cohorts. "This is Fleet Ambassador Aliza Babatunde. My Aide, Command Centurion Harinder Abbatelli. Command Diplomatic Centurion Amir Ava Pleško, who will be *Aquitaine*'s ambassador to the *Consensus*. And I would like to thank you once again for the immense assistance and friendship extended by your Commander Kaur Singh, and the entire crews of both *Aranyani* and *Khandoba*. They made much of today possible."

He noted the eyes flicker to Kaur. Some were happy. A few calculating. He made note of which, assuming that all the folks around him were doing the same and they'd have a detailed chat later. Markus was lagging at the back somewhere, looking like a dumb sailor because that was a disguise that fooled a great many people.

"In light of the weather situation," Mishra said now, "the Speaker suggests that we skip much of the original proceedings and step into the next hangar, which has been configured for a reception with food and beverage."

"That would be most excellent," Phil beamed at the woman.

Nothing ever got accomplished during speeches. And Phil had a lot he needed to get done, with only a few years at most in which to do it. Pet would sell him more rope if he needed, but probably never enough to accomplish everything he wanted to.

Even if he hurried.

Mishra stepped up and took his forearm in her hand, turning to guide him as one might expect from a Herald. Markus appeared with a telescoping umbrella so primitive that it was just cloth and fiberbar, popping it open and handing it to Phil.

Mishra flinched a little and then smiled, even as the Speaker, still silent until now, moved towards the rear door behind him. Phil could see any number of people looking for anything to keep themselves dry, even in the twenty meters they would be exposed.

There was a reason he kept Markus around. That boy had looked at the weather and planned accordingly for today. He had all that gear, ready for anything. Phil had no doubt that Markus had snow claws for boots and a spare thermal jacket in an emergency vac-sealed envelope, tucked into his backpack.

Just in case.

Herald Mishra held him in place for a bit as the big shots got going. When a social gap appeared, she stepped him forward and his party followed the Speaker, with everyone else coming along later.

He could make this work.

NINE

CONSENSUS AMBASSADORIAL RECEPTION

Roshni Mishra guided the First Centurion across the rainy gap with pure delight, as she was dry while everyone else was going to be at least damp and a little miserable. Except the visitors, she noted looking back. More umbrellas had appeared, indicating that Kosnett's team was far more than just a simple embassy.

She noted the way that five quietly-armed combat troops also enforced a polite bubble around her and the party. None had any beam weapons obvious, but she knew they had them in backpacks where they could be accessed. That had been part of the negotiations ahead of time, and a deal-breaker from the *Aquitaine* side, according to Director Narang.

After nearly watching a planet be destroyed, Roshni would grant the strangers that level of concern.

In front of her, the tiny woman leading them walked like a predator, in spite of being no larger than Roshni's oldest daughter had been when she was twelve. All the strangers moved that way. Fierce and assertive, in spite of being all *bonhomie* and cheer right now.

At the same time, the man next to her had also declared something short of all-out war on the *Ingham Syndicate.*

None of their representatives were present. A few business offices remained open, but had been told to prepare for extensive and painful audits if they chose to keep doing business.

Roshni wondered, as the rain fell about her now with a roar, how many of her fellow members of the *Consensus* Assembly would be quietly divesting themselves of stock, bonds, and other financial ties to that Syndicate.

Or the others.

Each trade house had their own fleets, and there were thousands of owner-operators out there with a single transport to haul cargo around. The Syndicates had represented pools of money and expertise that weren't necessarily tied down with all the usual legalities.

At least until now.

The little panther opened the door for them, but did not hold it, instead immediately stepping through. A second trooper wordlessly caught the door while covering his side of the formation.

Combat team. Well-trained. Experienced. Probably extremely deadly, if push came to shove.

The First Centurion leaned a little of his weight on her arm and shoulder now as they entered the reception hall.

"At what point will we separate, madame Herald?" he asked in a voice barely audible.

She parsed his syntax for a moment before speaking. His Hindi was exceptional, but his terminology was much denser than she was used to, even from other politicians.

She was thinking of him a Senior Director, rather than the politician he obviously was. A mere commander of entire warfleets specifically chosen by the *Aquitaine* government to explore these distant lands. And bring trade, because the man had already passed several opportunities for casual conquest that would have made his job easier.

Vilahana was still a free world, and was currently in the process of building new graving yards and warehouses as quickly as money could be assembled, on the expectation that trade from the main galactic arm would pause at that planet, or transition to local hulls there.

Money. And the man had not demanded any special rights.

"Technically, I will remain in your company for the rest of the day, First Centurion," Roshni replied, answering the unasked question. "We will physically separate shortly, but it is expected that you will need a guide."

She felt his nod and they continued, having not even broken stride.

A server approached with a tray on one hand, filled with glasses. She watched the little panther wave her off immediately and gesture one hand in the air. Roshni didn't understand the language they were using. Still, it was a language, because the one male who had delivered the umbrella took it back now then handed them each a cold metal container with a screw-on-lid.

Roshni didn't recognize the writing on the side, and presumed from the image that it was orange juice.

"I make it a rule to never consume beverages on a planet that are of unknown provenance," Kosnett murmured to her now.

Roshni wondered if *Aquitaine* had a problem with assassination, or merely a low expectation of the folks they might meet on their travels. Either was possible, but this behavior allowed him to imbibe with them, while not being at risk.

"Orange juice?" she inquired as they began to be surrounded more and more by folks who had followed.

"Safe," he nodded. "I don't do much alcohol at things like this for the same reason. I had an exceptional teacher on the subject. Jessica Keller trained us all in her procedures."

Keller. Even in the Balhee Cluster that name was known. Narang had delivered more recent news and gossip that he had accumulated from the meeting on *Vilahana* as well as the crew of *Aranyani*, who had grown rather close to the strangers.

The woman Keller had defeated the *Fribourg Empire*, then the distant and legendary *Buran*, before even defeating her own government in *Aquitaine.* That she had not subsequently proclaimed herself emperor of the galaxy had left more than a few folks confused. And surprised.

Roshni understood, though. It was nice to be able to simply go home and put your feet up.

"And since I had utterly disrupted everything planned," Kosnett continued quietly, "what should we do first to help the Speaker keep everyone organized?"

She dropped his hand and opened the bottle. Cold and slightly carbonated from the way it hissed. The male servant immediately captured her lid when she looked around, sliding it into his pocket. Her saree was lovely, except that she had no place for something like that.

Kosnett was planning ahead, obviously, as were his people.

How far ahead?

"Normally, we would mingle now, having heard and exchanged all the usual welcoming speeches," Roshni said. "In an hour or so, the first batch of food would be ready and they will fill up those long tables on your right for everyone to serve themselves. What do you need at this point?"

It was a calculated risk on her part. Speaker Mhasalkar would have given an hour-long stemwinder all by himself, given half a chance, so the kitchen was probably completely unprepared right now for the mad rush of people. Roshni had read reports from *Vilahana* that suggested Kosnett preferred open receptions like this to formal meetings, so that he could just talk to people.

Not the style of a conqueror, that much was certain. More like an explorer, which was how he saw himself, according to Singh's notes.

"Would it work better for your people if I sat still and let them swirl around me?" he asked now. "Or should I ride the tides in and out of conversations?"

"The latter, I think," Roshni immediately decided. "Some will be shy, or strangers. We have ambassadors from all the other nations and many of the major worlds here on *Aditi*. All got invited, but they are used to us. I expect many will eventually deliver Ambassadors for *Aquitaine*, once they have a chance to meet you."

He had stopped moving, but Kosnett nodded now and offered her his elbow, rather than his forearm, so she took it and let him set the direction, where she was close enough to introduce people, and deflect them as necessary, while still being in a position to find out what Kosnett really wanted.

And why the *Yaumgan Domain* had gone so far as to send a personal representative.

That had been the development that truly crystallized Mhasalkar and the others to get serious.

Yaumgan kept only a trade representative on *Aditi*, and then only out of courtesy. Not even a full embassy.

But they had sent an Ambassador to meet the First Centurion.

TEN

Phil watched the people move around like shoals of fish spooking as they imagined predators swimming too close. He wasn't about to do any serious deals here, but the time he spent chatting and being accessible today would help when it came time for it.

Maps and accurate directions to neighbors back home would be available to anyone who asked nicely, too, because those would be the people who did most of the work for him.

It wasn't like he hadn't prepped everyone back home and along the way to expect these travelers coming.

So he wandered. His trio of marines stayed close, but others had split off with Aliza and Harinder. Director Narang had absconded with Amir Pleško at some point, but they had already met earlier and were on good terms before today.

That left him, the Herald Mishra, and Markus inside a small bubble of folks. He'd eaten earlier, so he stayed away from the trays of munchies circulating now. When dinner came along, he'd be joining others.

If you can somehow manage to poison the entire Consensus government just to get to me, I'm not the one with the problem.

He smiled and ambled. Some folks just wanted to see him

up close, but not actually talk, and Phil was fine with that. Xochitl Dar had actually been collecting business cards of folks interested in later conversations. She was amused by it, too, seeing the way she became extremely formal when accepting such offerings, heads bowed and hands forward exactly as the others might be.

There was a reason he'd specifically picked Dar for his personal team, in spite of every security marine commissioned in the last five years sending him their resume.

A figure emerged from the crowd now. Singular, which made him stand out, as most important people around here, Phil included, had staff around at all times.

The man looked more Chinese Diaspora than South Asian in the bones in his face. The eyes were more elongated out from prominent, sharp cheekbones. The skin a lighter hue and more tinged with gold. His hair was gray, but straight and heavy, when the others around him tended towards more curly and frizzy.

Outsider, in every sense of the word.

The man bowed.

Phil returned the bow, noting that while his own uniform was designed to be tight across the body, in case you needed to get into an emergency suit in a hurry during a space battle, this stranger wore robes in a more classically-Chinese style, compared to the kimonos that *Dalou* tended favor.

His was worn like a long tunic rather than the big, elaborate Mandarin style, with cloth knots instead of anything more sophisticated. Slits on the sides from knee to hip, with pants not as baggy as the Speaker's pantaloons but still drawn in at the top of knee boots. The sleeves were only down to his knuckles, instead of hanging to his knees and requiring them to be folded back to do any work.

The tunic and pants were both a soft color Phil might have called mulberry, with both lighter embroidery and darker patterns highlighting things. All he lacked was a big design in the center of his chest that identified his rank and social station, as the ancient Mandarins had done it. That and those cute hats they wore.

Phil even had a moment where this man reminded him of the outlaw Khan of the *Buran* colony *Trusski*, the Scholar Ul Banop Cheani Yuur. He had dressed in a similar manner, if more elaborate.

"Ambassador?" Phil asked.

Everyone here was an ambassador or a businessman, and their style of dress told them apart.

"Hu Yating Kai," he introduced himself. "Of *Yaumgan*. Hu is my surname."

Phil noted the slight gasp from Mishra. Dar had absorbed the man's presence and shifted inward just enough that she could intercept him if she had to, before turning pointedly away and watching the rest of the crowd.

Phil nodded to the man. He'd been briefed that they used the ancient styles of naming, with clan first.

"Philip Scott Kosnett," he said, returning the bow. "First Centurion in the *Republic of Aquitaine* Navy and *Ambassador Plenipotentiary to the West*."

His more-full title, leaving off all the weird stuff that the Senate has authorized for him to be able to say and do when *nobody* knew what to expect.

"Plenipotentiary?" Hu asked now. "Did I understand that term correctly?"

"That is correct, Ambassador Hu," Phil nodded. "The *Aquitaine* Senate expected that I would need to be able to sign treaties in their name without spending several years sailing back and forth to explain everything. Obviously, such documents will be fairly high-level when they occur, rather than getting into great detail, but they will form the framework by which such negotiations will subsequently occur."

"I see," the man nodded, mostly to himself. He stood with his feet slightly apart and his hands crossed at his waist. "And what brings ancient *Aquitaine* to Balhee, First Centurion?"

Phil studied the man. He was pretty certain Hu was a man, but everything about the man suggested an additional layer of ambiguity that was more androgyny than espionage. A softness of form and style, compared to the greater machismo *Gloran* or *Dalou* wallowed in culturally. Perhaps the other end of a scale, with the *Aditi Consensus* in the center.

"Primarily trade," Phil replied. "We have spent the better part of two centuries at war with our own neighbors in the galactic arm, but those have been resolved now, so we seek to discover what interesting things might be found beyond our own western border. Trade is the thing that drives our interactions with *Fribourg, Salonnia,* and *Lincolnshire* these days. We hope that there might be more friends we could make in this direction."

"Are you wars truly done, then?" Hu asked.

It sounded innocent, but everything did in these sorts of situations.

"That is my hope," Phil said sincerely. "*Buran,* the so-called *Holding of Man,* has been broken by *Aquitaine* fleets under *Fribourg* command, and their supposedly-deathless God destroyed once and for all. Closer to home, things nearly came to a civil war a few years ago, but the instigators were captured, tried, and sentenced. Most have had death penalties commuted to life imprisonment instead."

"And yet you bring warships to the cluster, Ambassador Kosnett," Hu countered.

Phil watched out of the corner of his eye as Mishra wavered between interrupting and listening. She was a high official of the *Consensus,* and everything being discussed would be useful to them, but at the same time *Yaumgan* was still a competitor in many ways.

"We could not know what to expect, Ambassador Hu," Phil smiled. "And in fact we have been threatened on more than one occasion by outlaw vessels that might have sought to do us harm. Additionally, *Aranyani* was forced to *Vilahana* to rescue an ambassador that had been kidnapped by such outlaws."

"Outlaws?" Hu pressed.

"The *Ingham Syndicate*," Phil said simply. "Their representatives attempted to destroy an inhabited world by mechanical bolide weapon. Under most of the legal systems I have ever studied, that is a capital offense. Certain members of the Syndicate have been proscribed and I intend to offer bounties for their death or capture. What the rest of the Syndicate does in response will determine how I proceed."

Might as well get that out and clear. Basant Utkin and Andrea Liefan could not ever run far enough to escape him. Or his crews. A few of Phi's people had been on *St. Legier* after *Buran* had attempted to kill the planet. Phil had spoken with folks who had been with Arlo through it, as well as the man himself.

Fribourg would seriously consider orbitally bombarding any planet that gave those two refuge. That's how pissed they would be. The peoples of the Cluster—ALL the peoples—needed to understand that some crimes were too great to ever allow any respite.

Hu reacted by withdrawing a bit, at least emotionally. Like he could detect the raw strength of Phil's anger.

"And past that?" he offered as a polite deflection.

Phil allowed himself to be deflected.

"I'd like to learn the history of the Cluster, personally," he said. "We're here to establish trade links and maybe some outposts, depending. You have technology that is radically different than ours in many ways, and hopefully those are things we can take home as well. How does *Yaumgan* interact with its neighbors?"

That even sounded innocent, didn't it?

But again, Kaur had prepared him. The *Domain* hid back in a physical and psychological corner, largely remaining within six core worlds and only allowing a little trade with the outside.

Yaumgan's tech was said to be in advance of everyone else. Supposedly, they had the ability to stop any attack or attempted invasion, but Phil suspected that more than a little of that was good public relations.

The *Aditi Consensus* was bigger, as he understood, and more powerful economically at least. At the same time, having a quiet neighbor would be useful.

Idly, he wondered how much time *Aditi's* various espionage services spent poking at soft spots in *Dalou, Gloran,* and *Ewin,* as those three were constantly turned inward in various campaigns and minor civil wars that prevented them from being a threat to the rest of the galaxy.

Unless Yaumgan was behind it…

Hu smiled, as if reading Phil's thoughts.

"We tend not to interact that much with our various neighbors," Hu replied. "We have some trade, but only a handful of merchants are credentialed to visit our systems. We remain in our quiet corner and think philosophical thoughts as much as we can."

"And yet, my arrival prompted *Yaumgan* to travel to *Aditi,*" he noted. "That hopefully suggests good things."

"Curiosity, First Centurion," Hu replied. "We do not see ourselves as the guardians of the cluster, but a threat to any of our neighbors by aliens represented a potential threat to everyone. Like you, we sought knowledge."

Phil nodded. Fencing verbally, where both sides seemed well matched and would have to dance until someone tired enough to make a mistake. Not that he needed to.

Not yet.

"So what are your longer term plans, Ambassador Kosnett?" Hu asked with a change of tone.

And direction.

"At present, I have an invitation to address the Assembly here," Phil said. "See the sights and exchange diplomats and hopefully scholars. At some point, my Survey Cruiser *Viking* will hopefully be off to explore sailing directions and chart things for future missions coming behind us."

"And pirates?" Hu prompted.

"*Viking* is built on an Expeditionary Cruiser design," Phil smiled. "Back when we were fighting to the death for the future of humanity against a *Sentient* system that sought to become our god. It is capable of protecting itself, if pirates were to attack. And I can always split my escorts up to send some along. We have no intention of attacking anyone."

Phil paused.

"No, let me amend that," he corrected himself. "*Ingham* is my enemy. Everyone else is just a merchant until they choose otherwise."

Mishra nodded and chose that moment to step in, taking his forearm like before and signaling an end to this line of conversation. Hu bowed to both of them with a sardonic smile and withdrew.

"I would rather everyone understand my position," Phil murmured to her once they were back in a bubble of silence. "Less chance of misunderstanding later."

"Understood, First Centurion Kosnett," she said, directing them now towards a group that looked like *Dalou* warriors pretending to be merchant captains in clothing they found a little ill-tailored. "There will be time for those discussions as well."

Phil allowed himself to be deflected. The day was young, and he didn't have to fix everything this week.

ELEVEN

AMBASSADORIAL QUARTERS, ADITI

Hu Yating Kai closed the outer door to his suite and removed his shoes, lining them up with several other pairs. It had been a long day and he was exhausted, but many important things had been accomplished, however much remained.

Roads never complete, save when they dead end and trap you.

Lin Na Tai had been seated on a low couch reading when the door opened, but she was standing by the time he passed the hallway into the first living room. He waved her back to her seat and settled in a chair nearby. A glass of wine would normally be called for right now, but he had taken various medications earlier to prevent his body from absorbing alcohol, and anything he drank would just mean another trip to the toilet.

It could wait.

"You look tired," she said.

He was.

Partly, he was feeling his age tonight. Sixty was still middle-aged, but they had been long years that weighed on his shoulders. Na Tai was only a little greater than half his age, but she had been an exceptional student in her teens and had never stopped learning and proving herself.

"I met the *Aquitaine* Ambassador," Hu began. "Talked with him without structure for some time. And without interruption. Most of the rest of the reception was fluff, but Kosnett is a man of serious mien and great mental stature."

"Is he a threat to *Yaumgan*?" she asked. "Or the *Consensus*?"

But of course she would think that. As Captain of a *Jùrén*, the colossal warship known as *Zhang Gualao*, her job was to think in military terms.

"He is not intent on conquest, I do not think," Hu replied. "But his mere presence threatens to disrupt the harmony of all things."

"Is that a bad thing?" Na Tai asked. "I am aware of how the timocrats back home would reforge the Cluster into a better place."

"One cannot force change upon the resistant," he quoted one of the ancient *koan*. "They must be seduced into surrendering their obstinacy."

Na Tai grinned and bowed her head. As she should. She tossed that one back at him often enough to remind him that she could be just as stubborn as him.

"The peoples of the Cluster are at balance," Hu continued. "Change measured in generations is acceptable. Kosnett threatens a century of so-called progress in a decade. The cluster might not be strong enough to survive, whatever he does."

"Would that be the worst outcome, Scholar?" she asked now, using his proper title.

Yaumgan intentionally raised scholars to the heights, with warriors answering directly to the government. Artists and Merchants, however either defined themselves, supported the whole.

Hu shrugged now.

"Much remains unknown," he grimaced. "The breakdown of the other societies is bad, because people suffer far more than necessary, but good because it prevents any from threatening the rest of us. Even *Aditi* is constrained by *Consensus* as much as geography, in their mission to bring peaceful trade and unity to the cluster. Any direction they would aim provokes the rest to resist. Kosnett is not so bound."

"Is his power that great?" Na Tai asked, her eyes turning to hard jade now as she focused.

"I have the reports from *Vilahana*, though I can scarce credit them with truth," he said. "That his ship pushed an enormous asteroid out of the path of the planet with just their engines, and did not suffer any great damage as a result. That the *Ingham* pirates were so forcefully man-handled by Kosnett's squadron, one even taking a firebird the size of a crane on their shields without damage. I suspect that *Zhang Gualao* might be at risk in a confrontation."

"But they only fly simple warships?" she asked. "Nothing more sophisticated?"

"Do not make the mistake of equating **other** to **worse**," he snapped at her. "They are technologically ahead of *Aditi* by a significant stride. That simple survey dreadnought is monstrously powerful, and our agents in the *Consensus* report that both of the larger vessels have beams that are far more powerful than anything in the cluster right now."

"Excepting *Yaumgan*?" Na Tai asked, sober now.

"We cannot know until we can measure them," Hu conceded. "We have always been more powerful, however quietly we went about it. The timocrats of *Yaumgan* derive better distance by projecting a calm superiority that intimidates, than *Gloran*'s martial songs or *Dalou*'s rigidity."

"So how do we measure this man Kosnett?" Lin Na Tai asked now, sounding more like a Captain. "Or do you need to bring him to *Yaumgan* itself and have all the Scholars adjudicate?"

"That is one option," Hu nodded. "But I can't help but fear that we might be inviting the camel into the tent if we did, and never be able to get him outside again."

TWELVE

SPEAKER'S HALL, ADITI

Roshni Mishra was admitted finally to the inner sanctum of the *Consensus*, having passed three distinct layers of security intended to keep out spies and assassins. The Speaker was already splayed out on a couch, but she wasn't surprised, since he'd had to be on his feet for hours and Jasvinder Mhasalkar was not a man given to walking much.

She took an overstuffed chair and nodded to the Sergeant-at-Arms of the Assembly, Madame Nilima Parvati Chaudhary. Others would be briefed later, but for now it was just the three of them. Not even aides were allowed in here tonight.

"Well?" Jasvinder asked as soon as she leaned back. "What do we know? What did you learn? What did *Yaumgan* try to get out of him?"

Roshni took a noisy breath rather than immediately answer. Jasvinder was her boss—everybody's boss—but she belonged to a different party entirely, not one of his factions. Her holding the Heraldship had been the deal for supporting his government this most recent pass.

"If you own any stock in *Ingham* or one of their subsidiaries, I would suggest you quietly liquidate it right now," she offered.

"And maybe accidentally backdate the sale when you file your reports later."

"He's serious?" Jasvinder demanded.

"Kosnett told Hu that any legal system he knew would execute the folks responsible for *Vilahana*," she said. "Implying that even the *Consensus* better be on board."

"Do we even have such a law on our books?" Nilima asked now, leaned forward with hands on her knees.

"I don't think so," Roshni offered. "We should check and if there is nothing, we can win a big public relations battle by loudly passing it. Nobody will vote against it, not if they want to remain in office."

"Yes," Jasvinder nodded. "But what about the rest of the Syndicate? Or the others?"

"Right now, he's mad at *Ingham*, for all the obvious reasons," Roshni replied. "But he might not be amused when he discovers just how deep some of our official and unofficial ties go with all of them, merchants or not."

Jasvinder leaned forward now as well. It was almost a minor seismological event to watch, as big and squishy as he was tonight with his girdle obviously removed after the party. Only having access to the best medical professionals around had the man survived this long, with such an unhealthy lifestyle.

"Who gets hurt the most if we suddenly have to cut ties with some of the more egregious Syndicates?" he asked.

"Probably *Vyaapaar Vaayu*," Nilima said. "The *Tradewinds* Party has always had one hand under the table accepting petty bribes to overlook certain things. We normally need their votes much less than their donors, but I think we could stay in power if they withdrew in a huff after you declare a new law-and-order push. Might require one of the fringe parties being brought in. *Forest*, or maybe the *Mountains and Clouds* Party could be offered a lesser ministry in trade for a seat at the table. Both are heavily critical of the Syndicates anyway, so a pivot to do something about rampant lawlessness that had gotten out of hand, or however we want to frame it, would play well with their votes and maybe we shift the core of the *Bhavishy* Party and the government a little to the left for a while if we end up having to call elections early."

Roshni leaned back now and listened as those two dove into the weeds for a bit on deals they might cut, favors they would owe or debts that they could call.

"You're quiet," Jasvinder accused her after a few moments.

"This feels superficial," she replied.

"How?" he demanded in a hurt voice.

But then again, Jasvinder was one of the most superficial people she knew, a chameleon who could be all things to all people, as long as you didn't follow him from meeting to meeting, tracking all the promises he might make. All the lies he might offer up.

"We break some of our ties with the Syndicates," she continued. "But we have not addressed the underlying morbidities that gave the *Zen-Mekyo Syndicates* such a prominent place in the Cluster. Nor why they seem so rampant. This response feels like wild dogs have gotten a little out of hand, and we're suggesting tossing fresh meat out on the edge of town to draw them off for a while, rather than addressing the problem of packs of wild dogs running around the village growling at people."

Both of them bristled a little at that, but it was the accuracy of her comparison, and they both knew it. The silent scowls confirmed that.

"Have you considered that maybe we could take this opportunity to actually enforce some of the laws we have on the books that generally get ignored?" she pressed. "I spoke briefly with Kaur Singh tonight, and more extensively with Danyal Narang earlier. She went to *Vilahana* to recapture a freighter that had been transporting one of our ambassadors to a new post. She was able to succeed because it was her cruiser against a single Picket, and all was good. She would have taken his ransom and sent him on his way, mildly chastened but only for a year."

"Yes, yes," Jasvinder said, implying the *AND?* without actually saying it.

"And First Centurion Kosnett decided to cripple that ship surgically, according to the reports I have seen," she answered anyway. "And would have possibly annihilated that Enforcer and his wolfpack if provoked, although nobody understood that at the time. Kosnett's not going to be happy just declaring a new moratorium on trade with those pirates. Right now, everybody will assume that the smuggling will continue barely abated. Nothing will change, except that a couple of ships will have to lose their command crews for new ones that aren't tainted."

"So what do you think will mollify the man?" Nilima asked. "How do we stay on his good side through all this, without completely chopping off our leg?"

"Maybe we need to break *Ingham* ourselves?" Roshni asked.

"How?" Jasvinder demanded, slamming a palm on the couch to emphasize his frustration.

"We've got representatives from most of the major nations here right now," Roshni offered with a wicked smile. "The *Ewin Principality*, the *Dalou Hegemony*, the *Gloran Empire*, and even the *Yaumgan Domain*. Maybe we ask each of them to contribute a warship and support to helping Kosnett go off and destroy some *Ingham* base that has been too powerful for any one nation to handle? And do you suppose we could we could actually get someone from *Dalou* to round it out?"

"Would they come?" Jasvinder asked in surprise verging on wonder. "Who might we trust?"

"There was a *Dalou* captain at *Vilahana* before the formal embassy that the Shogun sent later," Roshni said. "I need to look up his name again because I cannot remember it right now."

"Makara Omarov, of the Sugawara Clan," Nilima interjected sharply. "The Heavy Escort *Morninghawk*."

"Yes, him," Roshni agreed. "Not a battleship or even a true

cruiser, but not much lighter than our own cruiser *Aranyani*, as those things go. That could be a personal connection we could exploit in Kosnett's name and a way to involve Kosnett directly in *Dalou's* internal politics."

"I thought we liked the man," Jasvinder laughed. "Nobody deserves that."

Roshni laughed with him, understanding that the *Dalou* took *byzantine* to whole new levels of crazy, but it would distract everyone and give the ruling parties of the current *Consensus* government time and space to clean up their own houses before too many people started looking too closely.

She had clean hands, as far as connections with pirate Syndicates went, as did all of *Prakaash*, the *Beacon* Party. That was an iron rule under her leadership, not to make those sorts of deals. In the past, it had been purely pragmatic, as it let her party stand out in a sea of potentially-less-honest parties.

Now, it might be enough to topple the government if she maneuvered everybody just right.

And make herself the Speaker of the *Consensus*.

THIRTEEN

INGHAM ENFORCER TANGO

Basant studied the charts again. His people had surveyed the entire arc of stars claimed by *Dalou* though never developed. In that, the *Dalou Hegemony* was even worse than the *Yaumgan*, because the Domain had their core six worlds and were only slowly developing outwards, following an utterly precise and logical path.

Dalou and *logical* weren't words that one used together with a straight face.

Still, they claimed this entire zone and most folks honored that. The Syndicates tended to be the ones to enforce it for them, only because if *Aditi* or someone wanted to come along and plunk down a colony, they wouldn't be easy to dislodge later. Pirates came and went, for the most part. And tended to build big platforms in orbit rather than bases on the surface.

Harder and more expensive, sure, but way easier to get a running start if a battle squadron showed up to evict you.

Hell, the thing he was looking for today had been assembled from a pair of the biggest bulk freighters available, jury-rigged catamaran-style so that there were docks all over the place where you could hook up to power and air, in case you needed to repair something.

Best of all, it was still generally a secret, as far as Basant knew. Not the ship. The *Yarmouth Syndicate* was small, but *Aggregator* was well-known in the industry. The location of the vessel itself was secret, changing on a frequent basis that was only shared with friends and family, as it were.

"We in the right place?" Basant growled at Johanic now.

Nothing was showing.

"Supposedly," Johanic fired back, still typing and tracing a finger on a screen. "We might be out of the loop now, Basant. They might have moved and told people not to tell us."

Basant snarled quietly. A lot of his plans had hinged on *Aggregator* being here *now* for what he had in mind next.

He looked at the planet nearby in visual. Burned-out cinder of a world too close to the star to ever support life. Too big, as well, with the surface gravity supposedly being twice what humans preferred.

But being this close to the star itself made it difficult for scanners to pick up, because you were often either transiting or hiding in the glare.

Useful, for a pirate base.

"It has a moon," Basant noted, keying on something his brain wasn't quite ready yet to share. "Look in the shadow."

"Got it, Commander," Johanic replied with a tone of surprise. "That's what they did."

Basant *was* the Captain here. Best to remind everyone that he was still smarter and sneakier, and not just bigger and faster. One of these days, physical attributes wouldn't be enough to hold his command.

Hopefully, he still had it in him to lead all the friendly Syndicates into a civil war. And then take on *Aditi* and their new, alien allies afterwards.

"Mati, make a short jump to get us where we can talk in real time," Basant ordered. "I need to know what they think."

He leaned back and let his crew work. Across the way, Gauhar Aigul had her eagle eyes on everything. On a ship that was an Enforcer, she was the Enforcer as well. But as small as the woman was, she knew every martial art studied, whether with weapons or open hand.

Basant was just glad, meeting her eyes now, that she had no interest in command. Nobody on this crew could take her in anything remotely approximating a fair fight. And if he was going after her, he'd do it in a dark hallway with a half-dozen friends, all armed with beam weapons and willing to repaint damaged walls afterwards.

And even then…

She smiled. It was a knowing smile, focused on him.

Basant nodded as they hopped across JumpSpace almost as fast as he blinked.

"Message sent to the platform," Johanic said quietly.

"All weapons crews stand by, but don't arm the crane," Basant ordered.

He had his wolf-pack if he needed them. However, destroying *Aggregator* ruined a lot of options immediately. He was more concerned that news of bounties on his head and Andrea's would maybe have reached these punks and convinced a few of them to make a play. Or run immediately, like that thug *Cicada* had done.

Basant needed time to rally captains. To make them understand that the future that had arrived wasn't a friendly one. He didn't think most people saw the end of the Syndicates in that monstrous warship *Urumchi*. Basant wasn't fooled. Kosnett would hunt them all down, and do it methodically, until *Aditi's* style of trade and government expanded to fill every nook and corner of the Cluster.

Neck or crown, indeed.

Heather turned to look at Leyla again, certain that her Science Officer was playing a practical joke on her.

"That's a ship?" Heather demanded. "Not a station or some bizarre kind of art installation in orbit?"

"Art installation?" Leyla asked, even as other crew members quietly snickered.

"Alien cultures, Science Officer," Heather reminded her. "Do not assume that they do things the same way we do. Not better or worse, just different."

"Gotcha, boss," Leyla nodded and shrugged at the same time. "Yes, it appears to be a jump-capable starship. I'm getting maneuvering pulses from engines in the thing's legs."

Heather grunted and dialed up a new image of the thing, zoomed in closer. She'd taken it for a Rhodian Colossus. Or maybe the work of a modern Ozymandias, neither yet broken off at the knees and left to rot in the sun as a warning against hubris and offending the gods.

So, not a statue. Not a station, either. But a giant, androgynous, human figure flying through space. Had to be *Yaumgan*. Maybe the Ambassador's ship itself, looking at the scale.

Standing, it was longer than her corvettes would be, though not as big as *Viking*, to say nothing of *Urumchi*. Weird. She'd honestly thought it was a statue, or maybe some rich goofball had built an art museum and given it a weird shape.

You could do that with galactic-level technology.

Two long legs compared to the torso gave an impression of femininity since, like most of the women she knew, Heather had similar proportions. Two arms that looked more masculine. Or at least bigger and beefier. Hands that also included weapons, the barrels as fingers. Weird, but functional.

She zoomed in on the head, now turned in such a way as to almost be looking back at *Urumchi*. Again, androgynous. Pretty but not beautiful. Coldly cast in a golden color at odds with how everybody else built starships.

"Okay, people," Heather announced. "We're back at *Vilahana*. Sensors, I want a standard hard ping every six hours of the entire vicinity, starting in twenty-three minutes at the top of the hour. Warn *Viking* to sit quietly with everything turned on, and have all the corvettes do the same and route everything to us for processing, just like before. If that thing is a starship, I'd like to know more about it. In fact…"

She keyed a button on her console.

"Centurion Nagarkar," Nam answered immediately.

"Routing you an image," Heather told her. "Can you identify it?"

"Oh, wow…" came the response, which Heather took as a win. "That's a *Yaumgan Domain* warship. You almost never see them this far from home. How big is that thing?"

"Scans suggest three hundred meters, plus a little," Heather said.

"That's a Jùrén, then," Nam gasped. "Uhm, maybe their equivalent of a Ship of the Line or *Urumchi*."

"Too small," Heather pointed out. "Even *Khandoba* is nearly twice that size, Centurion."

"Understood, Commander," Nam gulped. "But they are said

to be like dancers in how they move and maneuver. And *Yaumgan* is supposed to be far in advance of everyone else in the Cluster technologically, so they could make smaller ships that were at least as powerful."

"Thank you," Heather said, rather than snap at the woman and her mythologizing.

They were in the Cluster, and *Yaumgan* had everyone else spooked. What Heather didn't know was how much of that was fact and how much was legend to keep the little children from bothering them.

"Leyla," Heather turned back to the woman waiting with wide eyes. "I want to know what kinds of armaments they have when you scan them. Assume anything you've seen, here or at home, and if it doesn't fit, try upscaling the output, like we went from Type-3s to Type-4s. Questions?"

"Why would someone do something that crazy?" Leyla sassed back.

"You won't mistake them for anybody else," Heather pointed out. "And those two arms give you pretty much a universal arc on a weapon, without having to change planes or roll at all. If he's flying right at you on leg thrusters, that's a small profile to have to hit, and I wouldn't be surprised if they could tuck up like an acrobat and do silly shit in combat to make people miss. The sharks wouldn't have cared, but I bet your average *Fribourg* Captain would be beside himself trying to engage something like that. Past that, route me your raw feeds as they come in, and cycle your team awake for a few hours to crunch some data for me. Phil will want to know what these potential allies represent as fast as we can."

"Allies?" Leyla asked.

"Talked to Phil last night after his party," she nodded, speaking loud enough for everyone to hear. "*Yaumgan* was at least as friendly as anybody else, and Ambassador Hu has been sent specifically to meet us. *Yaumgan* doesn't normally have an embassy on *Aditi*, just a trade representative and Consuls. I promise you they are as interested in us as we are them."

"Oh," Leyla replied, having apparently spaced on that last part. "Deep scan, coming up."

Heather thought about it for a moment.

"You have the flag, Leyla," she announced. "Get me information."

"Have we considered just hailing them to say hi?" Centurion Virág, her Pilot, asked.

"That's next," Heather assured him. "First, I want to know just how dangerous they might be."

FIFTEEN

ASSEMBLY OFFICE BUILDING, ADITI

Kaur noted her location against the numbers on the doors around her. The orders had brought her here, now, without any aides or even a recording device, her personal comm having been left with the most recent set of guards, back two airlocks and frames. Or however you measured buildings instead of ships.

She was at the right place. The numbers agreed. Kaur followed the other instructions and entered without knocking. It was an office. A few books on a shelf on her left. A table with a coffee service on her right. One chair on this side. Small, given the political stature of the resident.

Herald Mishra. One of the top civilian politicians in the *Consensus*. Only a few years older than Kaur was, but blessed with those genes that made her look a decade younger. Dressed more formally than yesterday's reception, with a muted jacket almost like a sherwani with so many buttons.

Kaur was in one of her better uniforms. Formal, but private. Well representing her ship and the navy itself, without looking like a peacock about it. The top-line dress uniform was almost as bad as a wedding *kurta*.

The Herald rose and shook hands across the desk.

"Commander, welcome," she said, gesturing. "Thank you for joining me today."

Kaur smiled. The instructions had read like orders, not an invitation to tea. She smiled politely and wondered what she'd done this time.

Or rather, which of her sins had finally caught up. All the gods knew she had made a number since chasing *Saluki* to *Vilahana*.

"I need a military opinion," Mishra said now, quickly turning formal.

"I am merely a commander, Herald," Kaur offered up, seeing if the woman would be deflected. "Surely there are Directors you could better ask."

The woman smiled like an indulgent parent.

"I have spoken to Narang," she continued. "But I don't feel that you would be surprised if I referred to the man as a politician in uniform."

Kaur pressed her teeth together to keep from grinning. Once, he had been a great Cruiser commander, but had certainly spent too much time in the *Rear Echelons*, as it were. Kaur nodded instead, hoping to keep the giggle out of her eyes before looking up again.

"This concerns First Centurion Kosnett, as you are again unlikely to be surprised by," Mishra continued.

"How may I be of service?" Kaur asked, wondering if the government was ready to call in all those promises and lies she'd had to spin at *Vilahana* in order to keep that situation as close to under control as possible.

"You assigned one of your officers to *Urumchi* as a military exchange," the Herald said now. "Why was that?"

"Kosnett and his crew have been exceptionally friendly to us, but I felt that *Aranyani* might be assigned elsewhere shortly," Kaur offered. It was as close to open and honest as she was willing to be without ascending a witness stand. "Thereby depriving the *Aquitaine* squadron of any sort of cultural advisors that might help them understand some of the more complex nuances that we as a people take for granted."

"And yet you had to have known that the *Consensus*, as well as everyone else, would be selecting ambassadors to accompany him," Mishra countered in a voice with just a few concealed edges.

"Those would be politicians, madame," Kaur said carefully. "Or officers like Director Narang. I thought that they would benefit from someone with a more recent military background, as Kosnett has made plain his distaste for certain facts of life that we have previous taken for granted."

"Piracy," Mishra stated flatly.

"Your words, Madame Herald," Kaur agreed. "But Officer Nagarkar was someone known to both sides, and a person I would trust to represent us well to the strangers. Plus, Phil and Heather will trust what Nam has to say."

"Phil and Heather?" Mishra asked archly.

Kaur cursed to herself. Was she already too close to the strangers to be objective?

"First Centurion Philip Kosnett and the Commander of his flagship, Command Centurion Heather Lau," Kaur corrected herself carefully.

Was this when she got struck down with lightning?

Herald Mishra fell silent for a long moment.

"I would like to have a conversation with you, Commander," the woman said now. "One that does not go beyond these walls ever. Are you interested?"

"Yes, ma'am," Kaur said.

She was already here under what were close enough to orders, and there were not that many people above the Herald in the *Consensus* itself.

"After *Vilahana*, there has been a conversation about not just welcoming Kosnett's mission of doing something about piracy in the Cluster," Mishra said now. "But helping it."

Kaur couldn't help the way her eyes got a little big at that. Mishra smiled in recognition.

Yes, this would not go beyond these walls, because a lot of folks might end up on the wrong side of history if they didn't move quickly. Kaur wondered how many of them this dangerous woman was setting up right now. If anyone ever found out that she knew ahead of time…

"Yes, you see," Mishra pounced now, smiling. She pulled a paper file from a drawer on her side of the desk and marred the empty perfection of the tabletop by laying it down now and opening it.

Kaur held her breath, recognizing a personnel file upside down. She had to update those for her crew at least weekly.

This one had her own picture at the top left.

"According to the records, you have been the commander of *Aranyani* for longer than the navy generally prefers," Mishra continued, just dangling that out there like bait that Kaur didn't wish to taste. "And according to these notes, should be up for a promotion to Director shortly. Certainly as a reward for how you so successfully handled an impossible situation at *Vilahana*."

Kaur nodded as shallowly as control of her neck muscles would allow.

Spider. Web.

But she'd also had this conversation with Arya on the flight home.

It was a time of change, in more than just their personal lives.

"How would you feel if you were kept in command of *Aranyani* for another year, Commander?" Mishra asked.

"To what purpose, Herald Mishra?" Kaur asked.

There were rewards that could be mistaken as punishments. And vice versa.

"Phil and Heather, as you name them, want to go destroy the *Ingham Syndicate*," the Herald said now in a dark, malevolent voice. "The *Consensus* is going to propose that each of the major players in the Cluster contribute a vessel of cruiser tonnage to the effort, working loosely under First Centurion Kosnett's Operational Command, as I understand the term."

Phil as Senior Director, which would make Heather his Vice, with everyone else slotted in and flying behind all his corvettes as the second line on an *Aquitaine* Phalanx. Kind of like how they handled *Tango* before he managed to get away from them there at the end.

"And my role, Madame Herald?" Kaur asked, still careful lest the prize be snatched back as she reached for it.

"*Aranyani*, under your command, is obviously the first choice of the *Consensus*, Commander Singh," Mishra explained patiently. "You've worked with them before, and one of your senior staff is serving aboard his flagship now."

"Should we keep Nam there?" Kaur asked, assuming everything was a done deal.

At least she'd get the cookie she had in hand when the cookie jar slammed shut. Hopefully.

"I think that would be most wise, Commander," Mishra explained. "Again, contact. Connections. Intelligence, if we can use such a crude term, though I do not expect your officer Nagarkar to engage in espionage. I want her to learn from them."

"Very good," Kaur said. "And after a year has passed?"

"Director Singh aboard a Ship of the Line like *Khandoba* might be more appropriate," Mishra said. "Because by then, we might be at war with all the Syndicates."

Kaur held her breath and her tongue.

Just as bad as she had feared. Only the fact that she still had her ship mitigated the day.

SIXTEEN

Phil had a break in the various meetings that the *Consensus* had arranged. They had been running about two to one, outsiders versus *Consensus* folks, but he understood that everyone had questions and nobody but him really had the answers.

As yet.

Give him a year and they wouldn't need him at all. That would be the ultimate mark of his success on this mission, when he could just sail away and nobody particularly noticed. He still had points beyond Balhee that he wanted to explore. Earth was over there somewhere, still too ruined for anyone to settle, but he'd like to just orbit the homeworld once before he was done.

Maybe he'd have to track Kigali down and hire the man for such a long sail.

Phil was in the conference room that had been assigned for his embassy. Or whatever he wanted to call it. *Aditi* was as good a place as any to centralize things, and he had feelers out to visit the other capitals going forward. *Yaumgan* had even invited him to visit.

He just wasn't sure he was ready to ride in what Heather called a giant fighting robot. Better, one that had apparently landed directly on the surface here to deliver Ambassador Hu and the Captain of the vessel, a woman he had been introduced to at the reception, but not spoken with since. Lin Na Tai.

But it was motion. And in the right direction.

Harinder opened the door now, having seen the last round of politicians off.

"Schedule still says two hours open right now," she said, with that particular gleam in her eyes. "Someone just suggested a working lunch off-site."

He rubbed his eyes once and figured it wasn't worth arguing. There would be time to sail off after rainbows later. Right?

"Who?"

"Roshni Mishra," Harinder smiled. "Just four of us. Her, you, me, and Nilima Chaudhary."

Smelled political. More political. Not bad political, but it felt like he was being set up. Still, the Herald had done right by him so far, and Kaur Singh had been in a better mood, last time he talked to her.

"Off-site?" he asked, sliding his chair back and rising.

"Private room in a restaurant just off campus," Harinder replied. "I know the place and they have a reputation for hosting power lunches like this. Good steaks, although beef is not always favored around here by the wider population."

He nodded. Hindi, if you went back far enough, although the cultures had rearranged themselves a number of times over the centuries. Millennia.

Ages of Man, if he wanted to be didactic. Phil Kosnett had no doubts that he was in the era that history would refer to as the *Age of Aquitaine*. Or maybe the *Age of Jessica Keller*, herself, depending.

Hopefully, he was the first paragraph of the chapter after that, when the galaxy turned to peaceful trade. And piracy stomping.

"Yeah, let's do it," he said.

He could ask, and get polite deflections, or jump in with both feet.

Centurion Dar was just outside and led the way without questions, so Harinder had obviously briefed the woman ahead of time. They slipped out a side door past the normal guards and security, to where a car had been drawn up nearby.

Phil was used to flitters and shuttles, so climbing into a vehicle that rode on inflated tires struck him as a little antiquated. At the same time, it also rode perfectly smooth and you didn't have any third dimension to deal with as you flew.

He could get used to this.

They left the campus of trees and entered a forest of towers. Tall, but limited to a certain height to let sunlight reach the central grounds. The car deposited them quickly at a curb where a doorman in a fancy uniform let them in as soon as he recognized Phil, to be met by another woman in a fancy restaurant uniform.

In and through what felt like back hallways. Like a video set where *Stunt Dude* would be at home. Not where the public saw things, except traversing down one long, glass corridor where he could be *seen*, which would no doubt help their reputation for exclusivity.

Phil had a grin on his face by the time he was admitted into a huge banquet room compactly set for four. Roshni Mishra he knew. Nilima Chaudhary he had met at the reception, but not since. She was part of the *Bhavishy Party—Future*—with Speaker Mhasalkar. His right hand, as it were, since Herald Mishra was from the *Prakaash Party. Beacon*, which in this sense implied the light of learning and knowledge breaking up the darkness.

Honestly and probity, but they probably didn't say that too loud. Phil understood politicians.

He wondered how close the two were, personally as well as professionally. They might be part of the same government, but Phil had a lot of experience with situations like this back home, and didn't figure things were that much different here.

They were seated and had hot drinks. Food got ordered quickly and professionally. Phil noted that both women ordered steaks in private, though he wondered what they might do in a more public setting.

Who we are at home, rather than who we are on the bridge of a starship, as it were.

They were alone, with all three teams of bodyguards outside. He wondered how often the room was swept for listening devices, or if he should just assume everything he said now would be played back on the evening news at some point.

They made small talk while he waited for someone to commit to the opening serve. Chaudhary had apparently drawn the short straw. Or not.

"First Centurion, your arrival and subsequent challenges have brought certain things to the cognizance of the *Consensus* Assembly," she finally said in a flowery, evasive manner.

He nodded and smiled, a mug of pretty good tea in one hand as he listened. Mishra watched the byplay. Harinder was currently memorizing everything to the point she could probably repeat it verbatim tomorrow in the correct accents, but Phil wasn't about to mention that to these two women.

"Given that much of these difficulties seem to have arisen because piracy has gotten out of hand here in the Balhee Cluster," she continued.

Phil figured she'd get around to her point, but he also understood that some politicians couldn't just turn off all the crap in public. Roshni Mishra had surprised him at the reception, but that was probably why she was silent now. He wondered if the other woman was being set up.

"I would agree that you seem to have a significant problem with lawlessness on your various frontiers," Phil said into the gap when she paused. "However, I also understand that a lot of said issues generally take place outside the lumpy sphere of stars and systems that you tend to claim directly as part of the *Consensus*."

"Correct, First Centurion," Chaudhary nodded. "However,

we think that your presence might give us the opportunity to do something greater."

"Greater?" Phil asked in a reserved sort of voice.

"We agree that what *Ingham* did at *Vilahana* is a crime of the highest order, but honestly, it is not something on the book in the *Consensus* directly," she said. "Mostly because nobody ever imagined that it would be needed. We will rectify that shortly, but in the meantime we have a proposition to put before you."

Phil nodded, wondering which way they would go.

"In the interests of *Civilization Itself*, we would propose that invitations go out to all of the nations of the Cluster," Chaudhary said, emphasizing the capital-C as she spoke. "And that each contribute a warship of roughly cruiser size to a squadron intended to go out and chasten the *Ingham Syndicate* thoroughly."

"Chasten, Sergeant Chaudhary?" Phil inquired, perhaps a little sharp. "There are four vessels that will be eliminated entirely. *Tango, Atlas, Maddog,* and the Salvager *Wulfa*. Plus anyone giving them aid and comfort once the nature of their crimes becomes generally known. I do not intent to *chasten Ingham*. My goal is to crush it entirely as a warning to the rest. Unless they deliver me up those people themselves, that is, but I expect that the results of this particular conversation will be more in lines with lights coming on in a darkened room and causing all manner of cockroaches and other insects to scurry for cover."

He leaned back now and watched. Chaudhary was good, but still blinked a little at the vehemence in his voice. Mishra just smiled, but she'd heard it before.

You cannot build a solid foundation for a government on a rotten footing. The Syndicates had probably been a good idea once upon a time. Independent corporate entities outside any one government, serving to trade with many players and lubricate commerce across any and all borders.

But they had been allowed to turn into pirates. And *Aditi* hadn't really done anything to stop them.

Hell, at *Vilahana*, once the ambassador had been recovered by Kaur and *Aranyani*, *Saluki* would have been put on a list that prevented them from trading with an *Aditi* port for one year.

Nothing more.

He scowled. Let them see that scowl, to judge how they took it. Chaudhary was the only one caught off guard.

"However, in the spirit of things, I think that it is a wonderful idea," Phil suddenly smiled. "I shall contact *Viking* as soon as I can and send Barnaby off on a mission to survey potential worlds where your intelligence services think we might find pirate bases. Do you think that the other nations would be interested in contributing resources of that scale?"

Again, the blink. Chaudhary wasn't used to someone turning her own trap inside out on her that fast. Mishra wasn't surprised. Or had come prepared. She leaned into things now.

"Messengers are ready to go out," she spoke up. "Once we were certain that you would be interested, which we could not assume. The *Gloran* Emperor is the closest physically, so we would expect an immediate and assertive affirmation, as they often consider pirates to be entirely dishonorable folks but lack the material resources to do much. *Dalou* will take longer, as the message will be officially received by the Emperor, but then filtered to the Shogun, who wields actual power. Selecting a ship to come would be interesting, as many clans might be interested in participating."

"If I may?" Phil interrupted.

Mishra nodded.

"Captain Omarov, of the Sugawara Clan at *Ishiokoh-jo*, was present at *Vilahana*," Phil said. "He made a favorable impression on me there. Perhaps inviting him directly and asking the Shogun for permission, rather than disturbing that Court, would make this quicker and easier?"

He liked the way the two women glanced at each other, wondering who had just won a bet.

"I also presume that you will contact Ambassador Hu and ask for one of their Dà ships, as the Jùrén currently in orbit is likely unavailable for such a mission?" Phil tacked on as things got settled.

"Would a warship of that scale be acceptable, if they offered?" Chaudhary asked.

"Either would be fine," Phil said, nodding to Harinder. "She can work with them if they have questions about size and deployment, as she is fully up to date on my strategic plans."

Again, a glance between the two women. What would it mean if *Zhang Gualao* came? What would that sort of a monster be like in combat? Or were there even weirder things that *Yaumgan* might offer in its stead?

But the ball had been dropped into the machine now. Like an avalanche, Phil suspected that it would gain momentum as it rolled.

He just had to be careful to leave the Balhee Cluster in better shape than he found it.

ENFORCER

Basant studied the rabble of captains gathered before him. This was the biggest bar room available on *Aggregator*. He might have preferred more captains sober for this conversation, but beggars don't always have that option, and he was here hat-in-hand today.

At least metaphorically.

Forty captains, which was a little better than he'd been expecting. Most flew Raiders and Pickets, with a few Salvagers thrown in. Only one other Enforcer here, and one he knew.

One he already knew would probably be a problem.

Captain Harper Zemke, off *Blade of Kunke*. *Nagi Syndicate*. Not exactly the enemy of *Ingham*, but not particularly friendly. *Ingham* tended to prey on *Aditi* shipping into and out of *Gloran* space, while *Nagi* worked the *Daloul Ewin* zones most of the time.

Aggregator, however, was neutral ground where captains and crews could meet, chat with old friends, and occasionally swap around if they didn't get along with a new captain that had taken charge.

Harper had been around for a long time. Too long? He was older than Basant by a few years, but still held his command as the Captain of an Enforcer, so he had the support of his Board as well as his crew, which wasn't something Basant could necessarily say about himself right now without lying.

He rose now and studied the captains he had called together. All had come, if only to listen to what he had to say about the rumors and legends already accumulating around the aliens at *Vilahana*.

"I come bearing news," he began in the ancient manner of their kind, letting his voice slide lower into weary and concerned to draw them down from whatever emotional high they might be enjoying. "Strangers from outside the Cluster have arrived, and brought with them new technology."

He paused to sip some weak beer and study the hungry faces. Strangers implied new people to rob. New technology suggested that someone might get their teeth kicked in trying.

Lord knows *Tango* had gotten the worse end of the bargain before barely escaping.

"*Vilahana* has already gone straight," he continued. "Governor Patte saw all that credit from new trade and convinced the merchants to kick us to the curb so they could present themselves as legitimate businessfolk, when we all knew better."

"Is that why you tried to blow them up?" Captain Zemke asked with a voice not quite sneering.

"Partly," Basant answered. He could tell no lies here because too many folks knew the honest truth. "I was aiming to get Kosnett and his people. And fully intended to make sure all the rumors that went out blamed him for destroying the planet like he was some freaking monster from beyond come for all your souls. I have a pretty good PR crew when it comes to that sort of thing."

"So what went wrong?" someone in back called.

"They pushed a twenty kilometer asteroid out of the way before it could enter the atmosphere and splatter the planet," Basant answered, waiting for the cries of disbelief to die down before continuing. "It was a calculated risk, backed by my Board, but we have a problem."

"*Ingham* has a problem, maybe," Zemke snapped angrily.

"We're pirates, *Nagi*," he snapped back at the man. "You think Kosnett's going to stop with just hunting down a few ships? He's said to my face that he plans to crush all the Syndicates that don't immediately start toeing a line and act like good little merchants. He might come after *Ingham* first, but he's not about to stop there. The only question is who he decides to roll up next."

"So what?" Zemke said. "*Ingham* gets destroyed. You think *Dalou* will suddenly turn over a new leaf and stop funding us to hit other people? Do you honestly believe that subsidies and bribes from *Gloran* merchants for us to capture ships for them will suddenly dry up?"

"I think that *Aditi* might decide to start doing something about piracy," Basant said simply. "How many of you would like to face new warships generations more powerful than anything flying right now? What do your quarterly numbers look like if convoys are suddenly invulnerable?"

That latter got through. Enforcers were to keep the Raiders and Pickets in line, and that covered three quarters of these captains, with the rest flying Salvagers and armed freighters best described as wolves in sheep clothing. If they couldn't cut out some freighter at the edge of a gravity well without getting their fingers singed, there would be hell to pay.

And quickly.

That calculation made its way around the room as Basant watched. Eyes got ugly. Murmurs to neighbors took on a hostile tone.

"And?" Zemke demanded now. "What do you think that you can do to stop it? Last I heard, your Board of Directors was just about split down the middle."

That drew the sorts of hostile laughs you might get out of a pack of hyenas. Which adequately described this mob.

"That's right," Basant agreed. "My Board is fighting itself. Half of them want to throw me to the wolves and pretend that they had no idea what all those armed vessels of theirs were really doing. They're actually talking about going state's evidence and hoping to cut a deal with someone for shelter and maybe exile, as long as they don't have to give up all the money they've accumulated along the way. How many of your boards of directors will make the same calculations when the time comes? How many will tell the cops where to find you in order to save their own hides when Johnny Law comes knocking at the door?"

He stopped there and took a longer drink. The beer was crap, but he wanted the liquid because all this emotion was parching his throat.

He'd never seen himself as a revolutionary. Just a punk kid bigger than most and willing to get ugly in bar fights when he needed to. That got him aboard an *Ingham* Picket along the way. Twenty years later, he flew one of their flagships.

But Basant had his doubts as to how much longer the *Ingham Syndicate* was going to be in business. And he didn't figure anyone would be willing to give him shelter later if they knew who he was.

Not that Basant Utkin was the name he had been born with, but it was the one that most of the Cluster knew. And hated.

The captains were getting ugly now. Angry, but rightly so. Piracy on this scale required all sorts of things, written down in legal documents because they really were just another kind of business. All his crimes were in a filing computer somewhere, just waiting for the hangman to catch up.

That described everyone in here, as well.

"So what stupid ass idea does Basant Utkin of the famous killer *Tango* have for us?" Zemke sneered now, making it plain that the man wouldn't support him.

Probably already had a secret mansion and mistress under some other name somewhere, hidden away where he could hop into a shuttle, drop off the screen, and go live out his days in idyllic isolation.

"There are a dozen major Syndicates," he offered. "We need to band together now, before everyone else gets their act together and calculates that being on Kosnett's side is a smarter idea and turns on us."

"Then what, smart guy?" Zemke laughed. "We go conquer *Gloran* or something and live like kings?"

"They would be my last pick, if I intended to overthrow anyone," Basant replied flatly. "Too honest, when you get right down to it. If we were going to do that, I'd go after *Ewin* and get us all made dukes or something. But I have a better idea. Instead, we go round up some of those secret colonies we have hidden back in a corner, fortify them, and declare our own pirate kingdom or something. If we go legit, and walk away from piracy, enough folks just might let us. We'd have a significant initial warfleet which would be too big of a nut for anyone to want to crack, so they might choose to deal. We'd have to sit like porcupines for a while, but the alternative is that *Aditi* convinces folks to arrest us when we show up somewhere, and then we all hang separately."

"I'm hearing a lot of might and maybes in that conversation for a dead man, Utkin," Zemke snarled now. "Personally, I think you're just a coward looking for someone else to do all the dirty work so you can hide behind Andrea's skirt some more."

Gasps and nervous laughs greeted that. Andrea turned bright red, but it wasn't embarrassment. No, that was the color of pure rage. If Basant didn't call the old geezer out right now, she might.

That would be an interesting thing to watch, but this was his battle. His war.

His soul.

Basant waited for the noise to die down.

"And Zemke, I think you're probably too old to care about anything that happens to the rest of us, because you'll be retired and sitting on a porch in a rocking chair, sucking a pipe and telling local kids lies about what a big, bad pirate you pretended to be, back before it became dangerous and you had to get out to save your precious ass."

Suggesting cowardice was a sure way to challenge someone to a duel. Calling him old and washed up was a close second. And hit closer to the mark, because Basant had tried to kill an inhabited planet. Granted, *Vilahana* and not many people would miss it or feel bad, considering its reputation.

But he'd also fought the aliens twice, and knew just how dangerous they could be. Saying that Zemke would run away now was even better. Basant was willing to fight for their future.

Harper Zemke's face turned a dark, deadly red now. Basant just smiled, because he'd been expecting this from the moment he saw *Blade of Kunke* docked across the way.

Oh, yeah, he and Zemke went way back.

"You know?" Basant asked now. "*Nagi* aren't all punks, but they sure seem to be led by them."

Zemke growled and stood up now. He was as tall as Basant. Heavier, but that was muscle sliding down into fat now, as he really had a good life and didn't worry about beating a challenger for his captaincy. Just a few years from retiring, likely, and his crew already knew that so they would wait.

That made a man soft.

"I'll cut your heart out," Zemke snarled.

A long trestle table separated them, so it was a hollow threat. At least unless the man wanted to climb over it to get to him.

"Do they even let you carry anything sharper than a butter knife these days?" Basant sneered back at him, salting the wound.

"Basant Utkin, I challenge your words," Zemke said now, invoking the old formula. "You would lead us, and I think that would be a mistake, so I will place my name in to command as well. We will let combat settle this."

"I accept your challenge, Harper Zemke," Basant answered,

staying to the script. "I will lead us to a better future than you offer, and prove my right in the ring."

They nodded at each other. As the challenged, Basant had the choice of blades, and would go for something short where Zemke would have to get in close if he wanted to win, rather than letting the old man rely on guile to snipe with a sword from the edges.

Like a coward might.

The other captains rose now, witnesses to history to see something rarely played out.

But they also understood that their own future was probably on the line.

EIGHTEEN

Heather leaned back and processed everything that Leyla had to say.

"That's insane," she finally offered as an opinion.

"Same thing I said, boss," Leyla replied. "Plus a few extra profanities unfit for current company."

Heather studied the faces around her. They were down in Phil's flag bridge, for the better display electronics and space to stretch out. Her, Phil, Harinder, Leyla, First Officer Iveta Beridze, Command Centurion Barnaby Silver from *Viking* and his own Science Officer Sunan Bunnag. Nam was present, but pretending to be invisible right now sitting directly on Heather's right.

"That ship is smaller than one of our old *Founder-class* Heavy Cruisers, and has more power than my old battlecruiser *Jellicoe*," Heather repeated.

"Kilo for kilo, they're right up there with anything *Expeditionary* on a mass/power curve," Leyla agreed. "If they were feeling feisty, I don't think that anything else in the cluster could stop *Yaumgan* from kicking ass and taking names. Good thing they like living peaceful and contemplative lives of Platonic Scholars."

"Don't let that calm façade fool you, people," Phil leaned forward now and rested a hand on the table top. "Remember, they wouldn't build those ships for show. If they have them, then there is an expectation somewhere that either they need them, or they will use them. According to the notes, legend says they have eight of the biggest. Correct, Nam?"

Heather felt the woman cringe just a little, but this was her first staff planning meeting with the big players. Before, it had been political, but they'd just spent fifteen minutes hearing Leyla give a complete rundown on the scans she and her staff had taken of *Zhang Gualao*.

Scary scan results.

"That is our understanding, First Centurion," Nam said carefully. "Obviously, nobody has ever seen all of them, but rumors are pretty consistent. This is the first time a ship such as that has ever traveled to *Aditi*."

"There you go," Phil agreed. "Eight Immortals. Eight Jùrén, the colossal spacemecha they treat like dreadnoughts. I will presume squadrons of the smaller ones, although that's got to look weird in flight. Maybe like an army of infantry storming across a field to get to you. But they seem friendly. Do not assume harmless, but also don't provoke them. Am I clear?"

Nods, but Heather wasn't surprised. She'd have anybody's head if they did something stupid at this point.

"Okay, so messages have been sent," Heather turned the conversation. "We invited *Morninghawk* personally, but the Shogun might send someone else instead or in addition. *Gloran* will send something, because my understanding is that they live for combat as a culture. *Ewin* will take a while both in flight and picking someone. But we're in business, and we need to figure out what we're going to do with such a force."

She grinned and confirmed the smiles and nods around her. Everyone was on board.

NINETEEN

YARMOUTH CARRIER AGGREGATOR

Basant noted that the floor was a little rougher to the touch than others he'd fought on. Better friction when you needed to move and maneuver quickly.

Other duels he'd fought in his time had been on simple decks, with diamond grates raised. This floor had an extra coating of sand or something. He wondered if this was designed for fighting as some sort of spectator sport, but Basant hadn't really spent a lot of time on *Aggregator* in the past. Dock and resupply occasionally, but usually he'd been flying between *Ingham* bases. *Tango* didn't maraud. That was for Raiders and Pickets.

He enforced the will of the Board of Directors. And occasionally punished punks who got out of line.

Today, he was fighting literally for the future of their kind, because he knew that Zemke would go back to the old status quo and hold on as long as he could while everything burned around him. And then the ruffian would retire somewhere quiet and leave all the rest of them holding the bag like a pig in a poke.

That just frosted Basant an extra layer.

The temperature in here was turned up a shade from the rest

of the ship station. Lighting was better than normal as well, with floods and spots on all sides of the square room brightening things. The space was big enough to hold forty easily, but only captains were allowed at this event. Others would just have to wait for someone to emerge with the news.

Basant didn't figure they would both be walking out of here alive. Zemke was the kind of turd who would chop Basant's head off so he could collect the reward. Basant didn't figure it would be safe letting that old man run around afterwards poisoning minds with some conservative viewpoint about not changing with the coming future.

Fool.

They were both stripped down to shirts and pants. Heavy boots that seemed to be a standard thing among their kind. Basant was wearing gray. Zemke was in black.

That even felt right, all things considered.

Witnesses stood around the outside of a big circle marked on the floor with paint. Basant could hear wagers flowing back and forth. Not just winners, but time, blood, and whatever else they could put money on.

This was likely the biggest entertainment event any of them had ever seen. All had fought at least one duel. Some of them many, depending on how well they could command a crew.

But this would be two captains. Two Enforcer captains, at that.

And it would be for the future of the Cluster, as near as he could see it.

There was an avalanche just starting at the top of the hill. Like all pirates, Zemke seemed to assume that he'd be able to either ride it out when it arrived, or scamper off to safety.

Basant Utkin had seen the future. There was no place for the armed Syndicates. The law and the merchants just needed enough firepower to stop them. And that was coming. *Ewin* was already doomed. *Dalou* might be as well.

What would that leave?

Aditi and *Gloran*, but the latter was the piss-poor neighbor who would either rise to the occasion or fold. And nobody knew what *Yaumgan* was about.

Captain Dexter had been deputized for this one. *Aggregator* was his ship, after all, so he had the last word anyway. Not as big as the other two. Probably smarter, since he'd gone into the R&R business early on and just charged people for hotel facilities.

Basant studied the man and wondered if his own entire life had been mistake. Not a pleasant feeling.

"Captain Utkin, your honor has been challenged," Dexter called, getting the rowdies around the room to finally shut up. "Has Captain Zemke offered apology?"

"He has not," Basant called, turning his eyes on the old man with the knife over there.

"Captain Zemke, do you wish to apologize to Captain Utkin before this is settled in combat?" Dexter asked him now.

"I do not," Zemke growled.

"Captains, honor cannot be satisfied any other way than blood," Dexter announced. "I call on the audience to hear this challenge. Will it be to the blood, the wound, or the death?"

Basant just snarled silently at Zemke. Victory was victory, as far as he was concerned, but Zemke finally seemed to smell something different in the air.

The future, maybe?

"What will it be, Utkin?" he roared. "Are you a coward or a man?"

"You are the past, Zemke!" Basant answered. "Let it die with you."

Because if he was dead right now, the rest of the people in here would probably turn on Andrea and kill her, thinking that they could buy Kosnett off. Not one of them understood the truth.

Aditi might be satisfied. *Aquitaine* was a new order.

It was tomorrow coming.

"Captains, this fight will be to the death," Dexter announced in a grave voice.

But he probably had cameras on this from all sides and would be able to sell the footage on the black market tomorrow. Maybe the open market.

Was there ever going to be anything more entertaining?

Basant stepped into the circle itself, from where his feet had been on the line. Zemke joined him a moment later. They both had straight knives today. Longer than something you wore on your belt for bravado or as a tool, but not a dress saber or anything prissy like that.

Thirty-six centimeters of quality steel, give or take, with a honed edge on one side, a finger's worth of reverse blade on the tip, and a spine half as wide as his small finger.

A fighting blade that wouldn't crack off if you crossed them. But not a sword. No fancy dojo budo here.

Two men, with different dreams and wildly varying understandings of what tomorrow brought.

Basant shifted down and sideways into a fighting crouch. Watched Zemke do the same.

They were well balanced in size, in reach, and in intellect. Basant didn't think the old man really had the fire in his belly anymore. This was more like one last chance to stick it to an old enemy, with a grudge going back more than a decade now.

Basant moved like a crab, shifting forward with his left foot, and then bringing his right and his blade forward. Zemke did the same.

Blades made this more than just a wrestling match. You could grapple, but you better have hold of a knife-bearing wrist when you did, or the other man would open you up. Gut you to bleed out on the floor.

End you.

At the same time, neither of them were dancers. Not like Mati or some of his men, who relied on speed and dexterity.

No, this was a clash of two titans, waddling up and

hammering on each other. Swords and shields would have made it perfect, if that sort of thing was still used. And it would have been loud as hell in here, even as the captains around the ring started yelling encouragement and profanities at the competitors.

Basant drew close enough to provoke a slash from his enemy. He watched the flinch outward before the tip of the blade snapped in like a whip, but he was already withdrawing from the feint.

Okay, first tell.

Rather than mimic the man, Basant jabbed straight out with his own blade, point first and snapped it back. Zemke evaded by shifting down and back. Awkward and you sacrificed the initiative.

Basant crept to his right rather than pursue the man. Who knew what tricks the two of them might have accumulated in a lifetime of combat with blades?

Zemke crab-walked forward instead of circling, like he intended to press Basant into the edge of the circle, where hostile hands outside the circle would shove him forward again, likely onto a waiting blade.

Basant smiled and crab-walked backwards with an extra skitter to his step. Like he was surprised and fearful. After all, Harper Zemke was a big, bad pirate.

Right?

Another slash, followed up by a hand grasping. Basant pivoted in reverse, pulling his right hand and blade back by moving his hips, to keep them away from Zemke's hand. At the same time, he just jabbed the man in the eye with a fist.

Not hard, as he couldn't step into it and was left-handed anyways, but it was a stinger of a blow. Rocked the punk backwards a little, because it had probably been years since he's been punched in the face.

Basant kept the rotation and stepped across and back now. Zemke recovered his equilibrium and found that he was backed to the edge of the circle instead, so he scuttled away like he'd just seen an eagle overhead.

Basant smiled. Zemke was linear. That was a second tell. Relied too much on size and mass to intimidate, and hadn't ever learned speed.

Never had to spar with Mati on a mat to keep their reflexes and fighting styles sharp. Basant kept Mati around because the man wanted to fly, rather than command, so challengers came from below him and had to deal with Mati first if they wanted something. Not exactly regulation pirate behavior, but Basant wasn't exactly an old stuck-in-the-mud, either.

He feinted a hard lunge at Zemke as the man settled his footing, just to spook him a little. You don't watch the hands. They lie. You pay attention to the triangle of hips and sternum to see how he'll move.

Zemke's flinch rocked him back onto his heels a little.

Basant wondered how long it had been since the man had actually fought someone. He looked rusty. Tired.

And it didn't feel like a trap. They exchanged slashes again, killing air but not drawing blood.

Basant saw a flicker of something in Zemke's eyes now as they circled. Not fear, exactly, but tiredness. Had Harper Zemke's ego gotten him into something bigger than he was prepared for?

Or maybe the punk had seen the future, but didn't have an escape pod, because he'd been expecting to be promoted to *Nagi*'s Board of Directors before this?

He didn't feel pity in that case, because that was a dead end for too many captains. Let the Board dangle the hint of a promotion to safety and wealth in front of you, maybe while paying your crew to challenge you and take the captain's seat from you.

Death claimed too many in this business.

Basant lunged and nearly lost fingers when Zemke taught him a new block counter by crossing his wrists on the inside. As it was, Zemke claimed first blood by nicking the inside of Basant's wrist. Barely enough to feel because the blades were so sharp. Hardly anything to bleed because that was a spot with bone and muscle unless you got lucky.

Down the highway rather than across the street when cutting, as the old adage went.

Basant withdrew and glanced enough to make sure he was fine. The crowd's noise doubled as they saw a drop of blood fall. Old man scored first and bets got paid off.

Basant circled and watched that triangle. Hands flickered out on both sides as they probed, but nothing significant.

Zemke decided to get reckless. That was the only way Basant could describe it. Maybe he was feeling those extra years, but he lunged forward now, stabbing rather than slashing. Basant flowed to his right and stabbed back, managing to catch the man on the upper arm with a kiss before he could rotate away.

Even blood. But Zemke didn't abate. He lurched forward again, as if trying to drive Basant back to the line.

Basant let the man herd him a little, eyes still on the triangle.

Zemke opened up his hips to slash. That was the tell. His right withdrew as his elbow came away from his body, as a prelude to a whipsnap of the forearm that would get the tip of the blade wide and snap it across Basant's hands or stomach.

Basant lunged forward, left forearm up and blocking. He knew he'd get cut badly, but not deep and his medbay was up to handling knife wounds like that. And he got lucky, catching Zemke committed to a slash, and hung the blade just before it started inward by getting a wrist against the cross guard. No leverage other than edge pressing flesh. Bloody, but not dangerous.

Dangerous was the stab going into Zemke's stomach where he had opened himself too slowly. Basant felt muscles tear under his blade and then rocked it up and backwards to pull. Rather than grapple with the man now, he leapt back and to the side as far as planted feet would let him.

Zemke smiled for a moment before looking down in surprise. And then the man collapsed wordlessly to the deck, a pool of blood already spreading.

Basant drew a hard breath inward and realized that he'd gotten perfectly lucky with the blow. It looked like he'd severed the main artery coming down out of the heart. At the speed it was racing, Harper Zemke was already bleeding out on the floor, but nobody was about to jump in to save him.

This fight had been to the death, as they had agreed.

Zemke curled into a ball of surprised pain with a gurgle and Basant stepped another meter to his left, looking at his own cuts. Not even as bad as he'd initially thought, because he'd gotten the knife on the way out rather than tried to block Harper's strength slashing inward. Maybe a dozen staples and a tube of medglue, and he'd be in a working cast for a few weeks.

Way better than surgery to reattach muscles and tendons.

The noise had surged, but not fell to nothing. Shock that it was over that quickly, but that was the emotion. They'd been dancing for several minutes and Basant felt like he'd been digging gravel for several hours now as his whole frame complained.

The sand on the floor seemed to be absorbing the blood, but not fast enough as Zemke died. Dexter stepped into the ring now and waved his hands.

"Captains, challenge has been met and concluded," he yelled. "Honor has been satisfied. Captain Utkin, do you have any message for your fellows?"

Basant rotated slowly, making eye contact with everyone.

"Tomorrow, we're going to talk about what we can do to preserve ourselves from the law," he announced. "If you don't think they're coming for you next, undock tonight and run. If you think you can retire and hide, undock and run. If you think your Boards of Directors will somehow cut a deal with *Aditi* and *Aquitaine* that doesn't involve you going to prison for the rest of your life, undock and run. Otherwise, tomorrow morning we'll start planning our future."

He handed the bloody knife to Andrea as she stepped close and nodded to her. She was the one who Kosnett really wanted. The captain who'd tried to kill *Vilahana*. But she'd done it because he asked her to. Ordered, really.

And they would all hang separately when this was over, if they didn't watch for each other together.

TWENTY

Captain Makara Omarov, commander of the *Dalou Hegemony* Heavy Escort *Morninghawk*, was finally home. Home home, even, and not just back in Dalou territory. After the mind-boggling events from his various encounters at Vilahana, he needed some calmness.

A year ago, Makara wouldn't have believed any such a tall tale as a ship moving a small moon out of orbit on a collision path, using nothing but their engines.

And their supreme obstinacy that it could be done. The *Republic of Aquitaine* had reshaped all of the Balhee Cluster twice. First, by merely arriving. Then, by doing the utterly impossible so easily as to be frightening.

He was home now, hoping that he could recover his equilibrium. Today was not going to be that day.

Makara studied the summons again, as if a second reading would make any more sense than the first. It did not. He glanced up at the messenger, but that man merely stared at him impassively.

Imperial messenger, at that. Wearing black trimmed with the maroon of the Shogun's house.

Makara glanced around the small space, confirming that he was alone this morning, at his home port station, kneeling quietly in a small, private tearoom reserved for senior members of the Sugawara clan. Before him, a low table with a pot of tea on a candle and a tray of dim sum that had been delivered earlier.

Not all that far from his personal quarters, but remote enough that he could be alone. The ship was undergoing resupply prior to the next mission, and he had a few days to himself.

Or had.

Before this messenger had arrived with such disturbing news. The man was a nobody. A courier assigned the task of finding Captain Omarov and handing him a small tube sealed with wax in the ancient style and shipped across light-years to find him.

Makara nodded to the man and watched him withdraw quickly and silently, sliding the shoji shut and leaving Makara alone with tea suddenly too cold. Or maybe that was him.

He studied the calligraphy on the outside of the tube, almost afraid that it might bite him. He opened the tube again to check, but the single page of elegant handwriting was enough. It left him wondering if he was doomed.

How many captains received a sudden summons from the Shogun to attend them on *Ellariel?* Makara read it a third time, then unfolded his legs and grabbed a handful of dim sum barehanded, stuffing them in his mouth and chewing furiously as he wiped a sweaty palm on a napkin and organized himself.

He had been planning a simple day. Most of his crew had shore leave on the station as the vessel underwent maintenance, so he was in the Sugawara clan quarters section of the station. Better to be out of their way, both at work as well as at play. Close to his apartment.

Makara considered his attire. Pants and a nice, belted half-kimono, both black though far too informal for the meeting he needed to have next. It would just have to do. He ran a hand down his front to get off any crumbs and then wiped his hands on the back of his pants before slicking his hair back.

He was a grown adult. Why did he feel like a teenager called to the carpet for some forgotten prank that had finally caught up with him?

No answer. Not that he expected one. He stuffed the missive into the tube, then the tube into his half-kimono, and departed rapidly, heading back towards the main Sugawara palace section of the station. Not fleeing his fate, but not lingering in case anything was chasing him.

Makara quickly made his way to the hatch to his father's compound and paused to breathe before signaling the chime. It opened quickly and he was brought inside.

Had they been warned? Normally, he was an honored guest rather than family, according to custom that saw him as a grown adult son. He could have expected to be made to wait a time while Father got organized, even if Makara had been invited. To arrive unannounced might leave him in a waiting room for an hour or longer. Instead, Makara found himself being ushered directly into the arboretum. Not as grand or complex as Kosnett's, but still a greater statement of purpose, to have built and maintained such a thing on an orbital station.

Lingyi Omarov looked up from a small table where he knelt, next to the still pond, almost a perfect mirror of how Makara had been enjoying his tea not ten minutes before.

"Come, sit," Father instructed him, gesturing to a second pad on the small slab of stone amidst grass and low bushes.

Makara noted a second mug for tea, already poured and probably too hot to touch.

He knelt across the low table and composed himself.

"Thank you for seeing me," he began before faltering.

Lingyi nodded.

"There is news?" Father asked, with a decided twinkle in his eyes.

Makara swallowed and nodded.

"I have received a summons," he replied, trying to keep the emotion out of his voice.

Damn it. Forty-three and I feel fourteen again.

Makara crushed that moment and powered past it.

"It is from *Ellariel* itself," he continued. "Signed by the Shogun's hand directly."

"That is indeed interesting," Father observed. "What shall you do?"

"Call on him at Court," Makara replied simply. "One does not challenge the supreme authority without great grounds. I have none. But at the same time, I have no idea what might have brought my name to such a man's attention."

Lingyi studied him for a long second before smiling.

"I might have an idea," Father offered obliquely, waiting for another moment before continuing. "My own spies at Court sent a message that might have traveled on the same vessel as the one delivered to you just now."

"What?" Makara demanded, shocked almost senseless by the words.

"A messenger arrived from *Aditi*," Father said. "Speaking in the name of First Centurion Kosnett, the alien of whom you have spoken to me, the *Consensus* invited the *Dalou Hegemony* to join a force dedicated to anti-piracy measures against the Syndicate that attempted to destroy *Vilahana*. Specifically, they asked for *Morninghawk* and Captain Makara Omarov."

"But why?" Makara asked. "I was not particularly friendly with the man."

"Perhaps that was why," Father replied. "It may be that you impressed him in other ways. We cannot know without asking, so the Shogun has seen fit to demand the same answers from you, most likely."

"Do we have dealings with the *Ingham Syndicate*?" Makara asked now, concerned.

"We do not," Lingyi acknowledged with a wry grin. "There have been other deals with other groups, but none that will bring dishonor if you are asked to destroy this particular group of pirates."

"And the others?" Makara pressed.

"Ours is an internal prefecture in *Dalou*," Lingyi reminded him with a hard smile now. "We are far from that long wall of empty stars that surrounds us. Thus, we deal mostly with smugglers here, rather than enemy warships. As such, *Morninghawk* is an excellent ship for our tasks, and its commander part of my great pride in protecting Sugawara."

"Your pride?" Makara gasped. "Father, never have you spoken so."

"I understand," Lingyi bowed his head with a serious face. "It is perhaps not correct for a father to acknowledge such a thing publicly. Especially with a fourth son, who is always going to be considered unlucky, just as an eighth, had I such, would be the reverse. But I am."

Makara blinked and reconsidered his interactions with the man over the last thirty years. Had he always been proud and unable to speak it?

"I wanted you to know, before facing the Shogun," Father said now, smiling even.

"Father?"

"The Fourth is traditionally considered unlucky because in the ancient tongue *four* and *death* sounded alike," he said. "*Eight* and *luck* were also homonyms. But as you head to Court, I want you to remember that death can be a positive thing. You are a warrior, and this is a call to war, so you will represent Sugawara as well as Omarov. And perhaps even *Dalou* itself."

He fell silent at that and Makara did the same. Numbly, he reached for his tea, unconcerned at this point that he might burn his hand, only to discover that it was the perfect temperature.

As if Father had planned this morning like a military campaign.

But then, in his day the man had commanded the famous war cruiser *Wraithruin* itself to great acclaim.

Makara sipped his tea and wondered what other surprises the galaxy held for a Fourth Son.

TWENTY-ONE

Phil noted the latest in-system arrival with something of a grin and a snort when Heather forwarded Leyla's rather rude note.

****-Ewin sent something calling itself a light missile bombard. Didn't anybody warn those dipshits?-****

Not the most politic thing to say, but it was also something that would stay internal. He turned to the scan log attached, as well as notes from Kaur Singh's original description of the various naval forces of Balhee.

Light Missile Bombard. The name had chilling connotations, but not to an *Expeditionary* fleet such as his. It looked fragile, but the vessel was intended to stand off at considerable distance and unleash waves upon waves of missiles, each charging down at a target. In this case, twelve tubes in sets of four around the rim of the secondary hull.

Phil also wondered at the sly connotations of the name of the ship. *Shadowbolt,* which was an interesting euphemism for a wall of arrows, according to Kaur Singh from another note. As the *Dalou Hegemony* tended to use compound names for ships ending in all kinds of birds, they might take exception to arrows.

At the same time, Phil wasn't sure what *Morninghawk* might do against that many incoming missiles.

He hadn't heard back yet from the *Dalou Hegemony*, but Phil also understood that he'd thrown a fox into a henhouse just a bit by inviting Omarov rather than whoever was the Shogun's current favorite, as he had done with the others.

"What's so funny?" Harinder asked from across the table. He was out in the main flag bridge today, in between meetings as it was something of a weekend on the planet below and he didn't feel like doing the tourist thing.

Rather than speak, he just forwarded the note and listened as she snorted under her breath. He agreed with her assessment.

"But then, it's not like we said anything other than to send a cruiser-class hull to assist," Phil mused aloud. "*Gloran* did that, sending *Juvayni* to blow things up."

"Their idea of a Command Battlecruiser and mine are somewhat at odds, Phil," she noted in a tart voice, before dissolving into a fit of giggles that he matched.

"You almost said that with a straight face," he offered when they stopped.

"Almost," she agreed. "What do we do with them all? This isn't a battlefleet. It's a three-ring circus."

"True," he said. "But it gives us options. *Gloran* culture is all about rushing into combat, either solo or as part of a wolfpack of similar vessels, so *Juvayni* is geared for that. *Ewin* likes to stand off with missiles and small fighter craft like we used to do, so *Shadowbolt* could sit on a flank and provide cover for others or just overload a smaller ship. *Morninghawk*, if that's who we get, is more of a pure escort, so could sit close in like a phalanx vessel and either attack or defend."

"And *Zhang Gualao*?" Harinder asked.

"I'm still hoping we get something smaller," Phil grunted. "It's too big for what I have in mind."

"Which is?" Harinder pressed. "Today, I mean."

He grinned at her. Each time the situation changed, his needs and responses changed with it.

"They'd just run from a *Jùrén*, most likely," Phil said. "Remember, *Tango* is a big ship for them, and it's a light cruiser to us. *Juvayni* is probably their idea of our old *Admiral*-class battlecruisers, but a *Founder* Heavy could take it apart, one on one. If *Zhang Gualao* was there, I expect any pirate to just run like hell and damn the consequences. And I have no interest right now in explaining to these folks how to break JumpSpace with one of Lady Moirrey's supermines. Not while they still have a piracy problem as they do. That's like pouring a trail of honey from the anthill to the picnic."

Harinder shrugged. He shrugged as well. It was nice having the biggest sledgehammer around, but only if the nails would stand still to be driven into the wood. He doubted that they would be so helpful.

"Still, First Centurion's compliments and all that," Phil said. "Welcome them and send the standard information packet they need so they can follow along at home. Hopefully, our other two invitees will join us shortly and we can formalize a big dinner for everyone."

Wild cards. All of them. But he'd known that. This was an exercise in political treaty-building, as much as it was pirate hunting. However, if he could get them to see the pirates as enemies of civilization instead of a cost of doing business, Phil knew he'd be able to sit back and let them do most of the work.

And he had a lot of work ahead.

TWENTY-TWO

ELLARIEL-JO ORBITAL PALACE

Makara walked precisely, surrounded on all sides by the Shogun's Guards in their dress armor that somehow combined the most modern accessories with the most ancient appearance, down to the masks that obscured all faces, from *sōmen*-style to *happuri*.

The palace was someplace he'd never been. Even the system itself. The Emperor had a glorious compound on the planet below where his entire family lived in secluded comfort. (One did not call them hostages out loud.) The Shogun held all power, and presided over the Hegemony from the skies.

Morninghawk had been parked nearby, under the unwavering attention of two separate battleships and their escort squadrons. Overkill, but perhaps something of a political statement.

Who was this Omarov punk to have drawn the attention of the foreigners, and what dishonor has he brought upon the realm?

Makara kept his face calm and stiff. Unlike many of the courtiers he could see, he wore no makeup, and his dress uniform was positively mundane compared to the fine silk robes around him. His was merely a black half-kimono in silk and matching pants, all trimmed in emerald.

But he was a captain of a warship, and not one of these people. Hell, he was not even directly serving in the Shogun's armies, but instead was a the son of minor holder of a regional *Komyo* who owed allegiance and could be called up to service in time of war.

It was a style of government older than space flight, but it worked.

They came to a door. Up until now, the hallways had been ornate and pretty, but still functional steel decorated with art on the walls or objects on pedestals. But these doors were a statement.

This was a space station, so space was always at something of a premium, and the foyer into which he'd been led was seventeen meters tall at the peak. The twin doors that formed this airlock were four meters wide and at least nine tall, retracting sideways into the bulkhead as he stood at attention in the calm center of a dozen armed killers.

The chamber beyond belonged on a planetary surface. The seventeen-meter ceilings fled away upward into the gloom as he was led inside, until it was something closer to thirty-four meters above him at the beam, with great, arching spans of alloy holding things in place and obscuring balconies where one might watch from privacy.

The floor itself could have held sporting events, perfectly flat and stretching to what felt like infinity in all directions. Tiles had been painted in place, but the surface was still steel.

Much gold and some silver had been worked into almost every vertical surface, with the crimson of the Shogun's house —*Kugosu*—on the rest. Makara wore the Sugawara colors, black with green lacing and highlights, as befitted calling on the Supreme Authority. At the same time, he knew practically nothing about the man himself.

Supposedly a security thing, to keep the Court safe from assassins and other misfits. All Makara knew was that the man had ruled for more than ten years now, having inherited from his own uncle upon that man's death.

The troopers brought him to a spot from which loud conversation could be had, assuming good acoustics. The Shogun sat seiza on the cold, steel floor, alone at the center of a wide dais, kneeling with the pommel of a sword on his hip, resting up five shallow steps from the floor.

At some unknown signal, the dozen guards around him split, with half moving forward and pivoting to join the score at the bottom of the steps and the rest moving out to flanks. There were at least one hundred warriors around him now.

Makara Omarov found himself standing alone before his Lord and Commander, the only man in the room without a weapon on him. He bowed at the waist, held it the requisite amount of time, and rose, falling into a parade rest as a loyal soldier of the man.

Close enough, anyway.

The Shogun rose now, fluidly as one who trains on the dojo floor daily. Makara did not, but knew some of his own crew who did, and the grace was similar. The man wore dress armor like his soldiers, but without the helmet, letting Makara draw conclusions.

Fifty, give or take, with hair cut bristle short and more than half iron gray now. It was a strong, wide face with a big nose jutting out of the center, balanced by a jaw that might have been squared by a geometer with a plane.

Dark eyes bored in on him as the man took two strides to the front of the dais but did not descend.

They were perhaps six meters apart now, with a wall of crimson and silver killers between them.

"*Morninghawk*," the Shogun said simply.

Makara bowed his head as a nod of acknowledgment. That was his place in the greater scheme of things, at the end of the day. Fourth Son of an Omarov lord. Part of Sugawara Clan. A citizen of *Dalou*. One of this man's people.

But *Morninghawk.*

"Strangers come to our lands," the Shogun said now in a voice more conversational than Makara has expected. The acoustics in here must have been designed by a zen master, to achieve such utter perfection. "They have made many waves. Now, one asks for you by name."

Makara nodded again. He was here to answer questions, not to engage the man in a dialogue.

"What did *Morninghawk* do at Vilahana?" the Shogun asked now.

"Observe, Lord," Makara replied. "When the Syndicates and other nations sent diplomats to meet with the First Centurion, *Dalou* held itself aloof, so it was incumbent upon me to learn what I could of them and report such findings to the Hegemony."

And he had. Many reports. Scan logs. Observations. Official correspondence. Notes of meetings. Even the results of Kosnett's grand assembly of folks to talk trade.

"There are reports that *Aquitaine* is a threat to the Cluster," the man stated. "What say you?"

Makara had spent much time on the flight here asking himself that very question.

"Kosnett is more powerful than anyone else here," Makara replied. "He could be overwhelmed by sheer numbers, but might return later with sufficient force to have his way. I do not think conquest is his goal."

"And yet he proclaims the desire to eliminate *Ingham*?"

"*Aquitaine* remembers the ancient Great War," Makara replied. "And another such monster as the ancients attacked the *Fribourg Empire* capital world just under a decade ago. They nearly destroyed the planet with an anti-matter bomb beyond anything we could build. Kosnett was furious at *Ingham*, and will stop at nothing before he destroys them. That he has asked the Five Nations to join him I think elevates us to potential allies in a future he would like to create for the Cluster."

"One where the *Aditi Consensus* dominates?"

"Only by geography, Supreme Leader," Makara answered. "*Yaumgan* has technology other nations cannot match. *Dalou* has many stars into which we could expand, should we choose, that would make us the eventual match of *Aditi*."

"And the pirates who have claimed them?" the man scowled.

"They are your worlds, Lord," he said carefully. "Your subsidiary Clans lack the standing to grant those people permission to colonize one. Even *Aditi* does not establish colonies, even when they push other boundaries to establish trade and mining outposts. The worlds themselves remain pristine. We could make use of them, if we chose."

"But the pirates?"

Makara wasn't sure where the line of questioning was going. There were a handful of bureaucrats off to one side, but only watching. He and the Shogun might have been alone in here and not much would change.

"We trade with merchants," Makara stated, deflecting the conversation hopefully onto safer ground. "If some of them prey on shipping at other times, perhaps it would benefit all if such costs were eliminated. That way more revenue might then flow into your Treasury."

He had no idea how expensive it was to run the Hegemony, but he'd also never met a politician who thought he had enough money, his own father included.

The Shogun grunted but didn't say anything.

"This Kosnett asks the others for cruisers, even as he asks for you by name," he said abruptly. "*Morninghawk* is but a Heavy Escort."

Makara bowed his head again.

"I am a Fourth Son, Lord, and thus unfavored by the Gods," he said, as if nobody had likely done that much research. "My brothers have such greater commands, but *Morninghawk* has always been sufficient for my purposes, which are to protect

Sugawara shipping from marauders, rather than to engage in war games with others."

Who the others might be, he left off. Clans squabbled within and without. *Dalou* Daimyo and Komyo on the outs with the Shogun might retreat into the wilderness for a while, being rebels until they could make amends, form marriage alliances, or simply got hunted down.

And that broad swath of stars might include renegades from other places as well, with many Syndicates taking advantage of the quiet, just as *Gloran* rebels from their own Emperor often joined them there to plot.

Such was the mess of worms that filled the Balhee Cluster.

The Shogun watched him for a time. Makara stayed calm and watched the man back.

"I will send you to Kosnett," he finally announced.

Makara did not blow out a heavy sigh, but he felt it. This meeting, this interview could have gone any of several ways, including proscribing him as an outlaw and throwing him in prison for whatever sins the man imagined Makara might have committed.

The laws frequently were what the Shogun decided they were. That was why he was the Shogun of *Dalou*.

"Thank you, Lord," Makara bowed at the waist again.

"But I will sent a personal representative with *Morninghawk*," the man followed up.

Makara didn't let the fear or disappointment show on his face either. He had no choice in the matter.

None, whatsoever.

TWENTY-THREE

Phil looked up when Markus opened the hatch to his office and stuck his head on.

"Surprise meeting," the man said. "But you've got space on your calendar right now."

Phil studied his redneck for a long moment without commenting. Markus Dunklin was many things, but dumb wasn't one of them. If he thought this was something that needed the First Centurion's personal attention, he was probably right.

And Phil could always yell at him later if he'd guessed wrong.

So Phil was shocked when *Stunt Dude* walked in and came to something like parade rest, rather than just lounging in a chair. The man was a civilian, and occasionally took pains to remind everyone of that.

Markus closed the door like hounds were chasing him.

"Sit," Phil said. "I can't court martial you without first activating your commission, and it can't be that bad. Can it?"

Trinidad grinned and sat.

"Probably," the man offered ambiguously.

But then, they both knew ambiguity. If Heather had been

his First Officer in those days, Trinidad Mildon had been his Dragoon. And they were all pirates, with Markus thrown in.

"What drags you up out of your dojo and gym?" Phil asked.

"Rumors and innuendo," *Stunt Dude* replied with a smile.

"Spill."

"You asked folks to send you firepower to go hunt pirates," Trinidad said. "And you're getting some, from what I've heard through the rumor mill. But it got me to thinking about what you might be doing with it."

Phil had been reading reports and checking boxes. He slid his tablet off to one side now so he could rest his elbows on the desk.

"Oh?" Phil asked, wondering what news had made it to the lower decks.

Stunt Dude was one of the few people with the experience to understand and possibly anticipate things.

"Cruisers are designed to go a long distance," Trinidad offered. "As are all our ships. Lean crew and high automation from what we used to do when I first joined. But the pirates are all frigates and destroyers for the most part. And your big target is a light cruiser at best."

"Good initial assessment," Phil prompted when the man lapsed into thought.

"You could take just *Viking* and three corvettes and smash the shit out of any pirates short of a major sector base," *Stunt Dude* continued. "*Urumchi* could probably handle that task by itself, maybe with the other four. And that's just all wrong if you throw in five mismatched warships. Even if you could train them up to work as a team, they're too much. The pirates would just run like hell, and I doubt they are dumb enough to build a base without engines. Maybe a monitor or a drydock they could fly slowly."

"Yes," Phil agreed. "Hints and suggestions from *Aditi* suggest the same. They run from us."

"And they know the terrain better than we do, so they get

away unless you manage to do something like Keller's impossibly high-speed strafing drops out of JumpSpace at the edge of the gravity well and let the Type-4s light somebody up hard enough to force a surrender," Trinidad nodded. "Every fool and captain in the Cluster is going to do the same math and scratch their heads."

"So what does an *Aquitaine* pirate do?" Phil grinned at the man now.

"I think he adds a corvette to each of those five ships he recruited," *Stunt Dude* turned serious. "Keeps one back for *Urumchi* and another for *Viking*, and eventually sends out seven petite task forces hunting. You drop into a system and scare anybody away, while you have ships in nearby systems ready to pounce on someone who thought they got away. If you nail them the second time, the trick works until somebody's spies finally get word out. I assume during a resupply run, or something."

"You sure you don't want to come back into service, Trinidad?" Phil asked, serious now. "You've just about nailed it on the head. The only part you missed was where I ask everyone to stage whatever reloads they need on *Mexicali* and *Ensenada* so that we can handle food and weapons on the first cycle without those spies."

The man fell silent and Phil just watched whatever internal conversation he was having before he continued.

"No," *Stunt Dude* finally said. "But I think it would be a good thing if I did volunteer to help. You're going to have corvettes traveling with these cruisers, but you'd do better if you had someone aboard each ship as a liaison. Like Nam Nagarkar is doing here. I can do that."

Phil considered it. Thought hard. *Stunt Dude* had been part of that original team that *Lady Blackbeard*, Siobhan Skokomish, had taken when he sent them out to capture that first ship, *Queen Anne's Revenge*. The one that became the start of his pirate fleet.

"As a civilian?" Phil confirmed.

"Yes," *Stunt Dude* said. "It will remind them that we are not all warriors here. And my wife isn't even from *Aquitaine*, when you get down to it."

"Have you told Sam what you intend?" Phil asked now.

Sam Au would have to give permission, simple as that.

"I have," he grinned. "It was actually more her idea than mine, as she suggested that I could do more with my life than entertain her and train your marines."

"As long as I'm not going to get on her bad side by accepting," Phil confirmed. "Welcome aboard."

TWENTY-FOUR

AMBASSADORIAL QUARTERS, ADITI

Hu Yating Kai, Ambassador to the Barbarians though he would never say that out loud, regardless of what his peers at *Yaumgan* thought, considered his situation.

The First Centurion had done him a great honor by coming here, rather than insisting that Yating Kai call upon him in space aboard his great warship. Yating wasn't sure that it wouldn't have been better to tour that great ship again, but he had learned much in his time at *Aditi* and various meetings. At least as much as a stranger from *Aquitaine* had.

It was good.

They were relaxed, if you could say such a thing. Kosnett had left his warriors out in the hall, guarding even as Yating's own were doing the same. He had brought instead his Captain, the warrior Lau, rather than his right hand, the other warrior woman Abbatelli.

Hu Yating Kai had the captain of *Zhang Gualao* here, Lin Na Tai, but that was because she was assigned as his personal transport until he returned home. Indeed, she had just returned from *Yaumgan*, and brought with her the warrior that would be assigned to Kosnett's mission, the Dà or Skycruiser vessel *Li Jing*, under the command of Xue Dao Zhiou.

Captain Xue wasn't a woman he knew personally, but she came with a good reputation. And Yating still chuckled occasionally that the elders had picked a vessel commanded by a woman, when everyone else in the Balhee Cluster except *Aditi* tended towards a broad male chauvinism that was perhaps unconscious.

How could you build a society if you ignored half of your population?

They were seated casually around the great room now, the five of them, rather than at a table. Sipping a truly excellent scotch-style whiskey that Kosnett had brought him as a welcoming gift.

"First Centurion, if I may?" Xue asked now, as conversation had reached one of those lulls you got when intelligent people had rational discourse on a variety of topics and then paused to process what they had heard.

Kosnett nodded to the woman. Waited patiently.

Yes, that was what marked the man different. Even in *Yaumgan*, there was a tendency to talk more as one grew in rank and prestige, until you at times simply walked over one of a lower rank conversationally.

Kosnett listened. Lau did as well, though she might command the single most powerful vessel in the entire Cluster, not counting certain experimental weapon facilities back home that never left the *Yaumgan Domain* itself.

The strangers did not speak first, hardly ever. There was much to learn from that, as they themselves learned from the people of the Cluster.

Yating made a mental note to share that observation with Na Tai and Dao Zhiou later.

"You will hunt the brigands, First Centurion," Captain Xue said now. "*Li Jing* is more powerful than any pirate vessel. Do we need an escort?"

Hu Yating Kai watched the man formulate an answer.

"I was alone and trapped behind enemy lines," Kosnett said

now. "My JumpSails had suffered a spectacular, catastrophic failure that could not be repaired, but my squadron could not return to look for me, as we had just conducted one of the greatest raids ever on *Buran*. Heather and I, along with our crew, had to limp home on fragile backups, but we decided to first make a terrible war on our enemy, stealing his ships and cargo, as well as doing great material damage to his ability to threaten my allies."

Yating nodded. He had gotten parts of that story from Kosnett and his people directly, and others from spies in the *Consensus* who were still amazed. Astounded, truth be told.

"We will be off doing strange things, and moving quickly," Kosnett continued now. "I do not wish any ship to suffer the isolation and risk we did, especially as you will be hunting pirates and they might not welcome your appearance, however accidental it might be were you to suffer a similar problem. Here, at a minimum, someone can run for help."

"I see," Captain Xue said solemnly. "Will the pirates be greatly offended?"

"I intend to end their way of life," the First Centurion turned serious now. "If they choose to fight me to the death for the privilege, that is their right. Or their destiny. Others might simply give up the gun and return to trade, and thus most would be safe from my wrath."

"Most," Xue nodded. "How soon will we train with your ships?"

"I await only the representative of *Dalou*, but there is no reason you could not depart with *CB-502* and conduct some training exercises immediately if you chose," Kosnett said.

"I note," Yating spoke up now, waiting for all eyes to turn to him. "Of your escorts, one is called a type Command in *CC-501*. One is a minesweeper in *CM-507*. Four are Guardians with a CG designation. Why assign *CB-502*, the one called a Battle Corvette, to work with *Li Jing*?"

Kosnett smiled, as if he had been expecting the question.

"I want the biggest hammer in one place," he replied. "*Viking* and *Urumchi* are both quite heavy, to the point that my officers have side bets going as to whether or not *Zhang Gualao* is more powerful. *Li Jing* is likely the most powerful of the cruisers joining us, so it makes the most sense to have my heaviest corvette flying with them. Especially so as you are likely to fly into the heart of a battle almost as quickly as the *Gloran* battlecruiser *Juvayni*, under Captain Khan."

"You expect battle?" Captain Xue asked. "This much assembled firepower might be able to conquer worlds."

"Aye, but it could not hold them," Kosnett replied sagely, showing a greater wisdom than Yating had expected. "Jessica Keller actually conquered a *Fribourg* world in *Thuringwell* and held it, but I have no interest, even if I did have the resources. What is more likely is that one of the teams will stumble into a base of some sort and have the choice to attack or flee. *CB-502* and *Li Jing* are much better equipped to do that if they have an opening."

Yating smiled and nodded. This man had read many of the great treatises on military theory, that much was obvious. But he had also understood the oblique approach to fighting. Seduce your enemy onto bad ground, pivot him into a bad position, and attack him from a weak flank.

Yes, that would work.

"When this portion of your mission is complete, First Centurion, it would be my great pleasure to host you on a visit to *Yaumgan*," Yating said as the others nodded.

"I look forward to it, Ambassador Hu," Kosnett replied.

Yating wanted the others to meet the man in the flesh. To take his measure.

Philip S. Kosnett just might be able to pull all this off.

Then what?

TWENTY-FIVE

AMBASSADORIAL QUARTERS, ADITI

Yating had sent Captain Xue back to her ship, currently standing on a pad at the far south edge of the space port like a statue, with instructions to learn as much as she could about *Aquitaine* while training with this Command Centurion Erle Kuiper who commanded Kosnett's fiercest hound.

He was alone now in his receiving room with Na Tai.

Captain Xue was the older woman, but that was a mark of how exceptional Na Tai, Captain Lin, really was.

"You are having second thoughts?" she asked, sipping at more of Kosnett's excellent whiskey after the outsiders had left.

Yating shrugged.

"He is not a barbarian, for all that he likes to present himself as one occasionally," he said carefully. "But he is not working to destroy the Cluster: ideologically, strategically, or even culturally."

"Is he not?" Na Tai asked now tartly. "What will we look like in a generation, if his is the impetus for the five nations to begin working together to end piracy and increase trade?"

"Perhaps a viable competitor to *Aquitaine* and *Fribourg*," Yating answered. "It is the time between now and then that concerns me. *Dalou* might survive such a cultural earthquake.

Gloran and *Ewin* will likely implode. That leaves *Aditi* to absorb them and grow perhaps large enough to be a threat to the *Domain*. Then the wider war we have been quietly trying to prevent draws us in, because it only takes one lucky charismatic leader rising to turn the *Consensus* from a trade federation into a predatory empire."

"We could defeat them," Na Tai said.

"Today, I would agree with you," Yating replied. "But what happens when *Aditi* synthesizes outsider technology with their own? When they build something like *Urumchi*, but it is not a survey dreadnought? And mind you, Kosnett has been open about how much firepower was removed from that design to make it a diplomatic courier. One only has to walk through the arboretum and imagine it filled with generators and emitters. The possibilities that they might have sent that other ship, the true dreadnought Kosnett called *Kongō*, that is what frightens me. Add in a Shield Generator to the thing called a Bubble Gun. Mount an entire suite of the Type-4 beams. Or worse, whatever that thing was that *Aquitaine* used to kill the ancient god *Buran* by cutting an orbital platform apart. What are we facing then?"

Na Tai shrugged, but she was a commander. An expert on combat and not a particularly technical officer. Nor one yet old enough to envision just how terrible a future could be.

That was his job.

"Will we have to conquer the cluster at some point?" she asked pointedly now. "Extend the *Domain* to encompass the others? Take *Aditi* before it grows large enough to be a threat? Break the others into fragments that represent no threat and no resistance?"

Yating grimaced. They were alone. The room was scanned for listening devices on a regular basis, using tools even *Aditi* wasn't aware of, as far as *Yaumgan*'s spies had been able to identify.

This conversation should be safe.

And yet…

Yating emptied the last drops of his whiskey and rose silently, holding a hand out to Na Tai. She drank quickly and rose, taking his hand in an uncertain way.

He led her deeper into the suite, into the areas where only his barely-visible aides and servants, all of them brought from home, were allowed to tread.

He even drew her unresistingly into her personal chambers, which would have been a gross breach of conduct without her assent, but he had no interest in seducing the woman. At least not today. That was not to suggest he wouldn't consider it when their roles were different.

She was an attractive woman, with a triangular face dominated by large eyes and prominent cheekbones. Short and muscular, like a swimmer or a gymnast. Brilliant enough to command one of the eight immortals at such a young age.

Yating dropped her hand now and gestured her to sit in the chair, while he moved to the end of the sleeping mat and sat as well.

Her face had gone through a wealth of emotions, settling now on a polite concern that was short of indignance that he had brought her here, so she was wise enough to understand how private this conversation must be.

"We are strangers to the Balhee Cluster originally," Yating reminded her. "Outsiders like Kosnett, but ones who came to conquer and hold our six worlds. If the locals our people originally captured are suppressed, they also have opportunities to excel now. But we have found that realm sufficient."

"And *Aquitaine?*" she asked now, showing more emotion.

"The combination of Kosnett with *Aditi* might pose enough of a threat that the *Domain* had to turn to a war footing again," he said simply. "Break all of them while our technology is still better. Whether we pick up the pieces later or not would be a conversation far above your pay grade, Captain. Those are the things I would talk about with the other timocrats, over good whiskey or wine."

"Do we trust Kosnett?" she asked.

"I don't know," he replied simply. "On the one hand, all players working for a common good makes the Cluster stronger, but as you noted, a generation hence we might be peers, and thus the Domain would be at risk of some fool with a battle fleet."

"Do we steal their technology?" Na Tai asked.

"Messages from home suggest that they are already preparing a formal embassy that will travel to the *Aquitaine* capital at *Ladaux*, specifically to open such conversations. They have leapt far ahead in the last generation, from where we remember them being a century ago or where they should be now. That suggests a technology breakthrough equivalent to a new Age on Human History, Na Tai."

"Can they be trusted with such power?" she asked, pressing her lips together.

"Can anyone?" he countered, falling into a Socratic method older than civilization. "Or will we be facing a war with them at some future point? The distance is great, and the entries into the Cluster are mostly known and defended, but right now something like the fabled *First Expeditionary Fleet* Kosnett mentioned could probably annihilate all naval forces in the cluster, including our own."

She gasped. But that was why they were in this room. Where things could be said in safety.

"What do we do?" she asked.

"We watch," he replied. "We send *Li Jing* with a reminder to learn just how powerful their new weapons and systems are."

"And then?"

"And then we prepare for the possibility of war with *Aquitaine*."

TWENTY-SIX

DATE OF THE REPUBLIC AUGUST 10, 411 RAN
URUMCHI, ADITI ORBIT

Stunt Dude emerged from the airlock to something of an honor guard and saluted them. Captain Xue was here, but her face was unreadable at present. Several of her officers as well, showing seriousness of purpose but not necessarily hostility.

He reminded himself that he had volunteered for *weird* with Phil, and the man had taken him up on it. Although, truth be told, Trinidad had expected to be assigned to the *Gloran* ship. Those folks were warriors first, heavy on personal honor occasionally resolved in close combat, but the famous *Stunt Dude* had gotten his start more than ten years ago training marines in the field.

Instead, he was aboard the *Yaumgan* Skycruiser *Li Jing* now, apparently named for some famous general in the ancient past of Earth.

"Welcome," Captain Xue said with a smile. Like she meant it.

"Thank you for accepting a stranger into your midst," *Stunt Dude* replied gravely, falling back into the formality he'd learned inside a dojo when he was twelve.

She smiled at that. Nodded even and gestured him to accompany her. They turned an arbitrary left and headed forward, although it took him a bit to wrap his head around the architecture. *Li Jing* was a fairly big ship at two hundred and sixty-some meters long. Or maybe he should say *tall?*

It looked externally like a humanoid, though the dimensions were off. Longer legs like a woman, but bigger arms like a man. Engines in the boots and a secondary set in what Trinidad supposed you called a backpack.

Someone had gone all in on the concept of building a giant fighting robot that could fly in space, and then liked it so much they had an entire fleet of them.

She led him to the bridge. He was still a little surprised that you put something like that forward, in the actual head, rather than deep inside the chest, but this was the Cluster. Like everyone else, they separated a boom section to land on planetary surfaces, except when *Yaumgan* landed their whole dreadnought somewhere to make a statement.

In this case, the head and neck detached, with fin-like ears telescoping as it descended into atmosphere for lift and glide.

Aquitaine shuttles were streamlined, but still functional. *Yaumgan* landed a head.

Everybody else did the same, they just didn't commit art in the process of building it.

They entered and Captain Xue put him in a chair immediately to her left. There were three here, so another person could be on her right.

Right Gunner Ju Tou was a lean and dark man with serious eyes. Left Gunner Ying Xa-Mu was something of a throwback, as the woman had light brown hair and fair skin, when everyone else native to the Cluster that he'd met was dark skinned and had straight, black or brown hair.

Those two sat on the wings of the bridge, closer to the ears he supposed. Between those two were the other officers. The Flyer Hu BooLa—what they called their Pilot—was a heavier man but had hands like a pianist with incredibly long fingers that danced over his controls. Next to him was the

Seeker, or sensors officer. Huie De almost seemed mousy next to the Flyer, but she was simply a small woman, compact emotionally as well as physically from what he could see.

Captain Xue turned a smile on him now. It transformed her face from her usual serious dourness. The woman wasn't pretty, but imparted a sense of utter competence and brains with that look, which was better, as far as he was concerned.

"All of your gear was delivered earlier," she said conversationally. "Are you prepared for our mission?"

It was a weird way to frame it. Trinidad wondered if the Hindi they spoke here wasn't the native tongue of *Yaumgan*, but something they spoke for outsiders. He'd had to go through all manner of linguistic perambulations to find Sam, after she went home. The *Holding of Man* spoke a variant of Mongolian that had a lot of Mandarin Chinese thrown in, but not enough, so he'd had to learn to speak like a native.

And hide like one, when some folks were still a little mad that someone had killed their god.

"I am," he replied simply, before raising his voice slightly. "My job here is to help translate concepts and answer questions as they might arise, so everyone feel free to ask me, in public or private, if something confuses you."

Captain Xue nodded at that. It had all been worked out at the top. He was just here as a Centurion Ambassador to make Kosnett's life easier.

"Contact Command Centurion Kuiper and let them know we are ready to depart," she announced.

Seeker Huie nodded and began typing.

Trinidad leaned back into a relatively comfortable chair and confirmed the names he had been given. *Yaumgan* put the surname first, so Huie De would be like him introducing himself as Mildon Trinidad.

But he didn't figure he'd be on much of a personal basis with anyone. He was an outsider. But *Stunt Dude* was also used to that, and it had been Sam's idea to get him out of the dojo and into the sunlight, as it were.

He was probably better prepared than anybody to ride on a stranger's bridge, but it still felt like that first transport he'd bought out of a junkyard, in order to cross the M'Hani Gulf and go find the woman who had haunted his dreams.

He could do this as well.

TWENTY-SEVEN
HEAVY ESCORT MORNINGHAWK

Makara was on his bridge, mostly to keep watch on the person keeping watch on him. He did not hold with that old sailor's superstition that a woman on a ship was bad luck, but he knew that some of his crew did. Of course, as a fourth son, everyone was already a bit concerned about where karma would take them.

And the Shogun had sent an Imperial Inspector who was female.

Mid-forties, he guessed, having not asked. Perhaps a few years older than him. And Samnang Sobol had not volunteered much information. Nor much of anything, really. She had credentials and all the right chops on her papers. Had arrived with little in the way of luggage.

And two sets of swords, or course. The wooden ones you used on a training floor. The steel ones you used…

Makara wasn't sure what social situation he would find where it would be appropriate to arrive with twin blades on your hips. After a few days in her company, she had genuinely struck him as a woman who worked harder work than anyone else. As if she needed to arrive at a station in life that was normally closed to her gender. As such, she was likely tougher than he was.

Meaner, too.

So Makara make a point of standing more bridge watches in JumpSpace than he might normally have. Sobol insisted on *inspecting* the crew and the ship regularly. At least not many of them were goofballs constitutionally incapable of being serious when they needed to, even if Makara Omarov was known for running a looser ship that his brothers.

Those three commanded cruisers. Makara was happy with a Heavy Escort. It let him go more places, because he could sail places that a cruiser or battleship might not be welcome.

Sobol was studying him now from her station across the bridge. He felt the weight of her eyes on his ear. Or something. Not burning, though he wondered if she might be trying to set him on fire with the power of her mind. The woman gave off that impression occasionally, too.

He turned an innocent, questioning look upon her now. It was his bridge, on his ship. He had ultimate authority.

She was still an Imperial Inspector on a mission to witness what this fool of a fourth son might have done when nobody was looking.

Sometimes, she made him feel like an unruly teenager being caught by his parents again, but today he was calm certainty. She would not be prepared to meet First Centurion Kosnett. Nor Command Centurion Lau.

Makara let a little bit of smile dance in his eyes at the thought of that eventual confrontation.

"We will arrive in a day?" she asked.

As if that information was somehow secret and not a countdown timer any crew member could call up.

He nodded. She'd been snitty previously. She was being polite now.

"We should talk," she said, rising from the station she had taken over. "In private."

Makara nodded and rose. He'd wondered when this particular confrontation would arrive.

She was about average height, while he was tall, so he tended to lurk over her if she was too close. Still, he wondered what orders had needed to remain secret until now.

"Keo, you're in charge," he said, turning to Rinat Keo, his Second-in-Command, scowling to remind the man that now was not a good time for any of his practical jokes.

As long as that woman was aboard, it would never be a good time.

Keo nodded and rose from the engineering controls he had been monitoring. The man was something of a giant, close to two meters tall, but his beard was already white on the chin, even though he was only in his mid-thirties. The hair on his head was also rapidly fading, though he still had all of it.

Still, the man turned serious and somber, so Makara followed the Inspector aft, walking on her flank rather than behind or beside her.

They went a ways back, until Makara began to grow concerned, but finally she entered the training space back by engineering. He sighed but only internally.

Of course, she would retreat to the dojo floor.

Nursultan Chey was waiting when they entered the space, but she merely bowed.

"Master At Arms, could I ask your indulgence to allow me to talk to the Captain in privacy?" she asked in a formal tone.

Chey blinked and glanced at Makara. Makara nodded and the man withdrew into his office, closing the hatch and leaving them alone.

The training room was wide and long enough for several people to train or spar simultaneously. Makara Omarov spent the minimum requisite time on the floor each month, but he did not pursue the blade like a religion.

Not like Sobol apparently did.

She turned to face him from the middle of the space, as

though they were already wearing the full training armor and holding blunt dowels with which to pummel each other.

Samnang Sobol was dressed in the simple uniform of the fleet. Black pants kept baggy then tucked into calf-high boots in black leather. Her belted tunic came to mid-thigh and was blue with the crimson and gold of the Shogun worked in as highlights and edging.

Not a relative of the man. Just an important and honored servant.

And a dangerous one.

Makara moved to the edge of the floor but pointedly didn't cross the line separating it from the rest of the ship. She could stand there as a political statement, but he didn't have to dance with her.

She scowled as she watched his feet stop on the other side of the red line.

"You asked for privacy," he reminded simply, standing relaxed as if this was a casual conversation in the corridor.

"What will you do when *Morninghawk* arrives?" Sobol asked in a voice a little short of a demand.

"Place myself under the command of the First Centurion and his staff, most likely," Makara replied. "They have invited us to participate in a fleet force show of arms intended to hunt some of the more egregious elements of piracy in the cluster, and the Shogun chose to allow it."

There. Previously-plowed ground. Safe enough. Hopefully.

"And if those orders threaten the *Dalou Hegemony*?" she pressed.

"It is my understanding that they cannot," he fired back sharply. "That the Shogun does not trade with pirates in any official capacity. Does not even allow them to make use of stars he had claimed but never colonized, such that any we encounter are trespassers who should be immediately sent packing and their facilities dismantled. Were you about to suggest otherwise?"

She fell silent and Makara supposed he'd just scored the first point of this whatever-it-was match.

"I have the authority to overrule you if I feel your actions threaten the welfare of the ship or the Hegemony," she stated, going off on some *really interesting tangent* from what they had been discussing when they started, all of ten seconds ago.

At least he hoped it was a tangent. And not that she was about to tell him that *Dalou* funded pirates outright.

He certainly had heard the rumors. *Gloran* and others frequently had access to *Dalou*-style ships that they didn't build in their own yards. When pressed, the official story had always been that they had either been captured in honorable battle, or bought on a secondary market that never seemed to actually be open whenever Makara Omarov inquired.

"We are hunting pirates," he reminded her. "Enemies of civilization."

And left it at that, just to watch her eyes narrow with what he suspected was a terrible rage, however contained. Makara was stating the obvious, but he might also be pushing just a little right now, if only to see where she might be driven.

"I will make that determination," Sobol growled at him now, answering at least a few of his questions.

But he supposed that everyone besides him was double-dealing under the table. Even Sugawara had complicated relationships with some of the intrepid merchants that called on their worlds.

"And I will remind you that we will answer to the *Aquitaine* forces once we arrive at *Aditi*," he countered deftly. "If your orders are at odds with what the First Centurion proposes, I will not accept responsibility for insulting or alienating the man. I watched at *Vilahana* as *Urumchi* moved a small planetoid out of the way of striking the planet and probably destroying it. I would suggest to you the wisdom of not challenging such powerful folks. Nor of making enemies of them unnecessarily."

Unnecessarily being the key point here. If the Shogun was

funding as many rebels and pirates as rumors suggested, all to weaken the other nations of the Cluster, Makara could see a painful comeuppance in the not-too-distant future. He just hoped that as a minor captain of a minor lord of a minor clan, he would be able to shelter in some safe harbor until whatever storm it was blew over.

Sobol fell silent at that and Makara assumed that the message she had intended had been sent. He would need to tread carefully so as to not challenge her authority and force a break. Neither Omarov nor Sugawara could afford to retreat suddenly into the wilderness to hide for a generation. Not if the rest of the *Dalou Hegemony* risked starting some sort of overt war with *Aditi* and their new allies.

But there was most explicitly a storm coming.

TWENTY-EIGHT

Phil had more or less ordered Barnaby Silver, Command Centurion of *Viking*, and Barnaby's Science Officer, Senior Centurion Sunan Bunnag, to a private meeting on *Urumchi*. It wasn't that he didn't trust his own signals encryption, but a message never transmitted electronically can never be intercepted. And never decrypted to read Phil's secrets.

They were in a small meeting room off of the flag bridge. Him and those two, plus Heather and Harinder.

In person, Barnaby Silver didn't look anything like his name suggested, with dark hair in a brushed back in a widow's peak framing a square face that gave the impression of being almost flat. Broad shoulders and a wide torso made him look like a granite pillar rather than a man. He spoke with a quiet baritone voice but Phil had heard him above a crowd when he needed to.

Bunnag, in contrast, was nerdy and slender, but she lived face down on various consoles, absorbing information like a firehose, filtering it in real time to organize the important bits, and then feeding them to the rest of her team.

Viking was a Survey Cruiser, and *RAN Ballard* had set an extremely high bar for those sorts of crews back in the *First Expeditionary Fleet* days. That *Viking* was built on an

Expeditionary hull herself just meant that much more power for sensors, and enough big guns that Phil didn't have any qualms sending them out without backup.

"You are going to be off the reservation," Phil said now, watching faces. "You and *CG-505* will follow up on some of the leads and hints that Nam and Kaur Singh had quietly slipped to us under the table, but I don't expect to keep *Viking* on any sort of leash. I also won't be in a position to back you up if you bite off something bigger than you can chew, so be careful."

"I can always haul ass back for the cavalry, First Centurion," Barnaby replied. "But there's not much out here that can threaten *Viking* and a Guardian corvette."

"A light missile bombard might be a pain in your ass," Heather pointed out. "At least until you ran far enough away."

"He'd have to be salvoing missiles that closed at different speeds," Barnaby smiled. "And I'd have to be sitting there like a ninny watching."

"Just don't get yourself trapped down in a gravity well," Phil pointed out. "Keller and Jež always used to say that we couldn't win the war against *Buran* in an afternoon, but we could lose it. Same goes here. We've got an edge nobody can match if we're patient."

"What about *Yaumgan?*" Sunan asked now. "Are they a significant threat?"

But then, she'd studied the technical readouts Leyla had compiled, and probably supplemented them.

"They went a different direction than everybody else, culturally and technologically," Phil nodded. "But I'd be just fine never having to shoot at them to find out how well matched we were. *Stunt Dude* went with them because he's used to thinking outside of any constraints that might limit anyone else."

"We'll find your pirates, First Centurion," Barnaby assured him. "But what happens then?"

"If they are mobile, they might get away unless you can take them all down at once," Phil said. "So I'll expect you to act like

Ballard used to, sitting out in the darkness and peeking over moons to get a view, when we used to expect *Sentient* computers that would notice any star being occluded."

"I want their bases," Heather interjected now. "The ships are scrapyard junk, more often than not, but there have to be bases or drydocks out there keeping them flying. Without those, they become far less mobile."

"Agreed," Sunan said. "To date, we've encountered nothing like the Salvager *Wulfa*, once that ship disappeared, but it is a type I'm watching for. Plus those old strippers that *Corynthe* still flies."

"Good," Phil said. "You've got the set of rendezvous coordinates where either I'll be at or will have someone drop by. Worst option, I leave a buoy like Kigali used to do and you can follow that, but I expect you to be leading me around, not the reverse."

"You can count on us, First Centurion," Barnaby said.

Phil just hoped it was enough.

TWENTY-NINE
YARMOUTH CARRIER AGGREGATOR

Basant had a working cast and was numb on his left arm from the backs of his knuckles to his elbow from some really exceptional topical pain cream. It would run out in a few hours, but he was clear-headed now.

He'd have liked to have said that he was angry, but that would be a lie. Anger had died two days ago with Zemke on that dueling floor. All he really had left now was fear. And that was one hell of a motivator.

They were all back in that bar again. Not many captains had chosen to undock and flee like whipped curs in the night. A few had. Fewer than he'd expected, honestly. Given some of the names, he expect that someone was going to run to the nearest police station and tell the cops everything they knew, hoping to buy leniency when they were sentenced.

Basant turned to Captain Dexter, sitting across the trestle table and down a little bit like just another captain, rather than the manager of the resort that was the carrier *Aggregator*.

"I know you and I talked, but that was in private," Basant said, lifting his voice enough for the other thirty or so captains to hear. "I did all this on your deck, and you had no opportunity to run if you wanted. What's your decision, Dexter?"

The man scowled, but that was because he didn't think of himself as a pirate. He was really more of a merchant. A fence who bought stolen and pirated goods. Who traded with a few legitimate businesses for the things he needed on a regular basis.

And provided the ships a place outside the normal chains of authority where crews could just relax.

"I hear your words, Utkin," Dexter replied. "And while I could probably make a go of it as a legitimate business, I have no interest in that. It might be that the age of piracy in the cluster is fully over, save for the dead-enders who have to go down fighting, but that's not me, either."

"We're likely to move beyond piracy," Basant reminded him. And everyone else in earshot. "This will be revolution, at the end of the day."

"A founding always is," Dexter replied, turning slowly to look at the other captains around him and raising his voice "We're going to become a nation of refugees and vagabonds, so the duel you witnessed two days ago is the final one. Am I clear?"

A few voices stirred. Growls from the back without words.

"AM I CLEAR?" Dexter snarled at the room. "When we do this—**WHEN**—then we have to become our own board of directors. No more challenges. No more blood. Basant Utkin will lead us, because he saw early what was happening and chose to make a stand before we were picked off one by one. Starting yesterday, his term of office will run for ten years. By then, we'll have either been destroyed, or will have succeeded and can figure out what we'll do next. Questions?"

Basant was a bit surprised. They'd talked six years yesterday, but apparently Dexter had decided overnight that it would need to be longer.

"Who's the initial board?" someone called from the back.

Basant caught the key word there. *Initial.* Those folks who would be there today, but could be removed later if they screwed up badly enough. Directors were only removed by a vote. That was the tradition.

Only captains paid the price in blood.

"Me," Dexter hollered. "Andrea Liefan off *Wulfa*, because she's the one with the biggest price on her head. Six others from you lot."

"We going to have to quit the day job?" another voice called.

"No," Basant interjected. "All captains remain in place for now. And no duels there either. A crew can vote to remove a captain if they think they have to, but it has to be the crew voting without any serving officers involved."

More grumbles, but a few cheers. Retiring was always a tricky business, as a man or woman wanted to hang on as long as they could, and then go out on a high note. That wasn't always an option, especially if you had ambitious officers below you, itching to take your spot.

"So what are we doing next?" one of the female captains called from a corner behind him.

Trust a woman to be the practical one, with the men too fixated on knives.

"We have *Aggregator*," Basant said, standing up now so everyone could see him and hear him better. "And *Wulfa*. Those are the start of a backbone, but not enough. We need a mobile chop shop that can become the start of a true base, so that when we get where we're going, we can survive."

"And where's that?" she asked.

Basant smiled at her.

Captain Ward was old in the business, a tall, stout woman full gray now and starting to turn white with age. Mean as a hungry snake, too, but only if you crossed her. Captained the Raider *Hollywood*, and that was also her nickname, because she'd been in vids when she was young.

Before falling out and ending up here.

"*Meerut*," he said with a grin.

Almost everyone here scrunched down confused at that, but Basant wasn't surprised.

"Where the hell is that?" *Hollywood* asked him now. "*What the hell is that?*"

"A highly secret *Ingham* base and colony world," Basant answered. "Tucked in along that fuzzy stretch of border between places *Ewin* claims and *Dalou*."

"So who's coming after us then?" she pressed, scowling.

Basant couldn't stop the smile taking over his face.

"Neither," he laughed. "Technically."

"How is that possible?" Dexter spoke up now. "*Dalou* is persnickety about that crap. *Ewin* might be a little incompetent, but they'll get pissy if someone tries to wedge open a border and plant a colony."

"Neither side claims *Meerut* because they don't know it's there," Andrea spoke up now.

She'd been largely quiet. Mostly that was to keep from stepping on his toes. They still weren't a thing, aside from the occasional weekend fling, even as they were turning into full business partners, which was probably even weirder.

Heads swiveled to look at her now.

"It exists inside the wall itself," she explained. "In that stretch of nebulae and new stars still too hot and unstable to have planets. Everyone thinks of the inner edge of the Cluster as solid, and it largely is unless you spend twenty times as long slowly wriggling along shallow fords in all those gravity wells packed so closely together that they mess up your JumpSails. *Meerut* apparently drifted in a billion years ago or something, after some supernova blew a pocket for it. Rich mining. Couple of giants filled with exotic gases. One habitable world with about a million colonists now and a bunch of factories turning out parts for space ships."

"How come nobody knew about this place before?" another captain yelled.

"*Ingham* found it about a century ago," Basant replied.

"Recognized it for what it was, and secretly started hiding people there when the bounties got to be too much. Or let them retire and bring families, as long as they understood that they could never go back to the outer worlds. Even the folks that live there rarely leave, as they've got a paradise on their hands."

"How do you know about the place, Utkin?" *Hollywood* asked.

"Because I was born there."

THIRTY

Stunt Dude wasn't entirely sure what day it was back home, and didn't feel like doing all the math necessary to figure it out. *Li Jing* ran on a twenty-hour day that apparently tracked the planet *Yaumgan* itself, with some fiddling he hadn't sorted out.

Hell, the only time that calendars were really critical was when you needed to calculate mortgages on ships anyway. Then you had a secondary computer somewhere keeping time with some banker's homeworld so that interest could be done to the minute on demand.

Yaumgan didn't have that sort of thing going. He'd been aboard about a week, but fallen into the same time fugue as the rest of the crew. He'd had a similar experience when he went looking for Sam. It was part of the reason Phil had sent him here.

Every other ship was using a clock more or less adapted from Standard time on *Aditi*.

Yaumgan was special.

Today, he was somewhere in a kidney, he thought. At least based on the number of steps. Crew quarters tended to be in the upper thighs and upper arms and along the ribs, with hands and feet dedicated to functional stations. Either guns or engines, depending.

There was a gymnasium with equipment for the crew to stay in shape, plus a small dance floor he had begun to treat as a training floor. It wasn't a dojo anywhere except in his head, but that was fine. Hard floor with bamboo strips that had a layer of enamel for stickiness. Walls painted an egg-cream kinda faded down to mustard by the lights in there, which were currently only set to halfway.

He was doing his forms. Slowly moving through the maneuvers in a dance older than spaceflight, going back some thirteen millennia to *Earth* originally.

He'd first gotten into it when he was twelve, and stayed with it. At eighteen, he'd earned sufficient rank to train others. By twenty he'd gotten hooked up with a group of older men and women, all veterans of the *Republic of Aquitaine* Navy, who were then teaching actors how to fight for movies. He'd even been in a few, as either a faceless minion for the hero to beat up, or later as a stunt double.

Knowing how to fall without getting hurt was the key to that business.

The hatch opened now and he paused mid-form to see who had entered. A few crew members came in to watch every once in a while and Trinidad supposed that he'd have actual students in another month, but this was Captain Xue.

Stunt Dude froze his form and looked at her.

"No, no," she said, waving. "It can wait."

He nodded and returned to his breathing for a moment before channeling himself inwards and letting the muscle memory carry him forward.

Finally, he completed the form and bowed to his invisible first instructor, falling back twenty-eight years to a man he had only seen sporadically in the last fifteen.

"Captain?" *Stunt Dude* asked as he stepped to where she had been standing.

"You were a ground forces trooper before you retired, that is correct?" she asked.

"I was," he agreed.

She'd read a bio that Sam had helped craft that covered all the salient points. Including an impossible romance that still worked.

"And the First Centurion assigned you to *Li Jing* because of that?" she pressed.

"I have the most experience with radically different cultures," Trinidad nodded. "*Aditi* is similar to *Aquitaine* in many ways. The other three are similar enough to *Aditi* with their own cultural variations created by the long pause in spaceflight and the primitive technology that let you maintain some level of trade in the cluster without really letting you out until the JumpSail arrived. You were all more or less one people, save *Yaumgan*."

"We are different," she agreed now. "I feel that you should know a little bit about that while we sail together. Some Kosnett already knows via Ambassador Hu, but I have secondary instructions from home he was not privy to."

Trinidad perked up. Sounded like wheels within wheels, but Kosnett had suspected that many stories would be told by all sides in an attempt to muddy the waters sufficient to obscure any truth that accidentally leaked out.

It wasn't that the First Centurion actively distrusted everyone. He just knew that they all had axes and angles in the situation, and that *Urumchi* was a bull in a china shop.

Best to send a quiet philosopher with the weirdest and potentially most dangerous folks, rather than one of those Jessica Keller knock-off warriors like First Officer Beridze.

He glanced at the hatch behind her, but it was shut. They were as alone as he supposed they would get.

"*Yaumgan* came from elsewhere," she said, confirming the rumors. "From farther west, as your maps would mark it. A long tendril spur off the next galactic arm."

"Much closer to *Earth*, then," he noted.

"Much," she said. "But we left five hundred years ago for reasons not to be discussed now."

He nodded. Probably chased out by someone bigger, then. It happened. You came close to getting conquered or something, and loaded everybody up on a convoy of ships to flee into what would have looked like endless darkness from there. It wasn't endless, unless you pulled the map back far enough, but broken with thinly-spaced stars. The Cluster, however, would look like a diamond on black velvet.

"We encountered people when we arrived," Xue continued. "Conquered them at the time, but they were thinly settled on one world well separated from the other central points that would eventually grow into our neighbors."

Again, he nodded. Heather Lau had suggested Doric Greece as something of a model. Or maybe Yuan China was a better example, depending on relative numbers. Trinidad had a lot of experience dealing with folks related to Kublai Khan by blood.

"That one was the foundation upon which we built the six worlds that became the *Yaumgan Domain*," Xue said now. "We have intermarried and the distinctions are much less pronounced than they were, but the combination of the two cultures also involved a technology exchange that created in the new *Yaumgan* something well in advance of the others. We did not conquer them then, and trade very little with the rest of the cluster now, but your arrival has altered equations."

"As we suspected it might," he acknowledged. "Especially once we knew that *Aquitaine* was far in advance of *Aditi* and the others, all of whom look upon *Yaumgan* with great jealousy balanced against trepidation."

She smiled at his words.

"As well they should," Captain Xue said with a sharp nod. "I wanted you prepared for what is about to happen."

"Oh?" *Stunt Dude* perked up.

"We have done some training with *CB-502*," Xue grinned.

"Shot at rocks and flown around to understand each other. But our spies have suggested a place where the pirates keep a small base, tucked in an area largely unknown to *Aditi*."

"But known to *Yaumgan*?" Trinidad asked with the sort of tone that suggested *Li Jing* or some other vessels had traded there in the past.

"We keep many spies busy," she said in a closed-mouthed kind of way. "As one must when surrounded by folks who view us with jealousy and trepidation."

It was Trinidad's turn to grin.

"So we're going to sneak up and watch them?" he asked.

"Oh, no," Captain Xue said. "We've already done that. I'm about to give the order to attack and thought you would appreciate a few minutes to prepare before joining me on the bridge. You need a shower."

He sniffed, and agreed. A good workout always left him warm and sweaty as everything flowed.

"I will join you as soon as I can," Trinidad said.

"Excellent," Captain Xue said, turning and leaving without another word.

The Dà class of ships weren't as big as others, but had two gunners where others only had one, with local teams handling the weapon mounts themselves.

He was looking forward to seeing this mighty robot warrior in action finally.

THIRTY-ONE

SKYCRUISER LI JING

Captain Xue Dao Zhiou was strapped in and ready for combat when *Stunt Dude* joined her. His short, graying hair was still damp, but like her, he was already in an emergency pressure suit for combat, with his facemask open so he could talk.

From behind, she would have thought him one of her crew, except that the man flowed when he walked. Others trudged. Or stomped. *Stunt Dude* reminded her of a snake's smoothness as it slithered. Impressive and dangerous, but the man had led his own piratical assaults on enemy warships during Kosnett's war against the God-Entity.

Warrior. Fitting that Kosnett had sent him here, where he could appreciate single combat as it was meant to be played out.

"All hands stand by for combat," she announced when Centurion Mildon was buckled in. "Signal Command Centurion Kuiper."

Around her, everyone withdrew their own helmets from drawers or picked them up off nearby desks and snapped them into place, pausing to connect the umbilicus to a handy plug to keep them on power and air as well as communications, should they lose pressure and the ability to talk.

"Escort is ready for jump," Huie De replied. "All stations report combat readiness."

"Flyer, move to JumpSpace," Dao ordered, glancing once at her guest.

Stunt Dude was paying attention, eyes wide but also opening up a passive screen on his console to watch. It echoed hers, which was fine. She had one screen blank for the tactical map that would appear shortly, with a second showing a target in the near distance that was about to become fighting range.

The distance was short. Only a few light-hours, as the pirates had settled in an uninhabitable system where early movement by gas giants or neighboring stars had torn apart most planetary disks, leaving only rubble clouds, like so many stars in the Cluster.

"Arrival," Flyer Hu announced as all her boards suddenly began to fill in with real-time updates.

"Seeker?" Dao called, but Huie De was already in motion.

"Station has not changed status," she said quickly. "Two Raiders and two Pickets at moorage. Power output suggests surprise on our part."

"Order them to surrender in the name of First Centurion Kosnett of the *Republic of Aquitaine* Navy," Dao ordered, glancing over to catch *Stunt Dude*'s flinch of surprise. She dropped her voice. "Technically, we are doing this under his authority."

The man nodded after he gave it a moment of thought. And if anyone got away, they would tell the most amazing stories, seeing a *Yaumgan* Skycruiser and an *Aquitaine* corvette threatening this small station.

"Station has launched defensive missiles," Seeker Huie called. "Six from vertical tubes turning now to engage. All are locked on *Li Jing*. Engage with eye beams?"

Foolish mistake, but that was their prerogative. Not that six would threaten Kuiper's warship. She had seen the reports from

Vilahana. And watched the effects of Type-3-Pulse and Pulse-Two weapons.

Everything *Aquitaine* had sent was what they called *Expeditionary*-style. All energy weapons. Beams of three classes from short range to exceptional. She supposed that made them more dangerous, as they didn't have to return home for reloads and their support ships could just bring food and replacement parts.

"Negative," she replied, knowing that Huie would transmit her orders now. "*CB-502*, engage as you bear."

Not that she expected Command Centurion Kuiper to need goading. Already the rear beam, the Zebra-turret as they called it, was lashing out at long range, smashing down missiles before they could accelerate and begin evasive maneuvering.

The whole squadron of Kosnett's corvettes could probably stand off and disarm an entire *Ewin* Sector Fleet in an afternoon without significant risk, even if they brought a carrier with fighters.

The first salvo got smashed quicker than she had expected, but Dao had not seen what Kuiper's team could do when pressed, and only had verbal reports of the first engagement with the pirates at *Vilahana*. It had not gone well for the pirates.

"Both Gunners, lock on the nearer Raider and open fire," Dao ordered now. "I want him removed from the field before he wakes up. Then we will go after the second one."

Grunts and nods. Left and Right would work with the Flyer now as their Seeker fed them updates.

"Mass launch from the station," Huie called in a burst of surprise. "They have just launched twenty-four missiles in a single salvo."

"Where from?" Dao demanded. "How?"

"Tracking," Huie held. "They have a box-pod in a turret mount."

"*CB-502*, can you handle that?" Dao asked.

"Affirmative, Flag," Kuiper replied a moment later. "You

might want to shift outwards on your flank some, just to open a curl in their flight path. Fools only sent six after me."

Dao started to say something, but watched as the front of the little corvette suddenly lit up with beam fire. Twin Type-3-Pulse, firing as rapidly as they could cool the systems, along with the Pulse-Two in the scorpion mount. Truly impressive. And deadly.

Flyer Hu was already dancing to his left without orders, but he had seen the wisdom of such a thing, so Dao only had to watch.

Li Jing's left fist—the super titan bolt cluster—fired now. Six torpedoes flashed across space to slam into the side of the Raider at rest. Four hit, which was above average at this extreme of a range. Navigational shielding failed and energy began to dance on the side of the hull.

Then the Ōdachi locked on. The *Yaumgan* Greatsword beam weapon. That was the one thing *Aditi* had invented that *Yaumgan* had taken internally. And improved. Their version could only fire three or four pulses of energy sequentially, hammering a target. The Ōdachi fired six before the weapon needed to cool.

Were *Zhang Gualao* here, they would fire it ten times in the deadly superweapon configuration known as the Sunsword.

Right Gunner Ju Tou with the serious eyes was holding a single point of impact, even as *Li Jing* moved like a ballerina. The first pulse struck the Raider well aft, behind the cargo bays that occasionally got converted into flight decks or barracks for boarding armies, and into the engines themselves.

Dao approved. If the Raider was lamed, they could only try to limp away from here, but if they lost their JumpSails as well —and they might with this shooting—they were stuck here under her guns. Without any power to respond.

On her flank, *CB-502* had twisted like an eel, slewing their bow around some so that they could sail in roughly the same direction as *Li Jing*, though they lacked the maneuverability of legs or backpack thrusters.

But the missile swarm was melting under the savage fury of the *Aquitaine* force. Even her eye beams could not have done such an exceptional job.

Hue Dao Zhiou made a note in her personal log to talk to her superiors about building a lesser Kuài, one of the fast aeromechs used as patrol craft, with both fists comprised of multiple eye beam installations that could allow them to crush a missile pod like that. She didn't think they had anything like that in the fleet right now.

Somewhere, a Zen-Mekyo scientist had thought that adding such a weapon pod to this station would make them safe against attackers. And they might have, had she not brought an *Aquitaine* escort to battle.

Dao also made a note to thank Kosnett for his forethought. She kept forgetting that he had only become an Ambassador for the recent mission, and had previously been a famous and terrible fleet commander, successful more than once against impossible odds.

"First enemy vessel has been crippled," Seeker Huie announced in a triumphant voice.

"Engaging second one," Flyer Hu announced. "He appears awake, but one of the Pickets has not joined him."

Dao checked her screens. The killer missile swarm was just an angry couple of horseflies now.

"*CB-502*, move to engage the first Picket as you can," she decided aloud.

They were both escorts, but the *Aquitaine* corvette was almost as heavy as the Raider she was currently fighting, so a Picket was a dead man walking if they didn't immediately flee for deep space.

A signal on her board from Kuiper acknowledged, but she also watched one of the bow installations shift to a new target.

Even at this range, they were scoring solid hits. Dao doubted that the Picket could reciprocate.

"Titan bolt cluster reloaded with standard warheads," Left Gunner Ying called. "Firing now."

The Ōdachi was still cooling and charging, but the Raider was only awake enough to start moving and bring up their shields to a level that might protect them. Like the station, they fired a set of four missiles from their wing mounts.

So, an *Ewin*-style missile platform. More power for maneuver and shielding. Greater risk of running out of ammunition in the middle of a battle.

She saw the wisdom of the *Expeditionary*-class. Even *Li Jing* would need to return to base to replenish their stocks of titan bolts at some point. *CB-502* could fight until they ran out of fuel for their reactors.

Yes, *Yaumgan* needed to rethink warfare. Up until now, no base had been more than a few days sail away. Kosnett had traveled for months to get here.

Six titan bolts raced across space. Ju had the span perfect, as the first one missed wide across the bow and the sixth one missed across the stern. Four slammed into the sides of the ship.

"Engage missiles with eye beams," Dao decided. "Have Kuiper keep punishing his target."

Four she could deal with, unless that pirate had invested in some expensive and rare variant warheads, such as adding armor or turning them into beam emitters that would fire before they got close, softening up shielding on an impact facing for the others that followed.

Flyer Hu turned his face to the incoming arrows and gun teams began to fire.

From the bridge of *CB-502*, it must look like a swimmer in water, hovering in place with bent legs and arms out. Head up and deadly vision blowing things into flaming clouds of plasma like a cartoon character.

But it worked on the psyche of the lesser nations to see

Yaumgan as tremendous supermen who could not be defeated. That battle was half of any war.

"Ōdachi ready to fire," Right Gunner Ju Tou announced. "Lock engaged. Firing."

The Raider was badly hurt already. The first pulse finished off the flank shielding and began to carve away pieces of the hull. This time, he was firing forward, so Dao decided that he was trying to decapitate the ship before the captain could decide what to do to escape.

The Raider design was fairly standard, so that sort of aiming could be done. Command and most of the crew forward. Engines and generators aft. Weapon stations on two wings and a bow mount, though sometimes they upgraded the Point Guns aft as a secondary measure.

The middle was all cargo bays. Ubiquitous. Depending on the Syndicate, maybe any number of other things, but *Yaumgan* had experience with pirates such as this. The least useful thing you could do was fire at the central section. It would just shake off the damage.

"All missiles destroyed," Seeker Huie announced.

Dao looked at her board in surprise. All of them? Yes. *CB-502* was even more deadly than she'd originally expected. Already, the Picket that was their target was being hammered by Type-3-Pulse, even as the second wave of missiles from the station got the deadly attention of the Pulse-Two gunners aft.

This could be fun.

"Hit the last Picket with eye beams," Dao ordered.

They were still asleep somehow. Maintenance cycle interrupted and all of their systems torn apart as they frantically tried to put everything back together? It happened.

CB-502's Picket had apparently decided to flee, as they simply vanished from sight, though still trailing parts and leaving behind a cloud of plasma like a pool of fresh piss on the rug. The ship turned to the second Raider now and began surgically dismantling the ship, even as Ying fired another spread of titan bolts into the flank.

"Raider One had shut down everything," Seeker Huie called over the chatter. "Raider Two is asking for terms. Picket Two is unresponsive."

Dao noted that the lone Picket remaining was hardly putting out any power now, down from even what they had before the battle had begun.

"Assume Picket Two will surrender when they finally can and order *CB-502* to an escort position between us and the enemy vessels," Dao ordered. "Tell the station to shut down right now or I will stand off and shatter them into scrap."

"Acknowledged," Huie said.

Dao relaxed. The last fifteen minutes had felt like barely three, but at the same time, like she had been on a rowing machine for an hour. *Stunt Dude* had taken a shower, but she didn't know if he would be as sweaty as she was right now.

High stress, but oh so awesome. Doubly so knowing that there were very few things in the Cluster that could threaten *Li Jing*. The pirates would need raw numbers to survive. Tremendous squadrons to have any possibility of victory.

"Thoughts?" she asked *Stunt Dude* now.

"Professional," he said simply, but she'd spent enough time with the man now to understand that to be a high compliment.

Aquitaine saw itself as professionals. Engineers rather than warriors, unlike most of the Cluster. *Aditi* were merchants. *Dalou*, *Gloran*, and *Ewin* were all about warfare.

And possibly *Yaumgan* as well, but in a quiet, defensive-posture kind of manner that didn't threaten their neighbors.

"So now what happens?" he asked after a beat. "They've surrendered, but most of them probably expect parole. Back home, we'd have put prize crews on a *Fribourg* ship, or locked everyone up on one of them with a lot of marines. You can't really do that here, can you?"

"We can disable their weapons," Dao said. "Those not

already destroyed. And take them all prisoner, possibly stuffing them aboard the Picket with all the food they can hold. The station presents more of a problem, only because I don't know how many people are aboard."

"So we should go over and talk to them?" he asked.

"We?"

"I'm here to learn about other cultures because I'm already something of expert," he said with a smile. "And a former pirate, when you get right down to it. What are your orders?"

Dao considered it. He was an officer. And expert at close combat in case somebody got out of line over there. And she could always play the Republic up as an even stranger boogeyman than *Yaumgan*.

Captain Xue Dao Zhiou held out a hand in the ancient style and he shook it.

"I think that would be an excellent idea," she said.

THIRTY-TWO

Stunt Dude was in a *Yaumgan* emergency suit with the helmet hooked on his left hip and out of the way. They'd given him a pistol for his right hip, but that was more a badge of authority than an actual weapon, as he was accompanied by Captain Xue and a dozen men and women with the cold, hooded eyes of professional killers.

They had docked with the surrendered station and boarded, goons first.

It felt weird being back with the officers and not leading the assault, like he'd done on *Queen Anne's Revenge* and *Packmule* in the bad, old days.

The station itself followed a fairly standard design. He'd spent enough time studying how they built ships and things around here to figure that this one had come out of a *Dalou* yard instead of an *Aditi* one, mostly from the way the corners and seams were welded and polished. Neither was better than the other, but you made choices based on what you were comfortable with.

The station commander was here, standing with a few of his officers, all of them more than a little shell-shocked. *Aquitaine* they had probably heard of by now, especially as this was an *Ingham* station, but to get their asses kicked by the strangers and a *Yaumgan* Skycruiser had to be especially weird.

The commander ritually held out a belt with a pistol and a knife attached as he and Xue approached.

Stunt Dude kept his commentary internal and his face neutral as he watched her accept their surrender and parole. Dealing with pirates should not be so formal and casual that there were generally accepted rules of behavior.

At the same time, he was old enough to remember the end of the *Fribourg* wars, before Keller beat them. That relationship had been circumscribed by codes of conduct that all sides honored.

It had only been *Buran* that took prisoners forever and worked them to death on gulag planets.

With a few friends, he had helped put paid to that, as well. Still had a big medal personally pinned on him by the Emperor of *Fribourg* as a thank you for all they'd done for her.

Trinidad studied the man who was now Xue's prisoner as one of his lieutenants led them back towards the center of the station.

Roughly his age, so forty give or take. A little paunchy around the middle, like a shopkeeper rather than a pirate warlord. Thinning hair turning gray. Frightened eyes.

Just to be cruel, Trinidad started talking to the man in *Buran* Mongolian. Not that he expected a response, but to unhinge the fellow that extra little bit. His crew also flinched.

"Ah, Centurion, I doubt that they understand you," Xue said now with a mirthful smile that suggested she might be on to his practical joke.

"Do you understand any Mongolian?" he asked her in a friendly tone.

She didn't. The way her eyes glazed over a little told him that, but she immediately turned to the pirate.

"He asks why we should not simply annihilate this station and all the inhabitants," Xue told the man in a cold, emotionless translation.

Stunt Dude managed not to giggle as he turned innocent eyes on the pirate.

Good Cop/Bad Cop? Let's go there.

The pirate's eyes got HUGE. Bogeyman.

"You…you can't do that!" the man sputtered.

"Are we just being evil now for the sake of evil?" *Stunt Dude* asked, still in Mongolian as he turned back to Captain Xue, wondering what she was up to.

"I presume that you will give us no problems?" Xue asked the pirate. "This man comes from *Aquitaine* and was at *Vilahana*. He has great anger at your kind. His warlord has proscribed any who give him further cause."

"Absolutely," the pirate said, gesturing. "Here, we are at the bridge. You can see everything. We have surrendered on honorable terms and will accept that. Please do not let them kill us!"

She turned back to smile at Trinidad and spoke slowly.

"They will be no problem," she enunciated slowly.

"Is good," he replied in the Hindi they had been speaking, forcing a hard accent onto his tones, just to be an extra shit.

"Commander, you have relinquished your station to us," she said. "*Aditi* and *Aquitaine* have ordered that all *Ingham* pirates captured must be returned to *Aditi* to face justice, but there is an exceptionally short list of names with death warrants attached, so you will go to prison instead."

"But we surrendered!" he cried out. "What are you doing?"

"Ending piracy as a way of life," Captain Xue replied in the sort of cold, angry tone a woman got when you've found her last nerve and set it on fire. "All of you will learn what that means. You will probably get out of prison first, for going in first. Troopers, take them into custody and put them aboard the transport without letting them talk to anyone else. Then send over all of the combat teams to help round up the rest. Plus some engineers to keep the station running for now."

The man started to howl and one of the marines punched him hard in the squishy part of the stomach, driving all the air out of him at once. Then two of them picked him up and dragged him out of the room, leaving *Stunt Dude* alone with Captain Xue.

"That was rude," he said with a grin.

She smiled.

"Most of the Cluster fears *Yaumgan*," she replied. "Now, the pirates will get the message that their time has ended. If my people are strange, yours will begin frightening those who do not have a good relationship with *Aditi*."

"Good Cop/Bad Cop?" he asked.

"Bad Cop/Worse Cop, perhaps?" she answered with a grin. "Now, I must talk to Command Centurion Kuiper."

"Why is that?" he asked, moving to sit at an unlocked station that seemed to have full rights as he monitored the current status of the reactor cores nearby. Everything was running in the green.

"Once we clear the place, we would normally just blow it up," Xue replied. "That is what we do when we find such things back home. Sometimes, we do not even clear them, but just annihilate the station and all the crew as a warning. That is one of the reasons we have less of a piracy problem than others do. But this system is in a zone claimed by *Aditi*, so they may want to send a crew and claim it. I think *CB-502* would be better to run to *Aditi* with the message, only because I am not sure they could handle a squadron of pirate ships that might return from wherever that Picket fled to. *Li Jing* is better equipped."

Stunt Dude thought about it and shrugged. A battle corvette might give anyone less than *Tango* one hell of a run for their money, but could be overwhelmed.

"Your call," he replied. "I'd say even money. However, you're in charge here. I'm just along to help communicate and frighten pirates."

She smiled.

"And you do an exceptional job of it, *Stunt Dude*."

THIRTY-THREE
ADCON CRUISER ARANYANI

Kaur had gone out on patrol with *CC-501* mostly just to get away from the politics of the home system as Phil worked his magic on various politicians and ambassadors. She kept expecting some Director to cut orders to remove *Aranyani* from the squadron, but so far she had been left alone.

Maybe the Herald had managed to box everyone else in and won her little war within the government? Yet another reason to remain aloof and on patrol, lest someone find out that she had known ahead of time and could have warned people what was coming.

Had she wanted to.

Kaur sat on her bridge and watched the depths of JumpSpace as her new Weapons Officer, Indra Korrapati, worked quietly on his systems. There wasn't anything to shoot at, but the man was prepared in case something happened. He wasn't as good as Nam if it did, but was also younger, and she had done a good job training him before she left. He might even keep the position when Kaur left, assuming Arya took command and Nam returned to be her First Officer.

Kaur grinned and considered how loudly Arya would bitch

if Nam went to some Ship of the Line with Kaur instead. Tomorrow's problem.

Jagadish Misra had the Helm today, as they were returning to *Aditi* for what should be one last quick stop for supplies before heading out on Phil's grand expedition. They hadn't found anything on their patrol, but she'd taken them to three systems where smugglers were known to make rendezvous, on the hopes of catching someone asleep. The alternative had been hitting someplace where she might bite off more than she could chew.

CC-501 was a capable ship, as was *Aranyani*, but the last thing she wanted right now was to suffer any sort of damage that would sideline her from flying out with *Urumchi*, and Kaur suspected that there were folks in Naval Command who would gladly send their favorite vessel instead.

"Time to arrival?" she asked.

"Fifteen minutes, roughly," Jagadish replied. "We're coming out high and wider than normal on this flight path, both to avoid the larger numbers of ships expected to be in orbit, as well as maybe land on top of some snoop sitting in the darkness."

"Continue," Kaur acknowledged.

Rather than sit and fidget, she rose and made her way to the coffee machine, just to refill her mug and stretch her legs. Nothing to do in JumpSpace but watch, and she was already having a hard time sleeping with the excitement.

This was even worse than those last few days before she had formally taken command of *Aranyani*. Kaur dialed up the decaf instead, and added a lot of syrup and coconut milk. The rush wouldn't bother her later, but the caffeine might be too much.

She dawdled and finally returned, sipping liquid heat and watching.

"Stand by to arrive," Jagadish said now, drawing everyone's attention from whatever they had been doing to pass the last hour of flight.

Stars appeared and Kaur watched her scanner boards fill up with various ships and flight vectors.

"Message from the flagship," Arya announced, referring to *Urumchi* rather than *Khandoba*, which made both of them smile. "Oh, shit."

"What?" Kaur demanded.

"Priority resupply orders for us and *501*," Arya said. "Apparently we were the last team home and they have news."

Kaur waited while Arya found her own coffee mug and took a drink, as it calmed her nerves.

"*Tango* and a pirate warfleet have just declared themselves an independent nation," Arya said with dread in her voice.

MEERUT

THIRTY-FOUR

ENFORCER TANGO

Basant was on his bridge in his best uniform. Pirates really didn't go all in on that military stuff, but enough of his people and friends had served in some navy or fleet militia along the way that they tended to expect uniforms. *Ingham* was old enough to have traditions, though every ship tended to interpret their own and do things different.

A new ship always brought crew with it from somewhere else, sometimes multiple ships, so they made their own along the way. *Tango* was no different.

Knee-high boots with a zipper down the inner seam and a broad heel for gripping metal decks. Blousy black pants tucked in to the boots, with two small pockets on the front rather than the outsides, so you could get to them seated at your station. A simple undershirt and a collarless tunic with a zipper up the front and four exterior pockets to hold things. His was bright blue as a statement of captaincy, while his engineers wore a slate gray that hid stains and fighters wore red when they got formal.

He'd even gone ahead and visited the barber on *Aggregator*, getting a professional cut rather than relying on doing it himself or asking one of the local butchers to cut his hair. There was a reason most pirates just shaved it daily or buzzed it weekly. Or just let it grow down to their waist.

"Mati, Johanic, where are we at?" Basant called, looking around. Everyone had gone ahead and dressed the part today, like this was a documentary or a pirate video that would be popular a century from now.

Because nobody wanted to look like a schlub in the history books.

"We're good for flight," Mati growled without looking up, ready to be in motion and done with all this posturing shit. But that was Mati.

"Battle squadron is standing by, Captain," Johanic replied crisply.

"Open a general channel," Basant ordered.

He took a deep breath and waited for Johanic to nod.

"All vessels, this is Basant Utkin, aboard the Enforcer *Tango*," he continued, leaving off the name *Ingham*.

In his mind, *Ingham* was no more. That, or it was a cluster of frightened old women, desperately trying to cut a deal with *Aditi* and Kosnett by lying about how much they had known ahead of time. Like he'd ordered *Vilahana* destroyed without consulting his own bosses, since he expected their asses to be on the line, too.

Nobody had expected Kosnett to decide to crush *Ingham* like a bug afterwards, but at the time, he'd already set up all sorts of false rumors that *Aquitaine* had destroyed the planet themselves in order to wipe out a nest of vipers.

Governor Patte certainly fit that bill.

But Basant's gamble had failed. They did that. Usually, nothing worse than a ransom and a blockade, but a ship like *Tango* never called on any *Aditi* worlds anyway. They only went to places where heads needed to be cracked together.

He took another breath and forced his voice down and cold.

"*Ingham* is no more, as far as I am concerned," Basant continued. "*Hamath. Gilas. Wisym. Jakro. Nagi. Yarmouth.* Any of the others. Those folks are now our enemy, because they will sell us out to save their own skins, forgetting that we have all the ships. Messages have gone out to some of my friends, calling them to help, but they won't arrive in time, because I didn't want to give them time to tell anyone what was coming. If we are to survive, we must form a new people. And take over a place where nobody has even a social standing to dispute us, let alone a legal claim."

Basant paused and looked around his own crew, people who had been through hell with him.

"And by telling you about *Meerut*, I have signed my own death warrant with my old Board of Directors," he laughed. "So all of you are now on the hook with me. But when we do this, you captains will become dukes. Others that join later could be barons, and they might just be granted citizenship to let them escape the sorts of rough justice that we all have coming. And we all have it coming."

His bridge crew chuckled at that, and Basant supposed that others did as well, listening on the nearly forty other bridges in reach of his voice. Mostly Raiders, but even *Blade of Kunke* had elected a new captain after Zemke had died, and the new woman in charge had decided to throw in her lot with the mission, so he had two Enforcers today.

Basant hoped it would be enough.

"We are going to come out of Jump hard and fast, my friends," Basant said. "This is not a sneak-and-hit raid, but a strike to slide past the harbor guns before they can bring things to bear to stop us. You have your courses plotted, and now you understand why nobody ever found *Meerut* before this, so make sure you land hard and then turn into that next jump running as hard and as fast as you can, or you'll be waiting for me in hell when I get there."

He drew a breath and turned to Mati finally.

"All ships attack."

THIRTY-FIVE

ENFORCER TANGO

Basant was belted in and ready. How someone had figured out this particular quirk of galactic geometry was something he'd never learned, but this one worked. And only he and Mati had previously known how to fly this course.

It had been that way since the beginning. Two officers, and only two, sworn to secrecy about the path to *Meerut*. And the massive, deadly guard ships defending it.

He wondered how many more centuries the path would remain open.

Two nearby blue stars, massive beasts, were burning as hot and bright as you could without going full supernova. Right in the middle of a cluster of other stars so close together that there was no such thing as true night on *Meerut*.

Basant had stood on the surface of other planets at night, always surprised when it was too dark to read.

The Blue Twins, as they were called, had warped space so weirdly with their linked gravity that you had a funnel in JumpSpace. Try to sail through the edges of it and your engines fell apart and lost all tuning in minutes. But there was a spot at the center where you could sail safely almost through, but only if you knew the exact vector.

Because right now, the gravity wells overlapped just enough that you could not sail through. You had to drop out and cross a goodly distance in physical space first, before you got to the far side of that gravity blip Basant always thought of as a speed bump.

"Stand by for real space," Mati yelled to get everyone's attention. "Engine room, give me everything and keep it at the red line. Not sauntering today."

Basant laughed. Mati never sauntered, but usually you didn't come out of jump under the immense firepower of six big fortresses orbiting that common point in space.

Starlight.

Now, shit was about to get crazy.

Six stations tough enough for battleships. Orbiting at optimum range for all their guns.

A single ship trying to run this corridor was asking to be destroyed. On the other hand, thirty-eight meant that the gunners over there almost couldn't miss. At the same time, they also had to figure out who to shoot at.

Which was why Basant had plotted a course with *Tango* not quite at the front of the line. Anyone lingering was likely to get his ass burned off, but the first one to emerge might be alone when all six of those monsters opened up.

Mati wasn't playing around. He'd come right down the center of the beam, expecting other ships to fly far enough out to be enticing to someone with an itchy trigger finger.

"Shields to max," Basant ordered. "Route any excess to whatever flanks don't have friendly ships around to absorb fire for us."

The laugh that greeted him sounded more like a pack of hyenas spying a wounded gazelle than anything, but they were his crew. His killers.

"Four ships ahead of us and taking fire," Johanic yelled now. "Return it?"

"Negative," Basant said at the same time as Mati. "Everything into engines and shields. We can't hurt those towers without getting smashed ourselves. All we have to do is emerge on the far side intact."

The night sky that was filled with stars when he looked at the screen. Basant was almost home, to the world where night never fell. Just clouds of glowing gases, baby stars just getting wound up, and young, blue giants lighting the night for everyone to read by.

The hull rocked now.

"We're taking fire from Three," Johanic said.

"I know," Mati snarled back. "Someone came through too slowly."

But then, he'd helped plot the courses that would have given *Tango* bodyguards on all sides right now. Hopefully, nobody had broken down at the last. Or taken that information and decided that he could buy off a prison sentence someplace.

"Who is missing?" Basant asked.

"*Karga*," Johanic said. "A *Wisym* Picket we didn't necessarily trust, after we hit their base earlier. Is why they were on that corner."

"Shift shields around to cover that flank," Basant said. "How's the rest of the force doing?"

"*Blade of Kunke* is back a bit but keeping pace and following us like a pair of battleships in line astern," Johanic laughed. "Got a *Gilas* Raider in between, in case she wanted to get even with us for Harper."

Basant grunted. It was a cut-throat business, but he'd made his best case to everyone that this was the only way he could see how any of them could survive outside of life in prison.

It helped that he was burning all of his bridges to do this thing. That would encourage the others that he wasn't setting them up.

He was, but not like that. He needed to capture *Meerut* and then reinforce the front gate against cops coming later. Then set up a new government that would take as many pirates as wanted to come, while trying to trade with the outside world as much as they would allow.

One world wasn't a threat to anyone today, but it was all he had.

More earthquakes rippled through his toes, and then silence.

"Gotcha, you shits!" Mati yelled so loud that he might be hoarse after this, but he'd done it.

JumpSpace.

They'd run the gauntlet. There was only one station over *Meerut* that had any guns, and those were maybe enough to hold *Tango* at bay, except that he would be dropping out on top of them with a battle fleet backing him.

Whoever had survived.

"Thirty seconds to drop," Mati called, voice raw but triumphant.

"Shift us a little," Basant ordered now. "Up and out from where the original plan called for us to arrive, just in case somebody decides now would be a good time to put a spread of titan bolts into our ass and take over themselves. Dexter might have laid down the law, but he's still stuck outside until we can talk to the guard ships, and anything goes until shit is settled for good."

"Way ahead of you, boss," Mati screeched a little. "We're dropping out in a spot where we should be able to hammer the shit out of *Kunke* if they get frisky. Lack of trust, ya know?"

"I know, Mati," Basant said. "But tomorrow all that changes and we start from scratch. Everybody listening? All debts remain, but all feuds are done. Clean slate on anyone you hate, because we will absolutely hang separately after this, if we don't hang together."

Starlight again.

Home.

Basant felt an emotion tug at him that was almost unfamiliar after that first day at *Vilahana* where Kosnett had offered to kick in his teeth and stomp on his skull if he didn't behave.

Was this what hope felt like?

THIRTY-SIX

Phil had been hoping to chase the pirates into a corner where he could break them, but bureaucracy was the enemy of speed. And apparently Utkin hadn't waited to see who was coming for him.

Now, Phil studied the man that had been brought aboard *Urumchi*, having surrendered with what he thought was a good enough deal that *Aditi* might even do some sort of witness relocation and new identity.

Having your old friends and coworkers spending the rest of their lives and fortunes sending killers after you for a betrayal meant it better be big.

They were in a forward conference room, because Phil wanted all the various ambassadors as well as all of his attached Command Centurions, whatever they called themselves, present for this conversation.

Captain Ehman Bahra didn't look all that impressive on first glance, but Phil had spent a few hours with the man yesterday to get the gist of his story and had come away with a distinct impression of a creative, almost artistic mind, carefully hidden away behind the face of a pirate.

Urumchi's tables for conferences were all part of a circle, with gaps to let stewards navigate the inner portion of the ring. Nobody was that close to each other, but you also didn't end up with those long, skinny tables where you bonked heads when you and the guy across from you both leaned in to hear somebody talking at the far end. He'd done that a few times when he was younger.

Lots of folks present, including Herald Misra, speaking for the *Consensus* itself. And Ambassador Hu. Big player time.

Phil rose as everyone was settled. All eyes rotated away from Bahra to him, as intended.

"Captain Ehman Bahra of the *Wisym* Picket *Karga* brings us a troubling bit of information," Phil announced. "However, he also brought with him the scan logs to back things up, and I've had my people do a forensic analysis of it. They are comfortable with the results. Captain Bahra, tell them what you told me."

Phil sat as the other man rose. This would be his fourth or fifth time through, so he had the details and the flow almost memorized, but most of the room was coming at this cold.

"Utkin managed to organize fifty captains into a revolution," the man said now, speaking quietly but micced up with his words bouncing out everywhere. "He killed the Enforcer of *Nagi Syndicate* in the process, and kind of made himself over into a pirate warlord, something we haven't had in centuries."

Phil noted the stirrings around the room. The pirates had been slowly bought off with bribes and support to break them up in the old days, and that had formed the basis of Syndicate culture today.

It was also why you didn't do deals with criminals that didn't involve jail time. It just turned them to preying on someone else without solving the problem.

"There is a planet called *Meerut*, located inside the Cluster wall itself and protected by a weird warping of JumpSpace," Bahra continued. "I didn't see it, because we intentionally dropped out early enough to see the battle take place, before turning and running here."

Phil rose again at the point and cleared his throat.

"Captain Bahra is asking for leniency and forgiveness for himself and his crew," Phil called out, turning to look at Herald Misra. "They are willing to accept exile on *Aditi* itself, and protection, in trade for this information. I cannot speak for the *Consensus*, but representatives who can do so have heard this information and are working out the fine points. They have accepted the deal offered in general."

A few gasps. A little rumbling, mostly from his people. Everyone, however, understood that this was one of those situations where you took *good enough* and didn't push.

"The last stop before *Meerut* involved flying down a narrow funnel generated by two blue giants and a couple of ugly gas clouds," Bahra spoke now. Phil remained standing and watched, figuring he'd interrupt more than once. "You drop into real space, fly a ways, then turn sharply and take a second jump that supposedly drops you into a clear pocket with an inhabited world. Again, I only had Utkin's story, because we watched the battle and fled."

"Battle?" Captain Xue of the Skycruiser *Li Jing* asked in a bright, clear voice.

But then, she and *Stunt Dude* had just gotten back from smashing an *Ingham* base far too close to *Aditi* itself to be a true secret. Phil was certain that the fallout from that would happen later.

"There are six battle platforms," Bahra said. "Arranged in a ring around the throat. You have to fly right between them to get across the reef that protects the inner lagoon. The squadron was taking fire immediately and at least a couple of ships were damaged so badly that they either surrendered or were destroyed after *Karga* left."

"Battle platforms?" Captain Omarov asked now.

He'd only been home a day longer than Kaur and *Aranyani*, but that was politics back home. Phil already knew the man's reputation as a fighting captain.

"The scan logs we recovered suggest that they have firepower better than an *Aditi* Ship of the Line," Phil called out. "Significantly better. Or a *Dalou* Battleship. They have a mix of missiles, firebirds, and heavy beam weapons, as we would expect from their location at the seam between *Ewin* and *Dalou* space."

"How does this change your planning, First Centurion?" Herald Misra spoke up now.

She'd spent the most time with Bahra besides him, but she was also the one willing to shelter him from the shitshow that Phil expected to be coming after the man. On the flip side, if the pirates saw that they might be able to be reformed, hopefully many of the rest would choose that over death in battle with a police cruiser.

"You have several options here," he said, turning to take in everyone. "The people of the Cluster, that is. You can let them go and hope that they stay bottled up at *Meerut* and stop bothering the rest of you. You can accept them as a sixth stellar nation, with all that implies, but I am loathe to speak for the *Ewin* king or the *Dalou* Shogun on this matter, as they would be the immediate neighbors. You can try to put a stopper in the opening, or maintain a patrol force outside the range of those guns where pirates might not be able to sneak out. Or you can do it the hard way."

"What would you classify as *the hard way*, Kosnett?" Ambassador Hu asked in a leading voice.

Phil smiled. Captain Lin was seated next to the man, and already nodding to herself, so she knew what was coming, as did all of his people. It was only the locals that didn't think in those terms.

But *Yaumgan* wasn't really a local culture. *Stunt Dude* had clarified previous suppositions, based on conversations with Captain Xue.

"We fly in there and eliminate those six platforms as a threat," he said. "However that needs to happen. Then you either build your own platforms, or drop enough mines and defenders in place that nobody can get out, or simply leave the pathway open for fleets to get in and out. Considering the forces defending *Meerut* right now, you would need a massive undertaking to destroy those pirates, but it could be done."

"Could the force you have assembled accomplish it?" Hu asked, speaking loudly enough that he might have figured out what Lin had.

"Maybe," Phil said. "We have five cruisers, one survey cruiser, and *Urumchi*, plus the seven escorts. That's a sizable force but not enough to take on thirty-something pirates afterwards, as we'll need repair and resupply."

Hu turned to look at Lin and Phil watched the two of them have a complete conversation without saying a word. They weren't lovers. The body language was wrong. Father/daughter felt closer. Not like what he and Heather had, but Heather was closer in age to him.

And had been out there with him against *Buran*.

"*Yaumgan* is prepared to supplement your force, First Centurion," Hu said now. "The *Jùrén*-class vessel *Zhang Gualao* is currently merely at moorage overhead, awaiting my eventual return to *Yaumgan*. That would add something roughly equivalent to another battleship to your force, to go with *Urumchi*."

Phil nodded at that, unable to speak at the sudden babble of voices that had risen as everyone spoke to a neighbor or themselves in surprise. Phil was caught a little off guard, but only a little. Captain Lin had telegraphed her willingness.

Herald Misra, on the other hand, apparently didn't want to be outbid, as she rose and rapped the table in front of her to get some silence.

"The *Aditi Consensus* would also offer the Ship of the Line *Khandoba*, First Centurion," she offered. "Given your current force, that ship's two usual Moat vessels would accompany it without disrupting anything."

Phil fought to keep his face stern as everyone turned to look at the other three, but he didn't have time for messengers to get back to the *Gloran* Emperor, the Shogun, or the *Ewin* King to tell them they'd been outbid.

"I think that such a fleet might be sufficient, my friends," Phil overrode everyone. "Three dreadnoughts, six cruisers, and nine escorts is more than Keller had with her. I'm no Jessica Keller, but Basant Utkin is no Red Admiral, either. Plus, if we are to do this, we must outpace the inevitable spies running back to *Meerut* to warn them that we're coming. If they manage to reinforce those platforms with a significant portion of their fleet, there is little I could do to dislodge them. How soon can *Zhang Gualao* and *Khandoba* depart?"

"Immediately, First Centurion," Captain Lin spoke up now before Hu could say anything.

"I will speak with the necessary people myself, Kosnett," Misra called. "They will be ready tomorrow, or there will be a new Director in charge the day after."

Phil turned to Heather and Harinder and caught nods from both women. He'd already been planning to start his sail out to hound *Tango* and friends, so everyone was loaded up. Both *Tecate* and *San Quintin* had forward staged supplies secretly before running back to Phil's Citadel base outside the cluster under command of Fleet Machinist Valeriev.

He turned to the group and smiled indulgently.

"We will sail in thirty hours," he announced, wondering how far away those echoes might be heard.

THIRTY-SEVEN

HOLIDAY ORBITAL, MEERUT

Basant didn't trust the locals, but he'd also arrived with enough ships and firepower, however badly dinged up from the suicide run, that nobody here could gainsay him when he announced that he had come to take over.

Pirates are, after all, experts at understanding *force majeure*…

So he had taken over the station and more or less arrested the governor and all his staff, leaving only the bureaucracy in place. That meant Governor Youtler was gone and Platform Administrator Markeith Darji was in charge for now, subject to Basant's authority.

Which was a nice way of saying *a lot of guns*.

Staff meeting. Sort of. Basant and Andrea. *Hollywood* Ward because she'd been the first ship through the gauntlet and the first captain to offer to join the Board with him. Istis Bellie, the woman commanding *Blade of Kunke* now that Harper was dead. Captain Sterry Jenker, Basant's old sidekick on *Atlas*, since Jenker had been his ally for years now and was someone Basant trusted.

And Darji, uncomfortable among the revolutionaries that had just blown into town and taken over. Basant smiled to put the man at ease. It might have even worked.

"We're here because we have nowhere else to run," Basant reminded the man.

"Understood, Governor," Darji replied diffidently. "And you are a native, so you understand that you've just overturned our entire history in an afternoon, deposed Governor Youtler who was installed by the *Ingham* Board, and are now more or less trapped in here with us, with maybe the entire rest of the Cluster just beyond the ring, trying to figure out how to get to you. The staff are understandably a bit unnerved."

"Yes," Basant agreed, summing all of that up. "But *Ingham* is done. Over. The Board members were already quietly trying to cut deals with *Aditi* and *Aquitaine* to leave the fighting captains out to dry. And nobody would be willing to offer us sanctuary, so I had to bring all of my followers here. Yes, your cover is blown and yes that means more ships and maybe even officials come calling. But nobody can claim this world, and most of them will deal if we stop attacking their shipping."

"And you and your crews are all done with piracy, Governor?" Darji asked. "Just like that?"

"We have no choice," Basant agreed. "It was this or the hangman's noose. So we're going to turn these ships into a defensive fleet, build a base big enough to handle us, and then put the word out that other ships can come retire here. It's not like you're going to run out of land on the planet below any time soon, and we'll need a lot of colonists to turn this into a thing that works."

"What about the ring?" Darji asked.

"I need to send a ship to whoever is in charge there," Basant said. "Someone they know and trust, to let them know that I've taken command of *Meerut*. And to let some of my friends through who weren't fast enough to make it on their own."

"Friends?"

"*Aggregator* is out there," Basant smiled at the man. "Dexter is willing to turn his ship into an orbital hotel and casino here, as opposed to being arrested one of these days. Others will come.

Some need to be allowed in. Others need to be stomped on by the guard ships. Who sends that message? And more importantly, we need to send couriers to the five capitals, letting them know that we're here, what we've done, and that we promise to behave in the future."

"Will they accept that?" Darji pressed. "We're all accessories to piracy, one way or another."

"They don't have the firepower to force the guard ships," Basant growled. "And if they just run the gauntlet, they have to face everyone in here. The sooner we can get all our ships repaired, the stronger our position will be, so that we can start cutting deals with *Dalou* and *Ewin*."

"You've given this a lot of thought, Governor," Darji nodded.

"The Age of Piracy is over," Basant said firmly. "Now, we have to figure out what replaces it, but there are a lot of men and women out there who don't have homes to go back to."

"We'll make it work," the bureaucrat shrugged. "Somehow. The first thing on Governor Youlter's original schedule this week was a review of industrial productions…"

Basant nodded and let the man speak. This group with him, plus a few more to come, would have to turn themselves into businessfolks. Law-abiding citizens with no plans to cause problems to their neighbors. And get those outsiders to believe it and leave them in peace.

Somehow…

THIRTY-EIGHT
HEAVY ESCORT MORNINGHAWK

Makara Omarov was fairly certain he was going to die when they got there. That his luck was going to run out and he would not live through the coming battle.

Of a certainty, First Centurion Kosnett had enough firepower to take down the six monstrous platforms guarding the gullet to *Meerut*, but *Urumchi* was designed and built for a much more dangerous war than anything the Balhee Cluster had to offer, as was *Viking* and those seven deadly corvettes, including *CM-507*, the minesweeper that had originally been intended as a wingmate for *Morninghawk*. The other ships were true cruisers or even battleships, while he was in a mere Heavy Escort, a vessel only a little tougher than the two escorts for *Khandoba*: *Matangi* and *Kamalatmika*.

Inspector Sobol was studying him from her station on his far right. He felt the weight of her gaze and turned to make eye contact. She nodded to the hatch with an inquisitive look, as though asking if he wanted to talk in private.

Yes, they might as well get this out of the way now, so that she didn't do something stupid in the middle of Kosnett's battle that caused his death to arrive any earlier than it had to.

Makara nodded and rose.

"Bulat, you are in charge for now," he said, waiting for the man to acknowledge. Keo was the Second-in-Command, but he was off duty right now and Shamil Bulat could handle just about anything while they were in JumpSpace.

Makara led, so that they didn't end up all the damned way back in the training hall today. Instead, he took her only as far as his day office, where he could deal with never-ending paperwork out of the crew's hair, but be close enough to react if something happened.

Rather than sit behind his desk like he was afraid of this woman, however, he took the farther chair and gestured her into the one by the door.

It was a compact space. Turned sideways like this their knees would touch if either moved, so he sat perfectly still and watched her for a sign.

"You seem pensive and withdrawn, Captain," Sobol began in a voice that was not as hostile as he had been expecting. "More so than usual."

Not hostile at all. Almost friendly, as weird as that was. This woman was an Imperial Inspector with a chip on her shoulder. Or maybe several.

And he was the unlucky fourth son of a minor lord brought to the unwelcome attention of great powers.

Makara took a moment to frame his reply, sanding off some of the rough edges he had been expecting to use initially.

"*Morninghawk* is a small mouse in the coming battle," he replied. "We are not a cruiser, with all the redundancy that implies. We are not one of Kosnett's deadly escorts, designed to higher standards than the Cluster knows. *Morninghawk* is not even like the two Type-1 Moat escorts with *Khandoba*, because those crews know they are expendable. Promotion in *Aditi* is to ships on the second line, where they are more likely to survive the battle."

"And you do not expect to survive this encounter?" she asked, turning hard and cold now, as he did expect.

"I expect to die fighting," Makara said cruelly. "Kosnett will have us on a wing, protecting his battleships, but there are no wings when you engage a circular formation, so we will be close to someone who will recognize a ship of the *Dalou Hegemony*, and perhaps seek to target us more than they might the strangers, as *Dalou* and *Ewin* are the ones they will have to deal with later."

"The escorts cannot protect you?"

"They will try," Makara said. "But we are one of the escorts here. I personally do not think it will be enough, so we will suffer tremendous damage in the battle. Kosnett is a fierce warrior. I watched what he and Lau did to *Tango* at *Vilahana*. *Morninghawk* cannot survive in that kind of environment, so we must prepare to sacrifice ourselves on the altar of the future."

"Those are not the words I expected to hear," Sobol acknowledged.

"Every battle might be your last," he said, quoting something he had been taught at a young age. "No tomorrow is ever promised to you. But you will be remembered in death for how you lived and how you died, so *Morninghawk* will fight gloriously against numbers that far outweigh us. I only resent that you will not be able to report to the Shogun that we died with honor when we go, because you will die with my crew."

She blinked and leaned back now, eyes still focused on him but all hostility gone.

"The Shogun thought you had been turned by Kosnett at *Vilahana*," she offered now.

"I suspected as much," Makara nodded. "But we were never important enough to bother with. *Aditi* was a far richer prize and *Aranyani* happily fell into his hands and his orbit. I still don't know what I said or did that impressed the man enough to ask for *Morninghawk* by name."

"Perhaps he saw in your soul that willingness to die well, when all around you were pirates who were, at the end of the day, mere cowards," Sobol observed in a serious tone. "Utkin would rather overthrow his own kind than face justice. The others joined him because they feared being sent to prison. Or worse, being forced to grow up. That is not your problem, Makara Omarov."

He shook his head ruefully.

"It is not," he agreed with her. "But when that battle comes, I must demand that you simply sit and watch. We will fight. We will likely die, but if you try to issue contrary orders in the thick of battle, the confusion will ensure it, when I might be able to find us a lucky path through. Will you promise me that? Afterwards, you can cast my failures at the feet of the Shogun himself and have me destroyed, but that will be later, if either of us make it home."

She was certainly taken aback by his words. Makara saw that. They had a working relationship, but he knew nothing at all about the woman on a personal level. Just the sharp edges and impossible hardness of her soul.

"Why do you only command *Morninghawk*, Omarov?" she asked, turning the conversation inside out on him. "Why not *Wraithruin* or one of the fabled cruisers of your Clan?"

"I am the fourth son of Lingyi Omarov," he reminded her. "In the ancient tongue, *four* sounds just like *death*, and is thus unlucky. You know this as well as I. No sailor is comfortable with an unlucky captain. Even this crew took time to build for that reason. But I have molded them into a force that is sufficient to the needs of Omarov and Sugawara."

"And Kugosu," she said, speaking of the Shogun and surprising the hell out of him. "Did you ever stop to consider that a fourth son might also be the *Harbinger of Death* instead of merely a victim?"

Makara sat there numb. Shocked.

He had not. Ever.

Was it possible to take that superstition and twist it to his benefit?

At *Meerut*, they would find out.

THIRTY-NINE

Heather had called her own command team together for a staff meeting, skipping Phil and Harinder, but including Nam for all the usual reasons. The woman hadn't qualified as a battery commander on one of the Pulse-Twos, but that was only a matter of time. wouldn't happen before this battle, but eventually. Heather had no doubts about that.

"What do we know?" she turned to Leyla.

"Ring of monitors," the Science Officer replied. "*Karga* didn't stay long enough to see much, but we're looking at batteries of those Power Taps that they use around here, as well as firebirds in the crane range. Each platform also has at least one of the biggest version, what they call a condor."

"Heavy enough to hurt us?" Iveta chimed in.

Always thinking. Always planning. That described Heather's favorite Jessica Keller clone. Looked nothing like the legend, with a heart-shaped face a little plain and dark hair. Actually looked more like the Mongolian ancestry that had populated most of *Buran*.

But she was Keller's daughter underneath the skin.

"Hurt us or *Viking*," Leyla replied. "Cripple any of the cruisers. Stomp any of the escorts."

"We can damage them with pulse weapons," Heather reminded everyone. "We saw that at *Vilahana*, and even if these are battleship-class main weapons, I'm willing to bet a Lev that each platform only has one. Six would be enough to overwhelm any fool coming in here. What about the Power Taps? *Stunt Dude* told me about the Ōdachi variant that *Yaumgan* uses."

"In between," Leyla said. "Four pulses instead of three, but otherwise they look like the same weapon. *Yaumgan* gets six and better power out of theirs, but I assume that the difference is in the capacitor frame behind the weapon."

"So we're looking at ten escorts bashing away at incoming firebirds with everything they've got to protect the core?" Iveta asked.

"Nine," Heather said.

Heads turned sharply. Centurion Hào Boyadjiev spoke up first. He was the Gunner around here.

"Who are we holding back?" he asked, mentally obviously counting things.

"*Morninghawk* doesn't have the ability to survive all that shit on the front line, so Phil wants him tucked in right in front of us," Heather said. "Anchoring the exact center of the formation, if you will, with us and *Viking* flanking him, the cruisers just ahead, and the rest half-moon around the front."

"We trust him?" Iveta asked cruelly.

"We asked for him by name," Heather reminded them. "Phil thinks he's the key to opening up a long-term relationship with the *Dalou* folks, but he's being his usual sneaky self about it."

"How?" Centurion Bozhidar Virág asked now. He was *Urumchi's* Pilot, the one who'd be flying them into the heart of darkness here.

"Go look up the Meiji Restoration sometime," Heather laughed. "*The Professor* thinks that he might be able to pull something off in such a way as to permanently weaken the Shogun, but that stays in this room."

That last spoken directly to Nam, who was the only one who might say something later.

"Ma'am?" Nam asked now, confusion scrawled across her face.

"The Shogunate is a thing presently, Nam," Heather explained. "Back on Earth in the early industrial age, the Emperor rose up one day and overthrew his own Shogun and the entire military structure. Phil wants to maybe replicate that, because once that happened, Nihon went from Iron Age to one of the most powerful industrial nations in the world in a single generation."

"Oh," the woman replied. "I'll need a book to read."

Heather turned to Iveta and the woman nodded. First Officer handled that, and Iveta would get her the one that focused on the end of the samurai and how they reformed themselves into something else, rather than a history of the civil wars that some folks fought rather than give up their privilege. Something that showed how they turned into something so much greater for a long time, before demographics eventually toppled them over.

"So I have a stupid question," Iveta spoke up now, a smile lighting up her face like it did when she was about to get dangerous.

"Talk," Heather ordered in her Command Centurion voice. "That's why we're here."

"I know I have a particular reputation…" was about as far as she got before the laughter and sarcastic abuse by her friends and teammates caused her to stop and blush for a few moments. "Okay, granted. Well-deserved. **HOWEVER**…Are we looking at this all wrong?"

"Define wrong," Bozhidar Virág stated in a hard, curious voice. Gunners were all alike in that way. Heather could speak from experience.

"Funnel shape in JumpSpace," Iveta replied, holding up her hands to demonstrate. "Killers back above the water line where they're safe against someone coming out of JumpSpace too close, like *Buran* used to do with Heather and First Expeditionary."

Heather nodded, not sure where her pet killer was going with this.

"Most fools come out central, thinking they can run the tube and get out the back," Iveta said. "*Tango* was going to do that with all their people, on the presumption that there would be too many ships to all get blown up. Let's take out one of them. They probably don't move all that much."

"How do you get to one?" Bozhidar Virág asked now. Pilot-talk. His ears had perked up immediately.

"Everybody sees that gravity well as a wall," she smiled. "It isn't anything in realspace. Let's drop out way early, form up an Armada, and deadsail around behind one of the fools. I got ten Levs says they have hardly any guns on the backside, and none of those killer firebirds. And most likely nothing better than station-keeping thrusters nowhere near powerful enough to turn one of those beasts around to engage us in anything less than a month."

"Support fire from the others who can see us?" Heather leaned in now, sharp with anticipation.

This was why she'd picked Iveta from all the other Keller knock-offs, when she'd had her choice of dozens. The rest had all been too…*linear* was insulting and wrong, but maybe *direct* was a better descriptor. Iveta had literally just turned the question inside out.

"Those firebirds are physical platforms filled with a plasma overload that they use to generate inertia, like the missiles we used to use," Iveta smiled. "Every kilometer they have to travel means less boom when they get there. Awesome at short range. Reasonably effective at medium. Nam, what happens when they have to travel too far to hit something?"

"They kind of go boop," the *Aditi* woman replied now. "The frame is hard to kill, but the energy is already dissipated. Outrunning one is the best way to not get killed, if you can."

"There you go," Iveta nodded. "Assume three of them can fire on us, but the three farthest away. At that point we're talking their equivalent of Type-3 beams and maybe some Power Taps at extreme range from the other five, so they might not be able to hold the lock or the focus. I'll assume some idiot fires missiles at us, but nobody has manufactured enough to get Galia Abbasi and her team worked up."

Heather smiled. Pirate thinking, when you had to sneak around, even with a preponderance of firepower, because someone could always bring a bigger hammer if they heard you in the cupboard.

"Game it out," she ordered. "Nam, you'll take charge of the six platforms, and assume three or four different weapon configurations, one of which is everything pointed inward and another is the ability for the whole platform to rotate around to face us as we approach."

"Why would they do that?" Nam asked.

"Why wouldn't they?" Heather fired back. "But you are as close as we can get to local thinking, so let's take advantage of all your habits and assume that the pirates think like you do. Everyone turn over half your duty rosters to your backups for a couple of days while you do this, so we can fill everyone in at that last coordination drop."

Heather got them on their way and leaned back with a smile on her face.

It might be Phil's mission and his glory, but this was her crew built up from folks she had also approved, and not just Phil and the First Lord.

Pirates, as it were.

Which was just what this sort of thing called for.

FORTY

Phil leaned back and listened as Iveta and Nam completed their presentation. He'd known Heather was up to no good, but hadn't appreciated just how evil the rest of her people could get when given a blank piece of paper and a problem.

"You're completely nuts," he observed now, looking at them. "And I mean that in the best possible way. Gold stars for all of you."

The three woman smiled at that.

"What happens if they do move into line abreast to *Cross Our T*?" he followed up with his own evil smile.

Curiously, Nam leaned forward.

"They don't have the size for the weapons we've seen demonstrated," she grinned. "Generators are smaller than engines, but to actually move, the ships would have to either be bigger, or have fewer weapons than we've seen. Plus, Bozhidar Virág really messed me up on one of his attacks by just deadsailing all the way around the back over the course of a week, until he came out the far side of the gravity well of that monster and hopped straight into *Meerut* without ever firing a shot at me."

Phil turned to Iveta and caught the grin and nod. So, that

woman was growing up as well. He'd been fearful to have a Keller worshiper holding the guns, but had trusted Heather's intuition.

It was paying off.

"*Morninghawk*?" he asked.

"Safe as a puppy in a rug," Heather replied. "Unless they decide to kill Omarov and ignore the rest of us while we stomp them into the mud. Not a lot I can do at that point."

"Don't tell him why," Phil said. "Just put him in the spot for a Heavy Escort just ahead of the capital warships and tell him to use his own firebirds defensively. We know that they can shoot firebirds at each other?"

"Something about the plasma causes them to actually bend inward," Iveta spoke up. "Nobody really knows why, but you have to fire them off with just a little lag, or keep the launchers themselves well apart. That's why *Dalou* has two or three good spots. Forward from both engine pylons and sometimes on the bow itself. And why *Yaumgan* uses titan bolts for their left fist instead of firebirds."

"Okay," Phil decided. "I'm sold. Give me tonight to review your initial assault plan and various contingencies, and I'll let you know tomorrow. That gives you a day to refine things before we tell everyone."

They heard his words as the dismissal it was and rose to depart.

"Heather," he said and she plopped back down to wait until the other two were gone. Markus stuck his head in, got a shake, and closed the hatch. "We need to see how many other little bays and coves there might be out there like this."

"Already been trying to identify how we might interpret sensor logs," she nodded. "This one was about as weird as you can get, because of that little line that forms a lagoon. I also wonder if maybe they have a back way that nobody knows about. It's not that far to the outer edge of the cluster if you had spent enough time looking for places you could sail carefully."

"That will be Barnaby's job when we're done here," Phil acknowledged.

"What happens after we get in?" she asked. "You aren't the type to do a smash and grab."

"The pirates see themselves as above the law," he said. "Or outside it, which is just as bad. *Karga* used their information to buy leniency, but every ship in there chose to run away from responsibility. They need to be broken. *Meerut* needs to be brought into the fold so that there isn't a planet out there thumbing its nose at everyone else. I just want Utkin and Liefan, plus about a dozen other officers who issued those orders. But if the entire Cluster joins together to do this, it becomes a political statement and forces everyone to admit they have a problem."

"We can't change the galaxy, Phil," Heather reminded him.

"We can try, Heather," he fired right back with a smile. "I'd rather be known for failing than not trying. You know that."

"*zu* Arlo learned that," she laughed now merrily.

Phil nodded.

"I think he already knew," he said. "Kigali did and would have communicated that to everyone else along the way."

"So what do we do afterwards?" she asked, changing gears on him.

"We have an open invite to *Yaumgan*," Phil said. "But *Dalou* is close."

"I told my team about Meiji plus Iveta has Nam reading some history," Heather replied.

"I'd like to see if we can pretend to be Perry," Phil smiled in a hard way. "Especially with an entire squadron of so-called enemy ships being escorted into harbor by *Morninghawk*."

"Got him covered as well," she nodded back.

"Saw that," Phil acknowledged. "Really good work on your part, as well as your team, Heather. Thank you."

"Doing my job, Phil."

"Yes. Better than anybody else could achieve. Remember that."

FORTY-ONE

ADCON CRUISER ARANYANI

Kaur looked over the plans that *Urumchi* had transmitted to everyone, noting that the names of the planners included Senior Officer Namrata Nagarkar. At least Nam had made a difference over there. And a good impression, or they would have sent her back at some point.

The plan of battle was so completely insane that Kaur wondered if the entire thing amounted to a huge practical joke. The contingencies mapped out were even worse.

"Are they kidding?" Arya sniped from her station. "That will never work!"

"Why not?" Kaur asked as every head turned that direction.

Arya blushed profusely.

"Shit," she muttered, having apparently forgotten that she was on the bridge and not in her office. "What's to stop them shifting around and all hitting us at once?"

"Appendix Five," Jagadish spoke up. "Estimated technical readouts, extrapolating out from our own notes on a heavily-fortified gunnery platform."

Kaur found herself jumping to the end of the long document along with everyone else.

Shit, indeed.

Known weapons. Known shielding array. Assumed minimum power requirements. *Aditi* generator specifications. Crew requirements. Total allowed volume, built to *Aditi Consensus* standards.

"So it's our fault?" Arya asked.

"Or our glory," Kaur reminded her. "I doubt that we built those platforms. Probably came off a *Dalou* yard that made a point of not including maker's marks or signatures anywhere that might later be incriminating. Not likely to be as good, so they can't just chase after us."

"Contingency 17-G," Indra Korrapati spoke up. The man replacing Nam on the guns for this battle. "We can presumably move faster than they can by at least two orders of magnitude, so if we draw them out of position, we can force them into a bad formation. I do not see where they would mount JumpSails, so we can escape that way as well."

"Pulled by a tugboat at some point," Kaur decided. "Probably just the one at first, and they have added the others slowly over time, until they reached what they thought was a sufficient deterrent."

"The *Consensus* would have to send a full sector fleet all the way over there to deal with…*that!*" Arya said.

"I might remind you that this is more than a sector fleet, Arya," Kaur smiled and watched the woman blink in surprise. "And includes everyone, so nobody is left out while the pirates are surrounded by enemies. This is Kosnett's declaration of war on the Syndicates. There is nowhere you can run where he won't come after you."

Arya shuddered and subsided, but Kaur understood. They'd literally been there at the beginning, when the future of the Balhee Cluster changed one afternoon as *RAN Urumchi* appeared in the skies above *Vilahana*.

And after this, Kaur would be a Director, with Arya taking over *Aranyani* as the new Commander.

Could they really end piracy as a way of life in the Cluster?
She found herself looking forward to it.

FORTY-TWO

HEAVY ESCORT MORNINGHAWK

Makara studied the plans and shook his head as the implications became clearer. He looked over at Inspector Sobol and caught her momentary shock and watched it fade into…what?

He had an idea, but didn't want to necessarily speak the words aloud, for fear of which *oni* and other demons they might accidentally summon onto the bridge of *Morninghawk*.

She nodded at some internal conversation and looked up, making eye contact with him now and smiling in a way that he would have found vaguely terrifying as recently as a week ago. More terrifying. The woman was still dangerous. Would still file a report with the Shogun that would determine his fate.

"Fourth son," she said simply.

Makara watched that observation ripple across his crew. Both Keo and Bulat flinched, but they were just as superstitious as any sailors underneath.

But she wasn't meaning it in the context of unlucky. Her smile said that.

"Keo!" Makara said loud enough that the man turned this way to look.

Bulat and the others did as well, but Makara had added that something to his voice that got men's attention.

"Kosnett has us at the center of his formation," Makara gestured around them. "We will form an extra line of the phalanx they intend to assemble, behind the cruisers where we will have the ultimate responsibility for protecting *Urumchi* and *Viking*. Us and nobody else. You saw how dangerous *Urumchi* was at *Vilahana*. And those deadly corvettes. Kosnett is putting *Morninghawk* directly in front of him as a statement to the pirates of who we are."

"Who are we?" Keo asked in a voice that came out almost in a squeak.

But then, Captain Makara Omarov had already written a poem to encompass the death he had been expecting. Already made peace with dying well in the service of the Shogun and the Emperor.

And now the strangers from *Aquitaine*.

"He put us there because we will become Kosnett's harbinger of a new order," Makara pronounced his fate over his entire crew now. "We will become the First Centurion's *Herald of Doom*."

Makara was just glad that Sobol shuddered as much as Keo did.

He intended to make this a death for the ages before a bunch of pirates dragged him down.

He did not intend to go to hell alone.

FORTY-THREE

Phil noted that Harinder had a smile on her face that was somewhat at odds with the seriousness of the situation, but didn't inquire. Probably just glad to be over all the weird political stuff and to a point where things got simple.

Her staff were all around the room, ready to relay messages to any vessel and handle communications by filtering things down to what Phil needed and nothing more. Everyone was a little hyper, as he glanced around. Well, Markus had an oversized vacuum flask of coffee latched down on the chair next to where the redneck was quietly reading in his pressure suit, but unless something went weirdly wrong, Markus wouldn't have anything to do except refill coffee flasks.

Good Lord willing and the creek don't rise.

At *Vilahana, Ground Control* had taken charge and solved the problem in the least military manner Phil could think of, but that wasn't going to be an option today. Well, it was, but he didn't want to slip inside that bottle without first removing the cork, in case something went wrong in *Meerut* orbit and he needed to flee afterwards.

We'll burn that bridge when we get there.

"Open a squadron channel," Phil said to Harinder as he centered himself.

If this was purely an *RAN* mission, he could have had holographic ghosts of his command centurions seated at the empty spots around him, but none of the Cluster ships had the capacity to do something like that, so he had settled for everyone as small images on a large screen.

It was a lot of faces. For a moment, he was back with Keller and *First Expeditionary*, when she was about to launch one of those massive, destructive raids that had been intended to disrupt the economies of entire sectors and not just chase off sharks.

Today was that kind of day as well.

Philip Kosnett was not the kind of leader to give his troops *Death or Glory* speeches to rouse them for action. He was pretty certain that Striker Solo of the *Ewin* bombard *Shadowbolt*, and Captain Adham Khan of *Juvayni* were going to be disappointed, but those two had been in competition to be fiercer, and more militant, than the other since they arrived.

And everyone else.

Captain Lin and Captain Xue were much calmer as he studied their faces. Which made sense, as *Yaumgan* saw themselves as a land of scholars and philosophers. Who just happened to build massive fighting robots that were exceptionally capable when it came to combat.

Captain Omarov met his eye with a hard stare. Not hostile. Firm. Dedicated to the coming action in ways that reminded Phil of Keller's lead berserker in the old days: Alber' d'Maine.

Hopefully, that level of utter brutality wouldn't be necessary today.

"All vessels, this is First Centurion Kosnett aboard *Urumchi*," he announced, beginning the ancient invocation leading to battle. "I have the flag."

Nods greeted him. His people were the best he could find, when he had the entirety of the *RAN* to pick from. The others had all shown promise in their own fields of endeavor, with both *Morninghawk* and *Aranyani* having been there at that beginning to witness the arc of history changing.

"Shortly, we are going into jump," Phil continued. "Into battle with an enemy who has never been forced to acknowledge that laws and rules of civilized behavior apply to them as well. I will not bore you with a recitation of their crimes, as might be necessary later, when the historians weigh in to judge my actions in leading us here. I will, however, state one thing clearly. One thing that I hope each of you will take home with you later for when others ask. Basant Utkin and Andrea Liefan tried to destroy an inhabited planet. And would have succeeded, but for luck on our part and the hard work of all of you in preventing it. And I include folks who were not there that day with us, as you have since chosen to raise your flag to support what we're about to do now, which will hopefully make the Cluster a better, safer place, and put you all on the path to turning into the sorts of neighbors that I would be happy to call friends."

He paused there and watched the impact of his words on the faces. *RAN* people nodded, stern and ready for action. The others had to pause and absorb what he had just said.

The fate he had just pronounced on the entire galaxy, when Phil Kosnett didn't think that anybody in the Cluster—maybe everybody together—could stop the *RAN* if they had chosen a different path than this.

If Imperial *Aquitaine* was already a thing, and not just a fear that he and Denis Jež discussed in quiet letters between *Ladaux* and *St. Legier*.

But he could make Balhee better. Give them the chance to turn the page on an age of piracy and embrace an age of civilization instead.

"*CB-502*, you have the vanguard," Phil intoned. "Ahead full acceleration and prepare for jump. All ships come to battle stations and conform to *CB-502*. Stand by for imminent battle. Good luck, and good hunting."

FORTY-FOUR

YAUMGAN SKYCRUISER LI JING

Stunt Dude was in his spot next to Captain Xue. Dao Zhiou, as she allowed him to address her in personal settings, like the wardroom or in her office discussing philosophy, ethics, and how to survive in the middle of a nation coming apart as their God and government had been destroyed in a manner that turned a dangerous nation into a failed religion.

He had a lot of experience at that, and Dao Zhiou reminded him occasionally that she wanted to meet Sam in the flesh. To understand his stories, as she expected to be living through it shortly.

But only if Phil was lucky.

Stunt Dude, however, knew the nature of Kosnett's luck. But then, he knew *Lady Blackbeard* and *Ground Control*. Had been there when the warrior representatives of the *Seventeenth Imperial Police Protectorate* had struck back at an evil god in the name of justice.

Nothing happening today was even in the same league, as cataclysmic as it might feel to these participants. Still, he didn't say that to any of them.

All the corvettes were across the front, ready to stomp on missile flights and firebird salvos. *Li Jing* was next to *Aranyani* on the left flank, ahead of *Zhang Gualao*. *Khandoba* and her escorts were on the right, along with *Juvayni* and *Shadowbolt*. That side would be launching masses of missiles, while this wing was direct-fire weaponry.

Phil would lean into his shield hand, as it were.

"You are utterly calm, for such an enormous battle," Xue Dao Zhiou noted, turning to look over at him.

"*Urumchi* and *Viking* are survey variants of ships I served with in the previous war," *Stunt Dude* said loud enough for the others to hear. "Perhaps a third of the firepower of *Vanguard*, or two thirds of *VI Ferrata*. Imagine an entire squadron of such vessels sailing into battle with a foe dangerous enough that it was evenly matched on the hardware."

"But you won," Dao Zhiou said.

"Jessica Keller won," *Stunt Dude* corrected her. "The rest of us were just there to help. That was a struggle between gods compared to what's about to happen here."

He noted the looks of mild astonishment on various faces, but they would have to meet the woman. Even Iveta, who was considered a close student of the woman, lacked that certain something that would make her a legend, but she was still probably better at this than anyone else on the field today.

No, that wasn't true. Phil would still win if he had to face Iveta on even terms.

And *Ground Control* could take anybody, once she was in the zone.

He'd seen that personally.

FORTY-FIVE

Heather was buckled in, suited up, and had had the requisite potty breaks necessary for a major engagement. Around her, her team was just as poised.

"Pilot, call the timer," Heather said over the last minute murmurs.

She had her A-team today. Everybody had rotated watch assignments once Phil settled on his attack time. Warships in space ran twenty-four hours a day, but tended to be settled on some planet from which they originated. In this case, they had been at *Aditi* long enough to adjust, so it was technically the middle of the night.

Not that it mattered.

Centurion Bozhidar Virág had the helm.

"Thirty seconds to emergence," he announced in a calm, professional voice.

"Iveta, you have Tactical," Heather continued, feeling *Ground Control* sneak up on her now and slip over her shoulders like a warm cloak on a cold day.

"I have Tac," Iveta replied.

The woman's voice had gone utterly calm. Heather was used to her being hyped up and excited as the big guns were about to cut loose, but the days of war-gaming this had reduced it to almost a mathematical exercise. Phil was bringing enough firepower to take down six battleships. They didn't have any escorts other than themselves, which was a silly thing, but the pirates had never been challenged before.

Never been forced to behave.

Never had to grow up.

Ground Control growled quietly to herself.

"Emergence," Virág announced to anybody who hadn't felt the transition from JumpSpace.

Some people said it felt like falling into warm water and emerging. To Heather, over the last few years, it had become something like a sixth sense, absent in the jump but appearing as she came into realspace.

"Leyla, light them up with a hard scan," *Ground Control* ordered. "*Viking* as well."

Technically, Phil's job, but he had put her in command of his flagship, and expected her to run it. And run it well.

Survey vessels had a frightening ratio of power available for their sensors, compared to anything else. Time to make use of it.

Leyla pressed a button that beeped. A warning to everyone that she had just turned a spotlight on her target.

"Confirm six," Leyla replied a second later. "Ring formation as before. We are long on target now designated number one, outside his plane of engagement."

Ground Control nodded. It was out of her hands now. She turned to Iveta and nodded.

"All sensors channel to max ECM," Iveta called.

Electronic Counter Measures. Snow and sleet on your targeting scanners. Doubly effective against missiles and firebirds. Three ships lit their beacons and blinded the stations with them.

"Squadron status?" *Ground Control* asked Leyla.

The two of them were largely out of the command loop right

now. Phil would handle the big stuff. Iveta had her hands on the gunners.

"Big and scary," Leyla said, turning to grin this direction.

Six monitors. Citadels more or less, but not as well armed as the station Phil had set up outside the Cluster as a base. Tougher than Bastions.

Totally out of their depth.

Seven corvettes. Two Moats. One Heavy Escort. Five Cruisers. Three Dreadnoughts.

Welcome to hell, bubbles.

"Attention enemy forces," Phil came over an open channel now. "This is the *Republic of Aquitaine* Navy and allies. You will surrender or be destroyed. The choice is entirely yours."

He didn't say "*Immediately or I will kill you all!*" but it was implied. Keller might not have been bluffing, but Phil would let them give up. Only after having been taught a few lessons, however.

"I have mass launch of missiles," Leyla called. "Four stations just let loose with the same sort of pods that *Stunt Dude* told us about."

"Pulse batteries, you are live," Iveta called out. "I want at least two of you protecting *Morninghawk* at all times. You have your assignments, and I expect you to adjust them as we maneuver. Handle that among yourselves."

Ground Control watched green lights appear on her board. Three Pulse-Twos each in four batteries. Front and rear, both extending well past hemispheres, plus right and left sides. You were **always** facing at least nine guns. Not counting the Type-4's. Everything, if Iveta rolled onto a flank, relative to the plane of battle. Which she would do if she had to.

Expeditionary war design. Hit them with every single gun you have at once, because the sharks were only going to be in range for seventeen to fifty seconds, and you needed to overload those killers before they fled. While being savaged.

"Science Officer," Iveta called now. "Give me an outer

effective zone designation for the Type-4s, based on most recent gunnery practice.”

A line appeared on Heather's screen, well in advance of the line of sail. Power Taps could still damage at that range, but getting a lock was tenuous, even before a survey dreadnought blinded you.

“All shields reinforce forward,” Iveta ordered as Heather listened. “Pilot, expect an order to bring the squadron to rest as we get within that ranging sphere.”

Ground Control nodded. Phil could pound on Station One with four Type-4 beams while the best the pirates could do would be to try to shoot back.

A massive cloud of Persian arrows was approaching. Not quite blotting out the sun, but damned impressive if you had a design like *Aranyani*, where they didn't have the Point Guns or defensive missiles to resist.

As she watched, the corvettes unleashed hell with their forward Type-3s. The Twos didn't range as far, but would come into play later, assuming Phil got close enough to dance with these deluded fools.

Heather grinned at the thought of Phil Kosnett pulling a circumvallation and using siege tactics on a castle. Was there a weirder way to fight a space battle?

But those weren't warships. They were battlestations that had been designed to prevent someone from sailing through the narrow gap. Forts on a hill over a narrow channel, when someone hadn't given a lot of thought to a legion landing well up the coast and marching around to hit you from the back.

Whoops.

She smiled and let it reach out and embrace her entire bridge.

“What's Station One doing?” Iveta asked as they watched the fireworks show.

Ground Control wondered if that burst of missiles was a one-shot thing. No. A competent commander would have two boxes.

Who could possibly survive that kind of firepower, anyway?

The Republic of Aquitaine Navy, pal. That's who.

"Station One is not moving," Leyla announced. "I am not seeing anything like red shift or blue shift from any of the stations that would indicate they can move around to engage us."

"All gun teams, scenario three for now," Iveta called.

Heather approved. They'd fought a number of various schemes, with Nam getting all sorts of different abilities each time, in an attempt to frame what the squadron needed to do to react.

If the ring was permanently stationary, they pirates were doomed. They just didn't know it yet.

Phil was about to sail a Trojan Horse right up to their walls and storm the place.

"Flag orders," Virág announced. "We have a stopping point assigned for the squadron. *Urumchi* and *Viking* shifting to the front, with just the corvettes. No, strike that. *Zhang Gualao* is going to join us."

Ground Control smiled. She wanted to know what the Sunsword could do. *Li Jing's* version of the Power Tap had range and extra capacitors over *Aditi*, but *Stunt Dude* had been under the impression that *Yaumgan* had upgraded the weapon for their *Jùrén*-class ships. The Eight Immortals, as it were.

Time for the titans to battle.

FORTY-SIX

ADCON CRUISER ARANYANI

Kaur was simply in awe, watching that swarm of missiles being annihilated. *Aditi* had Moat vessels like *Matangi* and *Kamalatmika*, but those were Combat variants, because Phil already had the corvettes. However, even Escort variants would have been hard-pressed to kill that much death coming at them at high speed.

What had those wars between *Aquitaine* and *Fribourg* been like? Or the war to the death with *Buran*? She had heard stories about the man Yan Bedrov, but what sort of twisted imagination came up with things like that?

"Orders from Harinder," Arya called. "We're to hold here and the big guns are sliding into extreme range to fight the stations."

"Jagadish," Kaur confirmed, but the man was already nodding.

Kaur had a ring-side seat to one of the biggest battles in centuries, and this wasn't even the main event, as frightening as that was. But she had much to learn about how *Aquitaine* really saw the galaxy, and this would be as good an example as one ever got.

She remembered that first engagement, when *Tango* and his

escorts had come out of Jump and threatened to seriously damage *Aranyani*. *Saluki* had broken bond and fired into her flank, but she had been unable to rotate her shield projector away from *Tango* to do anything else.

And then *Task Force 502* had stepped in.

Kaur still occasionally had nightmares about the surgical way *Saluki* had been dismantled by those guns, even after they had attempted to surrender. Phil hadn't been feeling benevolent that day, breaking that pirate vessel as a warning that the others had misunderstood.

Tango had managed to deescalate things once all his missiles were destroyed, and then got away later after Heather had flown *Urumchi* into the side of an asteroid to push it out of the way.

But Phil had been poised to use a level of violence that nobody in the Cluster really understood. Even now, whispers among the other Commanders had suggested that they underestimated Kosnett's crew.

This would be as entertaining as it was enlightening for some folks.

FORTY-SEVEN

Heather was directly on-line with Phil now, studying his face.

"Catapults, Phil?" she confirmed. Had he really used that word to describe the next phase of battle he had in mind?

"Catapults," he nodded. Grinned at her even. "We've got the sally ports covered well. There are walls protecting the infantry against counter-fire. I want you to take one of these stations down so hard that the others wet themselves before surrendering."

"*Saluki*," *Ground Control* noted.

"Exactly that," he said. "Make an example of them, but we need to conserve our resources, so I want all the others back. They aren't Expeditionary-class vessels, designed for this sort of thing. You have the flag."

"Squadron, this is *Ground Control*, aboard *Urumchi*," she said, falling into her other identity in ways that her people already understood. If this happened too many more times she might have to start letting outsiders call her that. "I have the flag. *Urumchi* and *Viking* move to flanking positions with *Zhang Gualao* in the center. *Morninghawk*, you were supposed to remain with the others."

"I'm your escort, *Urumchi*," Makara replied. "Deal with it."

She held back from saying something tart. The man was serious. As serious as any of the *RAN* corvettes handling the same duty in front of her. She could honor that.

"*Morninghawk*, come to this position and settle in to rest, bow centered on Station One," *Ground Control* ordered. "Stand by with your firebirds in case they try anything silly."

He flashed her a green light and dropped in just below and ahead of the spot where *Zhang Gualao* would be, like a horse the robot was riding. All the corvettes were pulled in closer now, zigzagged up and down like teeth in a mouth.

"First condor firebird launch detected," Leyla called.

"All scanners lock on and give me the power degradation curve against the cranes and falcons we've engaged before," Iveta spoke up. "Escort teams, I want slow fire on this first one until it gets to Pulse-Two range and then saw it apart."

Heather nodded. Learn what your foe has, and then how to defeat it. Those mounts were huge enough that nothing less than a battleship would mount one. Even *Morninghawk* only had one falcon and four of the defensive shrikes, the weakest type available. Condor, crane, falcon, and shrike in descending size.

She watched the thing come at them like a scarlet comet, a big ball of energy at the front and a tail of plasma behind it that was the leftover from the drive mechanism. You could pack a lot of punch into a small frame, but they did degrade over range, and Phil had intentionally stopped well out a distance.

The corvettes unleashed a patient, methodical kind of hell as she watched, slicing off pieces like a salami at the butcher. Metronomes keeping a beat.

Then it crossed the imaginary threshold that Command Centurion Galia Abbasi aboard *CC-501* considered *close enough*, because every gun with arc cut loose at once. Piranha, eating a cow that had fallen into the river.

Eventually, the doomed carcass more or less slammed into

Urumchi's forward shield array, but that hit almost like a tug arriving to push them into dock.

"Okay, folks," Heather said. "We have the first two rounds fired at us after giving them a chance to surrender. *Zhang Gualao*, stand by to lock on with your Sunsword. *Viking* and *Urumchi*, lock with the Fours and fire a single salvo now. *Zhang Gualao*, you follow up and hold it as we recharge."

"Gunner," Iveta called, bringing Hào's head around briefly. "I want us to make *Viking* look junior varsity right now."

Hào laughed, along with the others. *Ground Control* leaned back and watched. She had the flag, but that meant that she was almost as passive as Phil, until something happened.

"Multiple condor launch," Leyla sang out over the rest. "Three in the air, so I presume two stations cannot get their launchers to pivot that far."

"Escort teams, engage as you bear," *Ground Control* reminded everyone, but beams were firing.

Then Hào cut loose with the Type-4s. *Viking* did at almost the same instant, so four of the mighty beams slammed into a stationary monitor platform with almost no parallax. You could do that when you were both at rest relative to each other.

Even attenuated by the extreme range, the hits were solid.

"Damage report?" Iveta asked.

"Facing shield down eighty percent," Leyla answered. "Sunsword firing now."

Heather wondered if everyone else was holding their breaths, too. Nobody but *Yaumgan* had supposedly ever seen the infamous Sunsword in battle. Except pirates who weren't around afterwards to say anything.

Like the Power Tap, it fired a first bolt of liquid energy downrange, slamming into the target. From there, the scanners held a hard lock and the arm froze on gyros to hold a specific aiming point. *Aranyani* would be hard pressed to lock on with their Power Tap at this range, and their pulses would be feather soft. The Sunsword wasn't a full order of magnitude more powerful, but they got lock and the first pulse hammered hard.

"Shields to fourteen percent," Leyla called. "Eight. Two. Penetration. I repeat, shields down on the facing array."

"All guns fire," Iveta called.

Technically, Heather's order to give, but she would have said the same thing half a second later anyway.

The Fours hit bare metal. Ass side of the station, so she wondered what was over there. If she was building such a weird thing, this would be warehouses and docking rings for cargo ships coming directly from *Meerut* with supplies. Then crew quarters and general facilities for a station permanently moored in place. The generators and weapons would be on the inner facing, where they had the shortest distance to guns.

A few Main Guns opened up now. Not just from One but Two and Six as well. The range was extreme and Heather had the impression that they had to dial the mounts around to the edges in order to engage her.

Dumb design, but they were focused on that hallway they were guarding. Who would walk a war fleet up behind them and knife them in the kidneys?

FORTY-EIGHT

HEAVY ESCORT MORNINGHAWK

Makara was left simply mute. He had grown up in a land where the firebird was considered the pinnacle of weapons technology. A thing so dangerous that even the threat of condors and cranes kept fleets and pirates at bay.

Now he was watching Kosnett's forces melt them like snowballs facing a blowtorch.

Keo was on guns today, with Bulat flying. It was always a coin-toss with those two, but Makara didn't mind, as they were both exceptional at either.

"Shit," Keo said as that first firebird booped the front shields on *Urumchi*.

Nothing more. Just the sort of boop on the nose that he might have done to a niece or nephew when they were all younger.

Inspector Sobol gasped. Makara found that to be the most rewarding. She hadn't been at *Vilahana*, when *Tango* had fired their bow crane or wing falcons at the corvette task force. The target escort had survived without even losing their shields because of the rapid-fire beams they had used that day.

"Are we doomed?" she asked.

Makara didn't ask what she meant. Sobol had already moved

past the current battle to the changes that would befall all of the Cluster when new weapons technology became available.

When a firebird might be so *irrelevant* that nobody even bothered mounting them anymore.

"That is tomorrow," he told her. "We are forewarned. Keo, scan the three condors in flight right now. I assume one each for the forward ships, but I also assume that the *RAN* ships can handle theirs. Pick the one aimed at *Zhang Gualao* and concentrate on hurting it as it closes. We're in the central position to protect against anything that makes it past the corvettes."

Keo nodded. Makara still quailed.

He had two Main Guns on the front of his engine pylons, and six Point Guns defending all sides, as a good escort should. His firepower consisted of four suddenly-puny shrikes he could launch, but they had a much shorter range than those damned condors.

"Flight paths confirmed," Keo called back loud enough to be heard. "One each. Engaging number two with the Main Guns. What about the Point Guns?"

"Everything," Makara answered. "Sequence two shrikes and hold the other two for the last. Put the falcon into it after the shrikes."

Escort was a way of life. A way of thinking that involved approaching some problems sidelong, because you lacked fists to make your point. At the same time, you had to be able to intercept trouble and deal with it before more valuable ships were put at risk.

Sometimes by stepping in front of them to take a punch.

He watched his boards with one eye and Sobol with the other.

First Centurion Kosnett had obviously planned this battle as well as one could ahead of time, and was exploiting what were in retrospect obvious design failings. They were still, however, the sorts of things Makara might have done wrong as well, so

Makara realized that Kosnett had much to teach him and all his people on the true art of war.

Makara Omarov decided that he needed to become a better student.

Assuming he survived.

FORTY-NINE

YAUMGAN SKYCRUISER LI JING

"What's that?" *Stunt Dude* asked, leaning into Captain Xue's space to point at something on her board.

He'd seen it, and understood it, but he wasn't sure the others had quite grasped the significance.

"We've got a runner!" Xue Dao Zhiou called sharply.

Stunt Dude nodded. One of the stations, maybe Four from the direction of the red shift, had just launched a ship. Small, but headed up.

Inward, he corrected himself.

The natural tendency from the outside was to see the ring of six stations as a drain at the bottom of a sink, but Phil had brought the entire force around to the side, so they were currently on a plane with the six, behind one.

Up, in this instance, was somebody running to cross the gravity well and get a message to the pirates at *Meerut*.

"Engines, pivot us and maximum acceleration," Xue called. "Let *Urumchi* know that we're in pursuit. If they get away, the pirates will know we're coming. They might even try to reinforce things here."

Trinidad didn't have much to do today. He was the observer

along for the ride, trying to explain *Aquitaine* as much as he was understanding *Yaumgan* for others for later.

Technically, this was disobeying orders, but only because *Li Jing* had been told to remain back where it was safe from the titanic struggle taking place between the *RAN* ships and allied battleships against the stations. But nobody else was in a position to do this. *Li Jing* had that excess power that *Yaumgan* ships seemed to. Better tech, though not as good as *Aquitaine*. At least not yet.

So they were off.

He grinned.

"What's so amusing?" Dao Zhiou asked as the crew fell into a pursuit mode that didn't require her to issue orders.

"From the station, I wonder if we look like a giant human flying," *Stunt Dude* said. "Like those vids where somebody gains fantastic powers and puts on a costume to fight crime. Flying through the air to chase bad guys."

"Something you've done?" she asked, but it was more curiosity than challenge.

"You're tall," he replied. She nodded. "Many of the male actors I worked with in the old days were about my height. And my skinny build in those days, when I weight seven kilograms less. They all seemed to do at least one of those vids, and frequently needed a stunt double who could handle the close combat fight scenes in a wig. I went for years with my head shaved because it was just easier for costuming."

Her eyes got big.

"Truly?" she asked in surprise.

"The lone hero is a recurring motif in *Aquitaine* culture," *Stunt Dude* explained. "One man or woman who arrives in town, sees the bad things that have gotten out of hand, and decides to do something about it. I presume from your response that *Yaumgan* does not have this?"

"We have our champion figures," she shrugged. "But they tend to be part of an army, stepping out with their close friends to challenge another champion between lines in a single combat for glory."

"Always as part of a group, though," Trinidad said, understanding the underlying links that reminded him of the ancient Hellenes or the era when China was first finally unified.

"As part of a group, yes," she said. "Kosnett's behavior suddenly makes much more sense to me."

"Make sure you communicate that to Captain Lin and Ambassador Hu," *Stunt Dude* said.

"You do not mind?"

"We are here to learn from each other," he reminded her. "To do that, understanding of cultural antecedents is just as important."

"Are you sure you were merely a warrior in charge of other warriors, *Stunt Dude*?" she teased now. "You sound disturbingly philosophical for such."

"When we destroyed *Buran*, I had to walk into the fallen remains looking for Sam," he said. "Their culture was entirely organized on the creche level, as *Buran* and his incarnations tested each child and assigned them a place in society into which they were then put for the rest of their lives. The people I met were unused to thinking for themselves, but it had been thrust upon them when the thinking computers that controlled every facet of their lives died one day. I had to understand that, in order to navigate the ensuing chaos."

"All that to find one woman?"

"To find Sam," he corrected her. "That was a promise I had made to myself as I watched her sail away that last time. We are all about the lone hero walking into town and fighting bullies, you know. That's what *Aquitaine* does best."

"And how you see yourselves in the mirror," Dao Zhiou nodded in recognition. "One of these days, I need to hear more about your adventures in *Buran, Stunt Dude*."

"When this is all over," he promised her, watching out of the corner of his eye as *Li Jing* cut the corner on that freighter and began to close.

"Hu BooLa," Captain Xue said now to her Flyer. "Will he get away?"

"No," the man replied tersely.

Stunt Dude thought from the tone that the man felt a little insulted by the suggestion, but kept his opinions to himself.

"Gunners, start punishing him now," Captain Xue called in her command voice. "He might decide to jump early, just to escape us, even if such a random jump most likely makes it worse for him. I want him stopped. And the others when they come as well. In fact, send a note to the other cruisers to take up similar positions against multiple ships trying to get away."

Stunt Dude sat back and watched *Yaumgan* handle the unexpected. Moments like this were when you saw the truth about people.

And he liked these folks.

Phil liked what he saw. Station One was being punished hard. From this range, the three stations with facing were having a hard time because only their firebirds could see him. Any beam weapons risked shooting a friendly station except in a couple of gaps.

That was why Heather had assigned her people a Red Team/Gold Team exercise. Put yourself in the heads of the enemy and figure out what he'll do.

Keller was still the best at it, able to juggle hundreds or perhaps thousands of options in her head at once, find the shift she wanted, and follow it down a logical track.

Chess Grandmaster, though that was more Enej Zivkovic's thing.

Still, he didn't think she would have scored Heather that badly on this one.

On the big holographic projection at the center of the table, he spun the image and dialed it back a little as a freighter suddenly came under the fire of *Li Jing*. That was one spot his team had missed, and would make a good teaching moment later, but Captain Xue had pounced fast and hard, like a hungry bobcat, and now the other cruisers were moving into intercept positions as well.

If this kept up, he might actually have complete surprise when he dropped this fleet out of jump at *Meerut*. Wouldn't that be fun?

"Thoughts?" Harinder asked now.

Phil watched the ballet of death playing out.

"Have all the cruisers do a hard scan of the stations," he decided. "Let me know what jump-capable ships are left, assuming the stations themselves are permanent here. It's really tempting to end this battle halfway done and go jump on *Tango* and his friends in the pocket if nobody behind us can do anything but watch. We can always long sail around the back, assuming everyone has enough food aboard."

She nodded and turned to one of her Centurions to relay that order.

That first freighter had been crushed by *Li Jing*, and Phil hadn't said anything. He had offered them a chance to surrender at the outset. There would be another one later, after he'd made his point. However, there was still that point to be made first. If Captain Xue had used her big guns to stop a tin can from fleeing, that was just the risk in battle.

"Two others," Harinder said after a few moments. "On Two and Five. According to *Li Jing*, they look like simple resupply cargo carriers."

"Not surprised," Phil grunted. "Your crews always need fresh socks and cream as our old friend *Mendocino* used to remind us. Plus R&R opportunities back on *Meerut* to keep them sharp here on what has to be the most boring guard duty in the galaxy."

He paused to consider.

"Can we get to either of them from here?" he asked a moment later.

Harinder pressed a button and the Science Officer appeared on his screen.

"Sir?" she asked.

"Cargo ships on Two and Five, Leyla," Phil said. "Are they visible from here?"

"Stand by."

She looked down but left the line open.

"Negative on Five," she continued a moment later. "We could shift up a little and reach Two, but that opens us up to the rear half of the ring being able to snipe at us finally."

"At this range I'm not worried," he smiled. "Ask Heather what she thinks."

Technically, he could assume the flag right now and order it, but she'd organized this battle and was handling everything according to a musical score in her head. The last thing she needed was him jarring everything with an unnecessary surprise.

Battles already had enough of those.

"Phil," Heather was suddenly on the tabletop screen that Leyla had been on a second ago. "You think it's worth doing?"

"Your thoughts?"

"If I can get the stations to surrender, stuffing all the crews aboard a pair of unarmed ships gets them out of my way and out of mischief for security teams we put aboard," she said. "With the cruiser team putting a cork in their own bottle, I'm guessing that they stay put now."

"Or run for open space," Harinder opined. "This is a tunnel with two ends."

"I'd like it if they ran that way," Heather growled with a smile. "They have to tell somebody where they came from, and then all the rest of the cluster knows what's up here. We're still in the high slot either way."

"Your call, Heather," Phil said. "Feel free to cut this short after One's demolished, so we can hoard our reserves. Or we can reduce this entire thing to rubble as a statement of purpose. Either way, they get torn down later. That or I send Barnaby off to find other paths into *Meerut*. They have to be there, just working on astrophysics, but I'm guessing the pirates were too lazy to locate other back doors, when they had this to intimidate people."

"Will keep you posted, Phil," she said and was gone.

Phil leaned back and nodded to Markus for more coffee. This was the hardest part of command, just sitting here while the people he had selected and trained handled things. Still, he had the best that a generation of deadly warfare had been able to produce, and had taken the free-thinkers from that group.

They'd solve this. And solve the piracy problem.

Whether anybody could solve the Balhee Cluster itself wasn't his problem.

FIFTY-ONE

ADCON CRUISER ARANYANI

Kaur watched the battle unfold with her heart in her throat. Missile swarms shattered. Condors reduced to ether. That one freighter hammered so badly that crews had jettisoned in their escape pods, where *Juvayni* was currently picking them up.

Li Jing claimed not to have the space for prisoners. Kaur assumed that they just didn't want the responsibility. The *Gloran* warriors would be brutal and rude, but probably not kill anyone unnecessarily, as these would be merely flight crews.

There was no honor in slaughtering civilians who have surrendered to you. Any *Gloran* warrior would be insulted at the suggestion.

However, the other two ships were refusing to budge. Kaur wondered if they were to be destroyed, but no order had arrived. While the stations were focused on Kosnett, they were better equipped to engage the four cruisers here, except that the range was exceptional.

She wondered if they had another set of missile pods that they might unleash.

"Get Heather on a line," Kaur decided.

Arya worked quickly and Heather appeared.

"I presume until proven otherwise that they have a second flight of missiles, being held until we rush them," Kaur told her.

"Safe bet," Heather nodded.

"At some point, they're going to get desperate," Kaur continued. "Perhaps launch them this way. The cruisers cannot handle that sort of thing. Well, *Shadowbolt* might be able to intercept them with his own missiles, but that empties his magazines before the battle even starts. Can we borrow a couple of your corvettes up here as a defensive shield?"

"Excellent idea," Heather said, turning on her screen to talk to someone. "*CG-506* and *CM-507*, withdraw from this line and circle around. Attach yourself to *Aranyani* for escort duties until we see where all this is going."

Some conversation occurred, and Heather turned to look at the camera again.

"Your group should back off another bit," Heather suggested. "No reason to tempt them when they realize what just happened and before help can arrive."

And then she was gone.

"Arya, let the other three know," Kaur ordered. "As much as they will allow it, I think Heather just put us in charge of this facet of the operation, so couch all orders as requests from the flag and let me know if anybody pushes back. *Shadowbolt* and *Juvayni* might not be entirely comfortable taking orders from a woman, though *Morninghawk* has been fine, down escorting *Zhang Gualao*."

"On it," the woman replied.

The stations were doing this all wrong, Kaur decided. But then, they had been invulnerable and unstoppable until this morning. She wondered if their tactical planning had gotten utterly ossified by entropy, or if maybe the new pirate overlords of *Meerut* had replaced all the commanders and unreliable crew members after taking over.

Either way, they were losing, and almost being embarrassed

about it, to watch regular Type-4 beams slam into shields and hulls so hard that she could actually measure the resulting quakes with seismological scanners if she wanted. Station One wasn't going to last much longer before it possibly came apart.

Then what?

FIFTY-TWO

Iveta had a running score in her head. Shots fired. Locations. Impact. Effect.

She hadn't understood it at the time, but one of her First Year instructors at the Academy had insisted that she understand the construction and architectural side of starships at least as well as an engineering-track graduate. Today, she understood why Professor Toskins had done so, and also why the woman had ended up being one of the few civilians to teach there, when almost everyone else had worn a uniform.

Iveta knew exactly where to place the next shot, because if she had done all the math in her head correctly, that one would be terminal.

"Gunner, hold fire," Iveta called. "Flag, have the others stop for now as well."

She could ask that. Iveta Beridze was in command of *Urumchi* right now, at least until Lau or Kosnett overrode her.

The Command Centurion nodded.

"This is Lau aboard *Urumchi*, I have the flag," she said in response "All ships cease fire."

Then the boss cut the line and stared at her.

"What's up, Iveta?" Lau asked.

"We're one good Type-4 hit from breaking Station One into two functional pieces," Iveta replied. "I can't be sure until we fire if it will actually separate, but those frames are weak enough right now."

"Purpose?"

"If the First Centurion wants to give them an option to surrender, there is nothing they can do right now except take it or die, Command Centurion," Iveta said. "The Sunsword absolutely cleaves them in twain if they hit right here. One Type-4 might do the same, depending on debris inside that I can't see from here."

She reached down to her targeting screen and drew a small line in what was already a crater. That would show up on everyone's screens to study.

Command Centurion Lau studied it for a moment and then looked up and smiled at her.

"Excellent, Iveta," the woman said. "Gold star for you. Hang on."

Iveta actually felt a blush take hold, which was so rare that she almost didn't recognize it. Except that Lau and Kosnett, working with the First Lord herself, had chosen one Iveta Beridze as First Officer of *Urumchi*, when Iveta knew that there had to have been hundreds of other candidates for the job.

She had to out-Jessica Keller all of them, but Professor Toskins had shown her how.

Know when to fight, and how, but also when to step back. Keller had more than once just annihilated *Buran* warships without touching the civilian shipping nearby, going so far as to remind them who her real enemies were. Later, when it had been necessary, she'd destroyed or damaged every ship that her guns could reach.

Violence as a surgical tool.

"Phil, Station One is ready for the chop," Lau was saying to the First Centurion now. "Orders?"

"Kill it and then I'll talk to the survivors," the man said in that voice that took her right back to the Academy.

Fleet Centurion Kosnett had been an instructor just before this. She had audited several of his classes once she identified this job, just to understand what the man would expect of his people.

"Iveta, all yours," Lau said now.

"Gunner," Iveta squared her shoulders. "One shot. Place it here, and see if you can draw the arc downwards and a shade to the right as you do. It feels like we have a frame partially severed already, and I'd like to cut it the rest of the way."

Centurion Hào Boyadjiev turned to look at her blankly, and then nodded. He'd been firing shots as she placed them, but this was the first time she'd had ever asked the man to commit art.

Or graffiti.

"Firing now," he said, pressing a set of buttons.

Iveta had a scan image up, updated regularly from the Science Officer and all the other scanners pointed at the stations for this battle. She saw the hit and knew the rightness of it in her bones.

Energy liberated as a plasma cloud, racing backwards out of the crater Hào's big cannons had previously blasted, but she also saw it emerge from the other side, inwards towards the center of the ring.

"Science Officer, confirm the damage," Iveta called, looking over at Leyla.

"Station One has buckled," Leyla confirmed a few seconds later. "There are a few connections on the inner top that seem to be holding, but there is a noticeable bend in the ship itself. I detect fires inside that the crew are fighting by venting sections to space."

"Secure the guns," Iveta ordered unnecessarily, but professionally.

Never leave things to chance unless you have to.

The other stations had continued to fire beams, missiles, and firebirds at them, but the escorts were handling that. Only one attempt had seemed dangerous at all, and Iveta had watched *Morninghawk* handle it sharply by using their own small firebirds as a counter-missile array before she'd needed to bring a Type-4 lateral to protect *Zhang Gualao*.

It was good.

"First Centurion, we are at rest," Iveta announced, just to finish the process.

She still had *Tactical* until Lau changed that, but they had moved to *Political* now.

Time to learn more from The Professor.

"Enemy stations, this is First Centurion Kosnett," the man said in a slow, somber tone that took her back to a news announcer she remembered from her youth. "You had a chance to surrender and did not elect to exercise it, so I had to kill one of your stations to make my point. This will be your last opportunity, because if you fight me after this, I will methodically destroy every single one of you and then ignore all your escape pods launched into space because you will have chosen to die gloriously in battle and I do not wish to come between you and whatever deities you have commended your souls to. In three minutes, my mercy will lapse and you will be annihilated."

Iveta remembered to breathe after a few seconds. That was a side of the First Centurion that she hadn't seen before. Butcher, talking to a flock of chickens about who will be next for dinner.

There had been about that much emotion involved.

Looking around, almost everyone else had been caught in that same spell, and was only now waking.

Everybody but *Ground Control*.

Iveta suddenly understood more of what made her boss tick. She made a note to ask Markus a few pointed questions, next time they sat down for a meal that wasn't a date. They weren't dating. Just enjoyed dinners or drinks regularly. And occasionally ended up in her cabin.

But not dating.

Ground Control was back. Iveta could see it in her eyes, like at *Vilahana* when the woman had driven *Urumchi* into the side of a planet in order to push it out of the way.

Legends, her and *The Professor*.

Iveta wondered what she needed to do to earn her own pirate nickname.

Because now she had a goal.

FIFTY-THREE

HEAVY ESCORT MORNINGHAWK

Makara watched his screens as the squadron slowly advanced into the sort of range where those condors and Power Taps would be dangerous, but nobody fired anything. Kosnett had truly instilled a new kind of existential dread into the galaxy today.

He turned to Sobol and felt better when her face was just as pale as his felt, jaw slightly slack, eyes bugged.

Two little cargo haulers remaining behind were slowly working their way around the ring, supposedly picking up the various crews to be transported back to *Meerut* for whatever internment would occur once Kosnett was done with the pirates in orbit.

On his screens, the stations shields had been reduced to the lowest setting, sufficient for stray rubble but not even enough to stop one of his shrikes from getting through right now. *Morninghawk* was just behind the corvettes on the leading wave, leading *Urumchi* in as both *Viking* and *Zhang Gualao* held damoclean swords over the hostages. At this range, he might face destruction, but Makara understood that the retribution Kosnett visited on the pirates would be terrible.

Final.

That took some of the load off his back.

"Inspector," he said to the woman, waiting for her to turn this way and focus.

Fish out of water and struggling to breathe. He knew that feeling.

She did. Blinked a few times. Seemed to come back to herself with a shudder.

"We're doomed," she whispered.

"We are among allies," he countered sternly. "Possibly friends, because Kosnett chose us to be here. Specifically us. To learn. To see the future that he was laying out and how it might unfold. The Hegemony will need to adapt. Must change for the better. Our culture of social isolation and quiet support of piracy must end, if we are to remain on the right side of history. *Do you understand me?*"

It felt odd, talking to the woman like a recalcitrant teenager, but Makara Omarov had seen the future in that instant when *Urumchi* shattered an orbital platform previously dangerous enough to engage a *Dalou* Battleship on even terms.

She blinked again. Drew a heavy breath that seemed to center her.

He watched her eyes flicker to his crew. Keo and Bulat were ignoring the woman, focused like diamond cutters on their respective tasks, but they would hear anything she had to say. Makara didn't think that she really grasped, however, that her secrets would be utterly safe with them.

Unspoken.

That was the kind of crew he had built for himself.

"Keo, you have command," Makara made a snap decision. "Do whatever Lau or Beridze tell you. Fire first on anything threatening us or any friendly vessels. I'll be in my office with the Inspector."

He rose and nodded the woman to her feet. He led. She followed, drawing strength from motion until she was pacing him at his side by the time they exited the bridge into the main aft corridor.

They remained in silence save footsteps, until the door closed behind her and he again took the seat in the corner, on this side of the desk, their knees interlaced but not moving.

"The Shogun feared that you had been seduced by the foreigners," she began out of the blue, but really she was continuing any of several conversations they had previously had.

"Frightened utterly silly, but I can see the confusion to an outsider," he corrected her. "We have nothing that can stand before them. Nothing. Today has just rammed that point painfully home to the rest of you."

"What would you suggest?" she asked now, sounding more like a bureaucrat and less like his superior officer.

"We need *Aquitaine* technology." Makara ticked things off on his fingers as he spoke. "Trade. Cultural exchange. Scholarship. At *Vilahana*…"

"Yes?" she prompted when he fell silent.

"I asked Kosnett at one point what he might do with that vast graveyard of old ships orbiting the planet," Makara spoke. "He suggested repairing some and putting his own crews on them, possibly recruiting locals to fill in empty slots. I had the impression that he had more crew members than he really needed for that very reason."

"What did you say?" Sobol pressed.

"The truth," Makara answered. "That I had been doing the same. Looking for old hulls that might be refurbished in an Omarov or Sugawara yard and sold for a profit, though I didn't specify to whom. What we need are second-hand ships from Kosnett's homeland. They will be old and worn out, and I suspect still better than anything we are currently building. I have been aboard *Urumchi* enough to understand that we lag there as well."

"The Shogun will not like that message," she pointed out, removing all trace of emotion from her voice.

"He has a tiger by the tail," Makara replied. "And not a paper tiger easily disproven as a threat. Kosnett has already introduced the tidal waves that will likely swamp many of the players on the board if they are not careful. *Ewin* is doomed until they reinvent themselves from scratch. *Gloran* might be able to handle it. *Might*. *Yaumgan* and *Aditi* will be laughing as the rest of us fall farther and farther behind them. How long do you think it will be until a leader arises at one of those two places who decides they have enough of a lead to simply conquer the rest of the Cluster?"

"The *Aditi Consensus* would never do that!" she snapped.

"No?" Makara asked. "They are not aggressively expansionist today, but that is partly the pressure of the pirates on all shipping. What happens when a vacuum forms because the pirates are no more? *Aditi* will flow into that and hold it. They do not conquer today, yet how many times have they built *trade outposts* in disputed systems? Ignored the empty planet below but held orbital space until we forced them to withdraw? And not every time are we successful at it, when the trade they bring to a region is sufficient to sway the locals in their favor. The Shogun and the Hegemony are too withdrawn for our future. They will hide from *Aditi* and their allies in *Aquitaine* and *Yaumgan*, until we are reduced to that small core of worlds we truly hold, letting all those mining colonies switch allegiance when we are not looking."

"Are you suggesting we fight *Aditi*?" Sobol demanded hotly.

"No, that's a foolish way to die," Makara said. "But we must meet them on that field of competition if we are to remain independent. We must trade. We must expand into those neutral zone worlds and make them ours while we still can. Otherwise, someone else will. Worse, if we continue to rely on archaic weapons, we won't be able to stop them from taking those worlds, or expanding into ours."

He leaned back now, heart hammering as he found himself leaned so far forward that he was almost breathing on the woman. That would never do. She could easily take offense at such a thing and order any manner of punishments.

But she said nothing. Just watched him with hot, hard eyes as he forced his shoulder blades to touch the back of his chair.

"I could have you struck down when we return to *Ellariel*," she began.

Makara waved that off like a fly that was annoying him.

"That just ensures that I do not have to watch the *Dalou Hegemony* fall," he snapped at the woman. "As I have no children of my own, they will not suffer, even as Omarov and Sugawara do. Pronounce your doom if you wish. You will go down with them."

She gasped. Makara wondered if he'd gone too far, but she needed to break free from the traps in her mind that were holding her welded and wedded to a past that had already failed. It had merely forgotten to tell anyone.

Yet.

"So I should return to my master and tell him to cast aside centuries of tradition and history on your say so?" Sobol sneered at him now.

"That, or watch helplessly as someone else does it for him," Makara countered, trying to rein in the anger in his belly. "I do not believe that it can be stopped at this point. Only controlled a little."

"And you would control it?" She laughed.

The laughter he gave in return had a chilling, killing edge to it that brought her up short.

"I am a fourth son," Makara reminded her. "The unlucky one that reminds everyone of death. Omarov is a minor holding. Even Sugawara is *Komyo*, a minor lord standing meekly before the greatness of Kugosu. My opinions matter so little that they will likely never even be recorded for historians to argue about later. *He* will listen to *you*."

The *He* was obvious. As was the threat inherent in the situation.

Samnang Sobol studied him closer now. Calmer, but in a penetrating way. Makara sat perfectly still, aware that he was technically too close to the woman if she chose to find offense. She was an Imperial Inspector on a mission. He was just the fool driving her around.

And standing nearby like a mouse while mighty samurai rode into battle.

"You have no spouse, Omarov," she observed out of the blue.

"Fourth son. Minor lord," he reiterated. "The geisha think well enough of me, but no allies saw fit ere this to sacrifice a daughter."

He kept the acid out of his mouth now. Left it in his stomach where it churned.

Makara Omarov wondered if he would still be the Captain of this ship when the day was done.

Then she surprised the living hell out of him by placing a hand on his knee. He looked down, and when he looked up she was much closer than she had been. Leaned forward as much as he had been.

"And when the Shogun accuses you of seducing me?" she asked in a voice loaded with emotions he couldn't parse into distinct flavors. "What will you say?"

Makara tried to find his tongue, but some magical pixie from one of the ancient stories had apparently stolen it when he wasn't looking. His jaw worked, yet nothing came out. That same pixie had paused to turn up the volume on his heart rate now, to the point that he wondered if the pounding was audible to her.

Or to the men on the bridge.

"You have, you know," Sobol observed, a sly smile forming on her mouth. "Without ever treating me like a woman. You merely treated me as an intelligent superior who was wrong, misinformed, and needed to be carefully and politely rerouted to the truth, that I would see it with my own eyes."

Words. Makara found himself filled with them, but none

bothered to find themselves a second word to connect to. Just static.

"I think that you have hidden yourself from most people, Makara Omarov," Sobol continued deliberately into his silence. "Let duty take the place to social intrigue. I suspect that I have seen more of the real you than perhaps anyone else, because you are *driven*. Not by fear, as I originally suspected. Or even lust or greed. No, you are impelled by a quiet patriotism and filial piety that allows you to merely command one of Omarov's lesser warships when the legendary *Wraithruin* might be yours. A loyalty to certain ideals and dreams that demands you save all of *Dalou from itself* rather than quietly positioning Omarov or Sugawara to rise in the coming chaos and civil wars that most of your compatriots have not yet imagined looms so closely."

Makara nodded, cut to the quick. Had his emotions gotten the better of him? Was he doomed?

But her hand was still on his knee. Not gripping painfully. Just resting. Possessively?

Was there a greater threat in the galaxy than this woman?

He nodded. What else was there to do? She had seen into his soul. That much was obvious.

"You will stand before the Shogun when this is done," Samnang Sobol moved inexorably forward with her words. "You will explain it to him as you did to me. You, Makara Omarov, will convince him of this truth."

"And if he chooses not to believe?" Makara asked. "Decides instead to have me put to death? Assuming, of course, that the man doesn't draw his own blade at that moment and handle the task with his own hands? There is absolutely nothing I can do to stop him."

"I will be standing beside you when you speak," she said. "I will support you in this, because Omarov is correct, and everyone else who seeks to gainsay you is *wrong*."

He tasted the power in her words. The certainty.

Shit, it might even work.

Makara had already been prepared to sell his life dearly in Kosnett's service, so not much would change if the enemy he ended up fighting for that future was Kugosu rather than mere pirates.

"And you?" he asked hesitantly.

If standing before the Shogun was a risk to his mortal shell, this woman felt like a threat to his very soul.

Her smile did not reassure him.

"They will be right when they whisper that you seduced me, Makara," she said, using his given name for the first time since he had known her. "And entirely wrong in the methods you used."

He processed her words. Found a combination that actually made sense in his scattered psyche.

Twice now she had used the word *seduced*, suggesting something far greater as well as deeper than merely allies against a greater foe.

And her hand had not moved.

He drew a breath and found that same fire that had sent *Morninghawk* surging forward into battle with the great ships this day as he leaned forward now.

Samnang Sobol smiled as he did. It was a warm smile, rather than the coldly predatory one he was much more familiar with from this woman.

Carefully, he leaned into her, wondering if he was sealing his doom in kissing the woman.

But she invited it. Did not flinch away. Did not strike him.

Kissed him instead.

Time passed. His heart rate did not recede.

A beep intruded. Broke the kiss.

Both combatants leaned back and smiled.

The beep was insistent.

"Captain here," he said, leaning over to trigger the comm on his desk.

"Orders from the flagship, Makara," Keo replied. "Figured you should be here for this."

"This?" he asked, shifting gears mentally.

They were still in the middle of a battle. This was no time to take this woman to bed. Or let her take him.

Right?

"Kosnett and Lau are about to unleash Phase Two, boss," Keo said with a grin in his voice.

Phase Two.

Going to *Meerut*.

And fighting a pirate fleet for the future of the galaxy.

FIFTY-FOUR

Phil watched somewhat impassively as the surrendered defenders rounded themselves up for him. He had no beef with them, assuming nobody gave him a reason at this point. They were just sailors hired to do a job.

That the job entailed defending a pirate kingdom from justice was separate. And they had fired on the fleet that had run the gauntlet earlier.

He presumed that Utkin had been successful. There couldn't be much in *Meerut* orbit to stop that many warships. The folks here had likely acknowledged a new boss and gone right back to what they always did.

Until today.

He smiled grimly at Harinder and dialed the scan down in tighter again. *Li Jing* and the others sealing the bottle by slipping past the Ring had ensured that nobody had a way out that didn't involve Phil Kosnett being a nice guy.

He could see a *Dalou* fleet slipping across their nearby border and spending a few weeks pounding this place into rubble, but Phil doubted that they would have had someone like Iveta to suggest coming in on the blindside.

Linear thinking. Lots of places taught it. Only Jessica Keller taught you how to think in oblong French curves.

"Where are we at?" he asked Harinder now.

She had everything at her fingertips. She was like that. He knew that Enej was proud of the woman and had personally called him to put in a good word, back at the beginning when Phil had first opened the slot.

"Six should be just about done loading all the crews into that last freighter," she said.

"Find out their logistical needs," he said. "We can always have one of the corvettes drop back to where *Mexicali* is staging with food, but I'd rather we got them to *Meerut* if they can hold out for a day. That way, they become somebody else's problem."

She nodded and Phil studied the situation.

In the old days, this would be the time to call on *Stunt Dude* and have him and his little team of crazy marines storm the place, but Trinidad didn't even take orders anymore. Plus, he was over on *Li Jing*, sending occasional updates suggesting just how much the man was learning. And how right it had been to send him there.

Phil located a button on his comm.

"Security, Opeyemi here," Temitope said as she came on-line.

"Got a mission for my Dragoon," Phil grinned at her.

"Been waiting for your call, First Centurion," she grinned back.

"I want you and Dar to take a bunch of teams over there in order to spike all their guns," Phil ordered her. "Leave the stations intact for now. I don't know if I'll want to destroy them later, or leave them, but it's not like they'll be effective after this, once people realize what we did."

"That will take a while," she observed neutrally. "Are you waiting for us?"

"We are not," Phil acknowledged. "You'll have assault transports that can jump back to the staging point when you're done. I'll send someone for you later. I'm only staying until you confirm that each platform is unoccupied. You'll be in charge of this part of the operation. Questions?"

"Do we keep one armed, just in case somebody gets by you?"

"Not worth the effort," he nodded. "And if they are running now, they probably won't ever stop running, and we'll find a ship's carcass someplace like *Vilahana* one of these days, where they abandoned it and took up new identities to get away. With seven exceptions, I win at that point anyway."

"We can launch in six minutes," she nodded. "It will take longer to stop at all the corvettes for bodies, but we'll be boarding inside an hour."

"As soon as you launch from the last corvette, we'll be moving inwards," Phil told her. "Then jumping when you give the word."

She nodded back and the screen went blank. He grinned. His Dragoon had been itching for something like this for months, but he hadn't gone out with any of the teams like *Li Jing* before he got the news that upended everything anyway.

"All ships, this is Kosnett, I have the flag," he announced, assuming that everyone had just been waiting for those words. "We will be launching marine assault teams to take command of the platforms and spike them. You have approximately three hours until we move forward on Phase Two, so everybody come down one alert level and make sure your crews get a little relaxation time. Maintain vigilance and formations, and remember that someone might wander out of the bottle without realizing what happened out here. No radio signal will make it to the planet before we do, however, so be prepared to take prisoners if someone appears."

He'd put that on a general, unsecured channel, so the folks aboard those two freighters would hear it as well. Being taken prisoner was always a good thing, assuming you didn't have a death warrant somewhere. And even then, most places might be willing to plead that down to a few decades incarcerated, if you come clean and were a good little model prisoner doing your time.

Phil wanted to break the pirates. At the same time, it wasn't necessary to turn this whole thing into an omelet of broken eggs in the process.

FIFTY-FIVE

Heather had only what rough astronomical mapping she and *Viking* had been able to do with passive and optical sensors at this range. It didn't help much.

Meerut was in a pocket, near as she could tell. Young stars and nebula packed together so closely that she wondered if the night sky on the surface was ever really dark. The two blue giants forming the tunnel entrance would go supernova one of these days. She presumed that the radiation from the first one might just scour the surface of the nearby planet clean at this range. And likely trigger the second giant to go supernova shortly after that.

There would be paths out the sides and possibly the back, but it was all star-forming nebulae, thick gases, and rubble around here. Scanners wouldn't work for shit to find such corridors, though. Or tell you which ones didn't end up in blind alleys that made you turn around and methodically work your way back out of the maze to try some other option. Just trying to sail out any other direction would be years in realspace.

She had to presume that the pirates probably wouldn't know them any better than she did.

Rats, trapped in a small room, fighting for their lives.

It was going to get ugly.

Alber' d'Maine would be licking his chops about now. Kigali would have a smile that chilled the soul to watch. Keller would bring her magic to the table.

They didn't have Keller. They had Kosnett. This wouldn't necessarily be a bloodbath, but Heather didn't figure it would miss by much when the shooting started.

"Team," she said loud enough to bring heads around.

Everyone had taken an extra potty break and had some food. Naps were for later.

Eyes tracked her from all sides. *Ground Control* took over her soul.

"We're the enemy they fear," she reminded her people. "Us. *Urumchi*. Everyone else is just along for the ride, but I doubt that they have nightmares about *Morninghawk*."

"More the fools them," Iveta said as the others chuckled. "Don't underestimate that man."

Ground Control nodded. Iveta had seen it, too, then. Omarov had a solid crew and a willingness to go for the throat where the others might hesitate.

"*Morninghawk* will be in our shadow, doing the right things," she continued. "We'll land in roughly the same formation we came out here at first, us in the middle and everyone out in rings, except that the escorts will be across a wider front and responsible for a full hemisphere of coverage. That means people rushing us can get close and try to do damage."

Ground Control could see orbital space above *Meerut* in her head, in spite of never having been there. Two Enforcers. The rest an even mix between Raiders and Pickets, with a few Salvagers and some others. One armed platform somewhere.

"We will be facing every possible weapon system they have in the Cluster," she said. "Main guns. Point Guns. Missiles. Firebirds. Titan bolts. Power Taps. The strength of the Zen-Mekyo Syndicates is that those designs come overbuilt with spots where you can pull one weapon out and mount something else in its place quite easily. We don't know who most of these ships are. Our escorts will be firing everything they have at anything that moves. *Morninghawk* will be doing the same, but he's not in their class, so expect him to be subtle about how he engages. We're going to use the Type-4s and the Sunsword to smash things. The cruisers are good at putting a lot of damage downrange, but not dealing with swarms of seeking weapons inbound. That's us and *Viking*, but mostly us, because I guarantee you that they're going to be trying to hammer us down more than they are *Zhang Gualao* or *Aranyani*. Pulse-Two teams, I expect you to overheat your guns and grind years off their lifespan today. We've got more crated up back at the base, and can have others sent from home. They are tools. Use them like it. Use them up if you have to. Anyone firing on us is an enemy to be killed until Phil says they aren't. He might have mercy later, but we will have none until he takes hold of the chain and pulls us back from savaging those pirates and tearing out their throats. Questions?"

Dead silence. Not shock. Nods. Commitment. These were her people. Hand-picked. *Hand-forged.* They would make the legend of the *Survey Expedition* the equal of *First Expeditionary* for future generations by the time she was done with them.

"Well said, *Ground Control,*" Phil's voice suddenly filled the air. He'd been listening. "Harinder, play that back for the entire squadron to remind them what's coming. I couldn't have said it any better on my best day."

Ground Control felt Heather wanting to blush, but she didn't allow it. They were minutes away from one of the biggest, nastiest battles she'd ever been part of, even back with Keller, and this was not the time for the softer emotions.

Tomorrow. Maybe.

She heard her words played back now for everyone. *Morninghawk* might blush, but Omarov didn't strike her as the type. Solid. He'd be the one she'd send into the corners after a puck, certain he would move heaven and earth to get it out to one of the pretty players to slam into the net for all the glory.

There was a reason hockey awarded two assists on a goal. To recognize that mean fucker who went into the scrum and won those battles. The ones that won games.

That won trophies.

"Squadron, this is Kosnett aboard *Urumchi*," he said now as her words finished up. "I have the flag. You are in formation, so I'll make this quick. Everything *Ground Control* just said. Simple as that. We aren't going to come out of jump firing like I used to in a previous life, but assume that it won't be long after that when you're taking fire, so be ready unleash all the hounds of hell on anyone giving you any reason. We'll sort them out later, after they get the snot beat out of them. I won't ask if there are questions, because I don't have answers. Just an expectation that all of you will give me everything you've got. They outnumber us. We outweigh them. Hold the line and break their teeth. Simple as that. *Morninghawk*, begin standard acceleration on your current line. All vessels conform to *Morninghawk* and stand by for jump."

FIFTY-SIX

Iveta let the calmness of *Ground Control*'s words envelope her. And *The Professor*'s.

"Pilot?" she asked the air.

"Sixty seconds," Bozhidar replied evenly.

Iveta turned to *Ground Control*.

"First Officer, you have Tactical," the woman said simply.

Iveta felt the surge of power roll through her.

Urumchi would be the heart of battle today. The center of everything that everybody had to try to escape the sorts of justice that the First Centurion demanded of a civilized land.

It would be her sword.

"I have tactical," Iveta replied. "Shields, full reinforcement forward and then keep the jump generators on line after we drop out. Assume Power tTps hitting the front shield before we even know where they came from. Everybody else will need a few minutes to charge things. Science Officer, we expect two Enforcers: *Tango* and *Blade of Kunke*. I need them coded separately so we can concentrate on the former. Pulse-Two teams, assume missile packs shitstorming us as fast as someone can type the launching code into the system and push a button."

Iveta leaned back and studied the scene as she envisioned it in her mind. A couple of stations, maybe armed, maybe not. Two bigger ships. A swarm of small and medium ones. Probably others that had been swept up in the tidal currents of a pirate civil war. Cargo transports, large and small.

Nothing like a shark that could threaten them and escape, though she had studied every one of Keller's battles closely to understand what the woman had done and more specifically the moment when she'd seen the need to completely upend her original battle plan to lunge on someone and eviscerate them.

Nothing fancy here. It would be short range unless every pirate ran, and then a chase where the little ones might not be important enough to prioritize.

"Type-4 teams, assume runners," she called out now. "Flag, you might remind the cruisers that long range fire would be a useful way to lame a Picket as soon as they redshift on us."

"Noted, Tactical," the First Centurion replied immediately. "Will transmit."

That felt good. Having an idea that the veterans accepted without qualm. Felt like she had arrived someplace.

Iveta didn't know where, because this was just going to be a mess.

And when she was done, it was likely to be a junkyard.

But that was fine. Today her job was to be a junkyard dog savaging people. Rip. Tear. Bite.

Only the ones that run might escape. And then only for a time.

Realspace.

Meerut in the near distance, but they'd come out a little higher in the gravity well than normal, assuming pirates might be hiding up here to jump someone coming out. Any of those fools were about to lose teeth.

"Science Officer, hard ping now and keep pinging occasionally," Iveta said. "Give me red shift as soon as you identify it. Everyone else assume blue shift as they rush at us."

Leyla's station beeped loudly enough to let everyone know. The music of battle, where you just listened as tones told you what was going on around you.

Three orbital stations, one on the far side mostly obscured, but the one in front of them identified itself as the Governor's Palace, so Iveta figured they were in the right spot.

A forest of purple dots on her screen. Ships at rest in orbit. They started getting transponder notes, but Iveta only cared about the ones that didn't turn green at this point. Those would be warships, while green were freighters that had no business in a war.

She would still kill them if they got mouthy, but they had to start it.

"Attention *Meerut* Orbital Traffic, this is First Centurion Philip S. Kosnett of the *Republic of Aquitaine* Navy," *The Professor* introduced himself now. "You will surrender to the combined forces of law and order, or we will treat you like outlaws in every sense of the word."

"*Tango* identified," Leyla called now.

Iveta watched a signal on her board turn gold. Long, long range. Way the hell over there, where he might decide to run away, thinking that he could skirt them.

Iveta wondered if they should have left some firepower back at the gate, but that would have been ships they needed here.

All the pirates were low in the gravity well. And cold, looking at the scan returns appearing on her board.

"*Morninghawk*, take us in," Iveta said.

Normally, Tactical was responsible for just the ship itself, with the flag handling the squadron. This required everyone to be on the same page, so Heather was letting her run things, with an eye towards that first shift in tactics that would occur when somebody did something unexpected.

Iveta wasn't sure she'd see it, but that was why you had a tactical officer fighting. Heather and Phil were watching everyone else.

"Gunners, hammer *Tango* now, before he wakes up," Iveta said.

Technically, she was supposed to wait for someone to shoot at her before going mean, but *Tango* had a bounty. As did *Wulfa*, though she didn't see that one on the scan just yet, so she wasn't sure where they were.

Viking joined in. Four Type-4 beams close to edge of coherence. But they had a ship with minimal shielding up right now. The kind that promptly collapsed like soap bubbles under the barrage.

"Second salvo," Iveta said, eyes tracking the rest of the field.

She was looking for an *Ewin* hull she knew had to be around here. *Tango* had brought some missile escorts to that first battle, before he discovered how worthless that style of fighting was now. They'd be in this mix.

"Multiple missile launches detected," Leyla said in a conversational tone. "Tagging."

Iveta watched the symbols appear. Did the math. Came to conclusions.

"*Morninghawk*, back your speed down a shade and let us close the gap a third," Iveta ordered.

His little pixie firebirds were amazing against corvettes and patrol boats, but exactly wrong for missile swarms. Omarov, however, would keep Pickets at bay quite nicely today, and that was what she really needed.

"Escort teams, as you bear," Iveta said formally.

Unnecessarily, as everyone had let loose with everything they had when they'd read the same targeting locks.

Sand castles and tides, watching those missiles get picked off one at a time. And more.

"Anybody surrendering?" Kosnett asked amiably.

Just chatting, almost. But then, he probably didn't expect it to be that easy. There were roughly forty enemy warships showing on her board right now. Frightening, except that they weren't a combined forces fleet like she was leading. Not trained together and working towards a common goal.

Rats, cornered.

Below her, ships started moving, but without any coherence. It was more like every command centurion ordered acceleration on whatever heading the ship had, while trying to charge weapons and raise shields. If they had been packed closer, Iveta was certain that she would have seen at least one collision.

"Let's go junkyard," Iveta mused to herself.

"What was that?" Heather asked.

Iveta realized she'd spoken louder than she intended. Or the bridge had fallen that quiet.

"Rats, cornered," she repeated the word in her head aloud now. Loud enough that everybody in the range of her voice would hear them. "Let's go *junkyard*."

"We're taking fire," Leyla called. "Main guns now."

"All yours," Command Centurion Lau said.

Iveta smiled. She tagged all the Raiders in normal range for her friendly cruisers to hit.

"All ships, prioritize these with long-range fire," she said. "Gunner, give me one more salvo into *Tango* and then start bashing downhill based on size and firepower. Anybody launching firebirds gets it first, but they take a bit to charge and recharge."

And Lord knows those pirates hadn't been keeping a proper orbital security watch of the skies above them, to let *Urumchi* and friends drop down this hard on them.

Beam fire began stuttering both directions. Lots of little things inbound, as every Picket had one mount for a titan bolt or firebird to go with a few Main guns. Uncoordinated, but coming from her entire front hemisphere right now.

As planned. None of her shields were likely to be overloaded as long as the woodpeckers didn't gang up on her.

"Gunner," Iveta called, tagging a new target. Leyla had

found the old missile Raider *Ironwolf* that had been there at the beginning. "Hit this one next."

Rats, cornered.

And a junkyard bitch killing them.

FIFTY-SEVEN

YAUMGAN SKYCRUISER LI JING

Stunt Dude watched all hell break loose. He was back in his training classes now, teaching the war with *Fribourg*, when things had still been snubfighters and missiles rather than the beam-heavy environment of the war with *Buran*. The missiles weren't a threat. That pirate Bedrov had made sure that his ships could deliver a stupid amount of damage in that short period when a shark was close, before they leapt away to safety.

Pulse-Twos just let you do that farther away. Type-3-Pulse even farther.

He didn't have anything to do at this point but pay attention and maybe point out things someone else missed. Or offer advice based on how an *RAN* officer would handle a situation, so they knew what to expect from Beridze.

"Right Gunner, lock with the Ōdachi and fire," Captain Xue ordered.

A Raider in the near distance was highlighted. A moment later crosshairs appeared.

"Left Gunner, put your cluster into this target," Xue followed up on another one.

Stunt Dude held his tongue. He'd always been told that you concentrated your fire on a single target, disabling it rapidly and then moving, rather than just wounding a bunch of ships.

At the same time, all these vessels were just now starting to get coordinated, so this might drastically weaken their ability—perhaps even their willingness—to fight at all. Useful, when you were facing a swarm of destroyers and patrol boats, rather than cruisers.

Speaking of…

Stunt Dude dialed his own screen around, looking for that second Enforcer. *Blade of Kunke. Nagi Syndicate.*

There.

Tango had gotten the sharp edge of a few tongues, but wasn't moving right now. That stood out.

Blade of Kunke was doing the same, which made no sense.

Unless their captains weren't aboard?

"Seeker, I am transmitting two identifications to you," *Stunt Dude* called to Huie De, marking the closer station as well as an enormous ship that was some sort of catamaran-style vessel identifying itself as *Aggregator*. "Scan them for a flag or transponder related to *Tango* and *Blade of Kunke*."

The woman looked up at him in confusion for a moment.

"Do it," Captain Xue ordered, hopefully seeing what he saw.

Or guessed.

"It looks like both have shuttle craft docked on *Aggregator* at present," she replied a moment later.

Stunt Dude grinned. Captain Xue had a concerned look on her face.

"The two Enforcers are not behaving correctly," he explained. "I wondered if their captains weren't aboard and the crews left were just now deciding to fight or try to get to them."

"Shuttles on the big ship suggest that, yes," Xue nodded. "Open a channel to *Zhang Gualao*."

"On Two," Huie De replied.

Stunt Dude had met Captain Lin a few times, but not spent much time around the woman.

Young. That was the impression she gave. Which suggested another Jessica Keller to a guy from *Aquitaine*.

"I am transmitting two locations on *Aggregator*, Commander," Xue said. "Could you destroy shuttles docked at these locations?"

That made sense. The Ōdachi didn't have the range, but the Sunsword did.

"Stand by," Lin answered.

Trinidad watched the side of that big whale called *Aggregator* light up suddenly as the first pulse of an overloaded Power Tap struck. The facing shield collapsed.

Civilian-grade stuff. No way to fight a battle in space.

The second pulse hit metal. Blasted a divot in the hull that rapidly turned into a cloud of plasma and escaping atmosphere.

Then the gunner over there rotated his shot. *Stunt Dude* felt his jaw fall open. It looked like a mechanical sewing machine running a stitch line down a hem. The fourth pulse struck the second set of coordinates and stopped.

Aggregator had developed a roll like it was indeed a 'gator trying to escape, but it was just the liberated energies demonstrating the laws of physics and thermodynamics to any interested watcher.

Aggregator was out of the battle, though it never should have been in the battle to begin with.

"Thank you," *Stunt Dude* said to everyone listening.

"What if he was aboard that shuttle craft?" Xue asked.

"Then a good chunk of the war is over," *Stunt Dude* replied. "If not, then that ship will happily surrender to us later, because he is in no condition to flee."

She nodded and went back to blasting Raiders and any Pickets that got too close.

The cockroaches were starting to scatter now.

FIFTY-EIGHT

HEAVY ESCORT MORNINGHAWK

Makara didn't have much to do. It was a strange feeling, to be sitting in the middle of a massive riot and only occasionally firing his two Main guns.

But Kosnett's people had put him in the safest single spot Makara could imagine. Right in front of *Urumchi*, with the other two battleships on his flanks and *Viking* above plus all the other escorts across the front of the formation.

Even the two Moats in front of *Khandoba* were engaging targets on their flank, but the bow of *Morninghawk* was like a snowplow pushing everything away in all directions.

"Warning, station just fired a condor at *Urumchi*," Bulat called now. "Front line engaging. Range is close enough to be a threat."

"Watch it and stand by to counter fire with the shrikes," Makara replied.

The whole battle had been like that. Paying attention, but not called upon to do anything.

"Everybody, we got a runner," Keo said now as he maneuvered. "Hey, that's not right."

"What?" Makara asked sharply.

Keo was normally the practical joker, but he could be serious when the situation called for it.

Like now.

"*Wulfa*, boss," he said. "That's the other target besides *Tango* that *Aquitaine* is hot and heavy after. They just showed up on my boards from where they'd been hiding close to the station. Hard blue shift, like they are coming almost straight at us."

Almost? Yes, Makara supposed that Keo might assume that.

Makara had already gone past such thinking. He'd watched the *Yaumgan* Jùrén *Zhang Gualao* blast the recreational vessel in medium orbit, but not understood why it rated the attention.

But there was a condor coming this direction and all the corvettes were shooting at it to soften the impact.

Wulfa was coming right in the wake.

"Keo, Bulat, *Wulfa* has the same target as the condor," he yelled loud enough to get heads turned around.

"What?"

"They are going to try to ram *Urumchi*," he explained.

Why else not turn tail and run like hell for the darkness at this point? Any number of ships would be able to get to the edge of the gravity well and make the transition to JumpSpace.

Then they would be free.

Except that none of them realized that Kosnett had left the door behind him open because he didn't have the force to hold both locations. They would expect that the stations had been captured and were being manned. They would expect to die if they tried to get away right now.

So they were going to die productively. Or something.

He didn't know what caused that realization, but it hit him like a brick and would not let go.

"*Urumchi*, begin evasive maneuvering," he said into the line to their bridge. "Sound collision warnings for *Wulfa*."

Tactical Officer Beridze appeared on his side screen, studied him for a moment silently, and nodded.

"Big guns, retarget and smash *Wulfa*," she called on her line, but he was already dialing the sound down again.

"Keo, Bulat, fire the falcon now," he ordered. "Right at *Wulfa*. Ignore the condor and put everything into the Salvager. Once she commits, sequence the shrikes and ask anybody with a line of fire to give me some wing shots. Even dead she will have inertia and *Urumchi* cannot maneuver that quickly to avoid rubble. Keep the Shield Projector centered on her, regardless of what she does."

They both acknowledged and Makara tuned the rest of the battle out. Everything was going to come down to that suicidal fool making a jousting run, which had to be the stupidest thing he'd ever heard of.

But they must be getting desperate now. If so, Kosnett had already won and it was just time to survive.

That was the problem. *Morninghawk* was a Heavy Escort. The ship that put itself in between capital ships like *Wraithruin* and trouble.

He took a breath. Held it for a long moment as he considered the hand that the fates had dealt him today.

"Keo, plot an intercept course and engage," he ordered.

Several people squawked and squeaked at that. Heads came around.

"*Morninghawk will be in our shadow, doing the right things,*" he quoted. "Lau said that. It is time to do the hard things. Stand by to ram *Wulfa* and keep them from getting to *Urumchi*. All guns go to rapid fire."

Sobol gasped. He looked over and saw her compose herself a moment later before nodding at him.

Seduced her, had he? Pity that he wouldn't be able to come to understand what that meant.

Captain Makara Omarov consigned his soul to hell and snarled his defiance at the fates that demanded it.

FIFTY-NINE

Heather shook her head in disbelief. *Ground Control* shook her head as well.

Le Beau Geste. The Grand Gesture. Two fingers in the air.

"Squadron, this is Lau aboard *Urumchi.* I have the flag," she said calmly. "*Zhang Gualao* and *Khandoba*, I need you to hit *Wulfa* with everything you have, right now. Every beam. Every weapon. Everything. *Task Force 501*, ignore the condor. I'll take it on my forward shields at this point and deal with it. Like Iveta said, time to go junkyard on these people."

Iveta hadn't even flinched when Heather spoke, but *Ground Control* recognized that her Tactical Officer had ascended to that special place you only found when you were in the zone.

The Pulse-Twos began to stutter. The Type-4s were like lightning bolts from angry gods in a terrible storm. *Khandoba* had three Power Taps and six titan bolts. All of them hammered a flank on *Wulfa* as the ship was only just starting to accelerate.

"Pilot, hold your line!" Iveta snarled above the noise. "*Wulfa*'s coming for us, and *Morninghawk* is going to get crazy. I need you nailing that bitch in place for them and everyone else."

Ground Control nodded. The *Junkyard Dog* had seen it.

Urumchi flying straight meant that *Wulfa* would as well, unless *Wulfa*'s nerve broke. Omarov's wouldn't.

Simple as that.

Morninghawk had a ramming course and was moving in for the kill. Five firebirds popped out, woodpecker style in a line of pulses racing madly towards their tree.

Li Jing suddenly spun like a ballerina and slid sideways like an ice skater. Or another hockey player going after a puck in the corner. Titan bolts and the Sunsword lit the night sky.

Zhang Gualao had been caught recharging. A few moments later eight titan bolts slammed into the side of *Wulfa* like an avalanche. The Sunsword spoke. Ra announcing the day, perhaps.

Captain Lin's Right Hand Gunner was an artist. *Ground Control* didn't have a better way to describe the shot.

She'd thought he'd missed high with his locking pulse shot, but *Wulfa* had sailed directly into it instead. The shields on that side had already been overloaded and crushed, so the man hit metal. High on the bow. Metal sublimed and a cloud of plasma formed.

Wulfa sailed into a hurricane made of gases blasted from its own hull. The energies being released were sufficient that physics got involved at that point, an expanding cloud of gases pushing the bow down and inducing spin as following shots began hammering down the hull.

Wulfa vanished into a cloud of white-hot gases only now cooling enough to be visible to the naked eye. The Salvager was out of control. That much was obvious. *Zhang Gualao* had induced a corkscrew roll, just like they had done to *Aggregator* earlier.

No Pilot was going to be able to regain control of that mess. And every ship that had a weapon with bearing was continuing to fire into the tumbling corpse.

Corpse?

Ground Control nodded. *Wulfa* was dead. They might slam

into the planet in a few days at this rate, unless someone rescued them, because the hull was starting to come apart in big chunks. Frames broken like someone ripping an orange apart without peeling it first.

"*Morninghawk*, sheer off!" *Junkyard* ordered now. "Target is neutralized. Repeat: **Neutralized**. Return to escort duties. All other vessels, you have your priorities. Follow them now!"

Ground Control smiled. Iveta Beridze had seen it, too. *Wulfa* had chosen to die in battle rather than being taken alive. She presumed that by the time rescuers cut living bodies out of the hull, Andrea Liefan would be dead, probably by her own hand if the bridge itself had survived that terrible onslaught.

Around her, Pickets and Raiders that could do so were suddenly turning and trying to run, but they still had to get to the edge of the gravity well, most of them, while she was closer.

"Squadron, this is Lau," *Ground Control* spoke now with a smile in her voice. "Cruiser force withdraw and haul ass to the Ring. I want anybody making it past us stopped there or broken so badly that we can chase them down next week."

Aranyani and *Li Jing* acknowledged immediately, but they probably saw it coming. *Shadowbolt* and *Juvayni* took a little longer, but they probably wanted to stay and hunt.

The hunting out at the Ring would be sufficiently bloody, if she had to guess, but the fire had just gone out of most of these ships.

Tango was still sitting there. As she watched, they struck their colors.

Ground Control wondered what had happened to Basant Utkin to cause that.

SIXTY

CARRIER AGGREGATOR

Basant had been meeting with a few of his new captains and subordinates when the alarms sounded.

Worse, someone had been asleep on the bridge, because there was an enemy fleet engaged in an all-out war just outside his conference room porthole by the time anybody remembered to tell him.

Basant had watched helplessly as ships started taking fire sufficient to rupture things.

He, Bellie, and *Hollywood* started running for the flight deck, but stopped cold when the entire ship shook and vacuum alarms sealed the frame in front of them.

Basant keyed the comm for the bridge.

"It's Utkin," he said. "What just happened?"

Around them, lights flickered, half of them staying off. Local gravity dropped twenty percent as generators failed.

"The law just arrived, Basant," Dexter replied in a heavy voice. "*Tango*'s taken severe damage. Other ships are reporting the same. Somebody just blew up your shuttle and Captain Bellie's with a Power Tap salvo. Not sure you wanted to be out in that mess anyway. It's ugly."

Basant moved to a porthole and watched what he could see from here.

Ships were just bright spots for the most part, even mooring so close together, but the sudden supernovae of beams hitting shields was visible to the naked eye. Or the explosions when they got through.

Aggregator was tumbling, from the way the planet suddenly rose up and engulfed his horizon.

"Dexter, is there anything you can do right now?" Basant asked.

"Negative, Basant," the man answered. "I'm still trying to recover control of *Aggregator*. They brought three battleships from the scans. *Urumchi* and *Khandoba* we know. Plus something that looks like *Yaumgan*."

"Why was there no warning from the defense stations?" he demanded.

"No idea," Dexter replied.

Bellie and *Hollywood* both just shrugged.

Basant fulminated, but kept it in his head. Somehow, Kosnett had snuck an entire battle fleet into *Meerut*, past all those defenses, and caught him and his people dead asleep.

Worse, if they were already attacking the unarmed ships, they must have defeated the rest.

A supernova erupted off the bow as he watched.

"Basant…" Captain Dexter started to say something, but his voice broke.

Dexter. One of the hardest men Basant had ever met.

"What?" Basant asked, letting most of the emotion go now.

He had gambled and failed. Whatever ship had just exploded was evidence of that.

"That was *Wulfa*, Basant," Dexter said in a husky, emotional voice. "Looks like they tried to ram *Urumchi* and got utterly destroyed in the process."

Basant nodded. Andrea going out on her terms. Never taken alive. Never face the hangman's noose.

He turned to the other two women.

"I need your help," he said. "Dexter, can you meet us back in the conference room immediately?"

"Why?" the man demanded.

"We need to negotiate our surrender."

Long pause.

"Okay, headed that way now," Dexter said.

"Let's go," Basant said to the other two captains.

It didn't take long. They'd barely gotten started before *Aggregator* had come under fire.

Dexter was there quickly, looking confused but ready to go out guns blazing with the rest of them.

Basant removed the pistol from his holster and handed it to *Hollywood*. She took it wordlessly. Enlightenment arrived a moment later and she nodded with a sad smile.

"Captain Dexter, I challenge you to combat," Basant said in a tired voice. "To the death, as my honor will not be assuaged any other way than by blood."

Dexter started to speak and stopped himself. Shuddered once. Bellie shifted to one side silently, drawing *Hollywood* in her wake.

"To the death, Utkin?" Dexter demanded in an equally tired voice.

Two outlaws at the end of the line.

"To the death, Dexter," he said. "I will accept nothing less."

Captain Dexter flashed a look of pain and resignation across his face before he settled and drew his own blade.

"Very well, Utkin," he sighed. "To the death."

"Thank you," Basant nodded quietly.

"Knowing you has been an adventure, Bassant," Dexter replied. "I hope you will have a glass of whiskey ready for me when I get to hell."

"I will, old friend," Basant nodded.

Then he slammed his mouth shut and shuffled forward, blade hand forward like the stupidest knife fighter ever born.

Dexter started to fall into that crouch that all successful fighters learn, but stopped himself and stood there, tears starting to run down his face.

But they both understood. The Age of Piracy was over. Had just died in *Meerut* orbit as *Wulfa* was destroyed.

Basant lunged awkwardly, wide open.

Captain Dexter stepped sideways and slammed his own knife into Basant's stomach, twisting it up and in.

There was surprisingly little pain.

And then darkness.

SIXTY-ONE

Phil was listening to the chatter. Most of the pirates were on unencrypted comms, because their panic had been so sudden and nobody had seemed to take charge of their flag.

"*RAN Urumchi*, this is Captain Milose Dexter, aboard the former *Yarmouth* Carrier *Aggregator*," a tired, sad voice came over in the clear. "Respond please."

Male. Middle-aged or later. Exhausted emotionally. Maybe broken.

"Dexter, this is First Centurion Kosnett," he replied.

"We surrender, Kosnett," Dexter said in an almost-explosive sigh. "Captain Basant Utkin is dead. I killed him in a duel for the right to command his forces. I am ordering all ships to stand down. This war is over."

"Over?" Kosnett asked.

"You destroyed Andrea Liefan," Dexter said. "I just killed Utkin on a dueling floor with my own blade. Who's left that you need to hang?"

Phil leaned back. If he'd have been like Keller, and made a list of all the possible outcomes of this day, this would have still been in the bottom three or five of all possible results. But he supposed that it made a certain sort of poetic sense.

313

Utkin had fought a duel with the captain of *Blade of Kunke* for the right to lead a rebellion against the rest of the Syndicates. If he was dead now, that revolution was indeed over.

Phil keyed an open line.

"Attention, this is First Centurion Kosnett, calling all pirate vessels," he announced. "You have a new leader and he has announced a surrender. If you honor those terms, you will be taken into custody and I will demand that all capital punishments be commuted to lesser sentences. Let tomorrow be a new day where you can earn forgiveness from your former victims and learn to become better people. If you run, I will declare you outlaws and order that no mercy ever be shown to you again by any civilized nation or planet. This is your only warning, and your only opportunity to survive. What will it be?"

He cut the line and went for the squadron channel.

Wulfa's death had seemed to knock all the steam out of everybody, with any ship that could running and being hounded.

"Squadron, this is Kosnett, I have the flag," he said, feeling that same tiredness descend on his shoulders like a cloak as he had heard in Dexter's voice. "Stand down on anybody that stops fighting at this point. Anybody who runs earns it, so kill them. *CB-502*, detach and carry this message to the cruisers out at The Ring, then stay with them to annihilate anyone who tries my patience."

He leaned back and watched green lights come on. Markus was suddenly close and more coffee was absolutely called for, so he handed his favorite redneck a forgotten, empty mug.

On his boards, one ship after another struck their colors. They would see prisons, but not meet their Maker just yet.

He supposed that the few officers on *Tango* that he had originally listed could fall under the amnesty, if Utkin was dead, killed by their pirate understanding of honor. They might have been killed when Iveta cut loose on the ship at the beginning, because it hadn't done anything at all after that.

Maybe a lucky bridge hit had ended all his problems.

Phil took a moment to locate the office he wanted and placed a call.

"Fleet Ambassador's office, Babatunde here," Aliza said immediately.

"It's Phil," he replied unnecessarily. "Aliza, I'm going to need one of your ambassadors to take charge of *Meerut* as governor until they sort out what they want to do."

"Governor, Phil?" she asked, perhaps a bit surprised.

"Neither *Ewin* nor *Dalou* technically have a claim on this system," he replied. "So neither of them get to make demands. If Utkin was the government, I need someone neutral to step in now and push everyone else politely back over a line that those ring stations originally enforced. That's the technical border of the Cluster, according to all the treaties and understandings. Until everybody, and I mean *everybody*, comes to a *Consensus*, my will is the law around here."

"Will do," Aliza replied. "Let me see who would be best of the folks we have around on deck."

She cut the line and he smiled at Harinder, quietly, professionally seated across from him being competent.

"Unless you want it," he said offhand. "You'd be at least as good as any of her people."

"Governor, Phil?" Harinder asked.

"I can do that," he smiled. "This is a former pirate enclave. Maybe *Aquitaine* signs a treaty with them to establish a forward operating base with extraterritoriality. Whatever. I just need this to not turn into the trigger of a wider war between *Ewin* and *Dalou*."

"Let me think about it," she replied.

Phil took that as a win.

He'd just broken the pirates. The cultures of the Balhee Cluster were going to be a while finding a new equilibrium, and he didn't need to be a bull in a china shop while that was happening.

There were already enough of those running loose.

EPILOGUES

CHAPTER 62

HEAVY ESCORT MORNINGHAWK

Makara held a glass of Kosnett's better whiskey in one hand and tried to reconcile the last three days into the sort of narrative that made a damned bit of sense and didn't come out like the start of some ancient legend. Around him, other captains, friendly and reformed pirate both, milled uncertainly, small clusters of nervous people.

If he'd felt like a teenager before, the rest seemed to embody it today, but the *Aquitaine* folks were being magnanimous and friendly. Victors on this scale could afford it.

Inspector Sobol—Samnang—had vanished into the crowd earlier, leaving him somewhat off to one side. Not a wall flower, but not one of the centers of attention over there, like Kosnett or Lau.

"You are *insane, Morninghawk,*" a voice intruded on his right.

He turned to look. Senior Centurion Beridze of *Urumchi*. Tactical Officer and the one that had been mostly responsible for the battle they'd won.

Makara shrugged.

"Would you have rammed *Wulfa?*" she asked, stepping close enough to make it a quiet conversation.

"Escorts are occasionally called upon to make sacrifices, Senior Centurion," he said earnestly, however tired he still was. "*Morninghawk* is far less valuable to the future than *Urumchi*."

"I doubt that," she countered.

"How so?" he asked, thinking back to her comment just before the battle when Heather had been speaking. *Morninghawk* did not give anybody nightmares.

Except the occasional smuggler.

"The First Centurion has been talking about a grand tour of all the capitals," she offered now. "That will include *Ellariel*. Possibly *Ishiokoh-jo* as well. We'll need friends when we get there. People who understand what Phil's trying to build. And have shown a willingness to help."

Again, he shrugged. Fourth, unlucky son. Minor captain serving a minor Komyo. Nobody that mattered in the grand scheme of things.

"Inspector Sobol has been talking to the First Centurion," Beridze continued, sipping at her own glass. Looked like wine. "You should look at it as a reward, not a punishment."

"I will do what I can, Senior Centurion," he offered as a way to deflect the conversation onto safer ground.

She took the dismissal with grace and withdrew. Just as well, as Samnang approached now, a warm smile on her face. Their serious conversation in the middle of battle had been left unfinished, in spite of the days that had passed. Perhaps being aboard *Urumchi*, in the Ambassadorial section, had loosened her up, because she was not the dour, hardened, bureaucratic warrior killer he'd been dealing with previously.

Sobol stepped closer than Beridze had. Into his personal space, which was unlike the woman.

"Kosnett has proposed awarding you an *Aquitaine* medal for valor," she murmured. "He has that power from their government."

Makara shrugged again, wondering if such behavior on his

part was likely to become a habit. He was not a hero. He was simply a captain tasked with certain things.

Potentially dying in battle just happened to be one of them.

"You do not care?" Samnang asked now.

"I am not sure what to think," he replied carefully. "Much has changed in the last six weeks."

He left that dangling. She had come aboard his ship just over a month ago.

She smiled knowingly.

"It is a good thing," the woman assured him. "He asked permission to present it as part of a reception at the Shogun's Court, where all could see. I agreed."

Makara blinked. Shocked.

"Yes, Makara Omarov, I have that power," she said now. "I am an Imperial Inspector, yes, but the Shogun himself charged me to speak in his name, were it necessary when dealing with the outsiders."

"Oh," Makara replied, stunned.

If that was the case…

"We had a conversation earlier," he began carefully. Oh so carefully. "In my office. Talking about the future."

"And the fact that you had seduced me with your commitment to honor and the reputation of the *Dalou Hegemony*, yes."

Not exactly how he remembered it, but Makara wasn't going to argue with this woman on the topic. Perhaps not any topic.

"What does it mean if a woman of your apparent stature and rank finds herself seduced by such a minor player?" he asked, wondering if she was about to destroy him for his audacity.

She probably could.

"Minor player, Captain Omarov?" she smiled. "You continue to underestimate yourself, but I am not fooled."

"Oh?"

"No, Makara, you are the *Harbinger of Destruction*. Never doubt that. I wish to be on your side of any battle that erupts."

Yes, he supposed she might. The future had changed.

CHAPTER 63

Phil watched the crowd swirl and eddy. He preferred these kinds of battles. Social over military. Easier to defeat someone in such a way that they could be turned into friends later. Not all of these pirates around him were likely to see prisons, in the long run. Letters of Marque and Reprisal, however forged or bribed to acquire, could cover a multitude of sins, if the man or woman holding them was willing to adapt to a new reality.

Especially now that the future had dawned.

One of them approached him now. *Hollywood* Ward, Captain of the Raider of the same name.

She was as tall as Heather but far stouter. Fully gray, with maybe a decade on *Ground Control.* Hard to tell. Rough woman, but still feminine as she approached.

"Captain Dexter wished me to ask you a question, First Centurion," she said as she stepped close enough that his security team considered bristling at her. "For various reasons he is planning to keep his distance from you and everyone else, but Basant trusted him, so the other captains have accepted him for now. At least as long as they can hold on to what they might otherwise be about to lose."

Phil nodded. *Aggregator* wasn't a warship. It was a floating hotel and shopping mall where crews had been able to relax away from their duty, swap lies, and maybe recruit crews.

Neutral ground.

"I'm serious about the war being over," Phil reiterated. Everyone had asked that question. "Everyone I wanted dead is off the table. The rest of you get to decide where to go next."

Hollywood nodded at him.

"Dexter would be someone that the locals could accept as a governor, over the longer term," she said. "Once your people are finally withdrawn and *Meerut* is on their own. Basant killed the senior people in the *Meerut* government when he took over, and the rest of us belong to various other Syndicates. *Yarmouth* wasn't particularly an ally of *Ingham*, but Milose is somebody that all the outsiders know well enough."

"And your question?" Phil prompted.

"Who will own *Meerut* tomorrow?" she asked bluntly.

"Not *Ewin* and not *Dalou*," Phil replied, just as blunt. "The Ring is no longer a viable defense for the system, because everybody knows how to get around it now, but I expect a forward warehousing station and maybe one or two of those guard ships to remain out there. Possibly moved to the inner end of that tunnel, just so cargo can be transshipped there and folks don't have to make that sail. But I will guarantee the neutrality of *Meerut* for now. At some point, they can decide if they want to join someone else, or remain independent. There are few places that can honestly claim be free of the five nations of the cluster, so I see no reason to eliminate one as soon as everyone discovers that it exists."

"You'll guarantee?" she asked, perhaps a bit surprised.

"*Aquitaine* can do that," he said. "The Senate granted me plenipotentiary powers in the Cluster. If I have to, I'll sign a treaty with the *Meerut* government establishing an *RAN* naval base here, or out at the mouth, just to make my position painfully clear."

"And the pirates?" she asked.

Phil got the impression that she'd finally gotten to the question she wanted answered.

"You aren't pirates anymore, *Hollywood*," he told her with a hard smile. "You have all retired and taken up peaceful trade with the systems of the Cluster. As long as that's true, I don't care what you do with the rest of your lives. Retire to *Meerut* and take up politics or gardening for all I care. Hopefully, none of you have been so bad that anybody out there feels the need to send assassins after you personally, because there's not a lot I can do at that point. Warfleets will be met with superior force."

"Superior, Kosnett?" she said in a voice almost a sneer.

"I brought *Urumchi*, Captain," he retorted, his voice turning hard. "That's a Survey Dreadnought and heavier than anything in the Cluster. I could have just as easily taken command of a Heavy Dreadnought like *Kongō* and an Expeditionary Fleet instead of merely Explorers. If someone gives me a reason, I can change that decision. It is my hope that nobody else decides that they need to go out like Andrea Liefan did."

She flinched under his tone, but she was merely the messenger. He understood that. Dexter was keeping a polite distance as a potential successor. *Hollywood* had been there to watch Utkin die, and Phil had seen the tape of the event, as short as it had been.

The man had boxed himself into a corner, but decisions like he had made were always a Neck-or-Crown kind of thing. You won or you died.

Basant Utkin had chosen to die in such a way that everyone else had a chance to live.

Phil would honor the man *exactly* that much.

Hollywood nodded and withdrew. He let her go. The important messages had been delivered both ways, and the pirates—*former pirates*—were still in shock.

He smiled as Heather appeared out of the crowd.

"You look like a cat with a bloody mouth," she laughed and

handed him a fresh glass of whiskey.

"*Hollywood* Ward had questions," he said. "I had answers. They get to ruminate for a while."

"We going to *Dalou* next?" Heather asked.

"I was speaking with Inspector Sobol, and that's an open invitation to pursue," he nodded. "Not tomorrow, as *Meerut* needs to calm down, and we're going to release the cruisers to return home bearing news, so *Ewin* will likely immediately file a complaint with our Ambassador and throw a fit."

"Do we care?" she smiled.

"We choose not to alienate them over such a little thing," Phil smiled back. "Not yet, anyway. I reserve the right to change my mind later."

Heather laughed. It was a warm, lovely sound. Part of the reason he liked having her around. That and *Ground Control*. Two sides of one coin, but the best two parts of any human he knew.

"What if they all want to go with us to *Ellariel*?" Heather asked as her mirth subsided. "That's always been something of a Forbidden City to outsiders, so they might want a chance to be tourists and spies."

"As long as they behave," Phil said. "I was just telling *Hollywood* that anyone really wanting to plague me might cause me to bring in *Kongō* and Fleet Centurion Raizō Tanaka. Not even The Eight Immortals of the *Yaumgan* fleet would stand a chance against the sort of warfleet event that the First Lord would send if that message arrived at *Ladaux*."

"I'll remind people to behave," she said, sobering.

"Do that," he replied with something of an order to his voice. "I'm going to fix this immediate problem, but then you and I are going to sail into Kyoto Harbor and demand an audience with the Emperor."

She nodded.

"To Revolution," she toasted.

They clinked glasses together and smiled.

READ MORE

Be sure to read the next books in the First Centurion Phil Kosnett series!

Encounter at Vilahana
Consensus at Aditi
Hegemony at Dalou

Available at your favorite retailers!

ABOUT THE AUTHOR

Blaze Ward writes science fiction in the Alexandria Station universe (Jessica Keller, The Science Officer, The Story Road, etc.) as well as several other science fiction universes, such as Star Dragon, the Dominion, and more. He also writes odd bits of high fantasy with swords and orcs. In addition, he is the Editor and Publisher of *Boundary Shock Quarterly Magazine*. You can find out more at his website www.blazeward.com, as well as Facebook, Goodreads, and other places.

Blaze's works are available as ebooks, paper, and audio, and can be found at a variety of online vendors. His newsletter comes out regularly, and you can also follow his blog on his website. He really enjoys interacting with fans, and looks forward to any and all questions—even ones about his books!

Never miss a release!
If you'd like to be notified of new releases, sign up for my newsletter.

http://www.blazeward.com/newsletter/

Buy More!
Did you know that you can buy directly from my website?

https://www.blazeward.com/shop/

Connect with Blaze!

Web: www.blazeward.com
Boundary Shock Quarterly (BSQ):
https://www.boundaryshockquarterly.com/

ABOUT KNOTTED ROAD PRESS

Knotted Road Press fiction specializes in dynamic writing set in mysterious, exotic locations.

Knotted Road Press non–fiction publishes autobiographies, business books, cookbooks, and how–to books with unique voices.

Knotted Road Press creates DRM–free ebooks as well as high–quality print books for readers around the world.

With authors in a variety of genres including literary, poetry, mystery, fantasy, and science fiction, Knotted Road Press has something for everyone.

Knotted Road Press
www.KnottedRoadPress.com